D0555450

LEGENDS
OF
LUST

LEGENDS OF LUST

Erotic Myths from around the World

Autumn Bardot

CLEiS PRESS

Copyright © 2019 by Autumn Bardot.

All rights reserved. Except for brief passages quoted in newspaper, magazine, radio, television or online reviews, no part of this book may be reproduced in any form or by any means, electronic or mechanical, including photocopying, recording, or information storage or retrieval system, without permission in writing from the Publisher.

Published in the United States by Cleis Press, an imprint of Start Midnight, LLC, 101 Hudson Street, Thirty-Seventh Floor, Suite 3705, Jersey City, NJ 07302.

Printed in the United States.
Cover design: Allyson Fields
Cover photograph: iStock
Text design: Frank Wiedemann
First Edition.
10 9 8 7 6 5 4 3 2 1

Trade paper ISBN: 978-1-62778-278-4
E-book ISBN: 978-1-62778-279-1

Library of Congress Cataloging-in-Publication Data is available on file.

CONTENTS

MISTRESS OF
THE ISLE

I am drawing my golden shuttle through the loom's warp when Hermes races into my home.

"Where is he?" Hermes takes off his winged crown, wipes a bead of sweat from his brow, and looks with an admiring eye at the elegant tapestries and ocean treasures adorning my luxurious grotto home.

"He's not here." Surprised by Hermes's visit, I rise from my stool and go to the cupboard. "Are you hungry?" I gesture to the table and chair. "Let me get you something to eat and drink. You've traveled a long way." Hermes had flown over a vast sea to get here, and hungry gods tend to be grouchy.

"Thank you, Calypso." Hermes sits down and quaffs the goblet of red nectar I set before him; likewise he gobbles down the ambrosia.

I stoke the fire and toss in logs of sandalwood and cedar, pretending composure. Hermes is here for Odysseus. And I'm pretty sure of the reason. "Why are you in Ogygia?" I bat my eyes and feign ignorance.

"Zeus sent me." Hermes runs his hand through his flaxen curls.

Swallowing the lump in my throat, I pick up Hermes's caduceus-tipped staff and trace the golden snakes coiling around it. "Well, get on with it. What's the message?"

Hermes yanks his staff from my hands. "Zeus demands you release Odysseus. The mortal is not destined to live out his days as your...slave."

"Why not?" I pluck off a wilted leaf from the spray of violets on the table.

"Zeus wants Odysseus to return home to Ithaca. Says his bad luck must come to an end."

"Zeus thinks his time with me is bad luck?" I flick back a lock of hair.

"The mortal spent ten years fighting in Troy, then his ship capsized on the voyage back home and all his men drowned. The last seven years you've kept him here against his will for your own lascivious amusements." Hermes jabbed his staff toward the bed. "Zeus fears the people of Ithaca have forgotten Odysseus's merciful reign. Even as we speak cruel men plot the death of his son. Odysseus's destiny is with his people, his family, and his friends. Not here. Not with *you*."

"You gods are a hypocritical bunch of liars!" I stand, every muscle taut with anger, snatch the violet-filled vase, and throw it against the wall. "How dare you come to my island and tell me I must give up the man I love! Wasn't it Zeus who caused the lightning strike that sunk Odysseus's ship and killed his crew? Wasn't it Zeus who carried Odysseus atop the waves and guided the wind to make sure he washed up on my island?"

"Calypso—"

"I found Odysseus on the beach half-dead. I took care of him, nourished him, and made him strong again."

Hermes points his staff at me. "And made him your sex slave."

"He is enthralled by me." I toss my hair over my shoulder. "He begs for it."

Hermes sets his winged crown back on his head. "Is that why he sits on the beach all day, sad-eyed with homesickness?"

"Get out!" I point to the grotto's entrance.

Hermes, unmoved by my outburst, pours another goblet of nectar, gulps it down, and wipes his mouth with the back of his hand. "Let Odysseus leave or suffer Zeus's wrath."

I cross my arms. "How? I don't have a ship or men to sail it."

"Figure it out." Hermes pokes his staff at my nipple. "And quickly."

Hermes is gone in a flash, leaving me trembling with anger in the entryway.

Ignoring Zeus's command isn't an option. At least not a smart one. I head toward the beach knowing just what I'll find: a melancholy Odysseus staring into the blue distance, his heart aching for the wife and child he has not seen for nearly twenty years. I sigh, my sorrow a breeze wafting through the branches, the leaves trembling for me. With a heavy heart, I stroll down the path shaded by verdant alder, black poplar, and cypress.

As always, Odysseus is sitting on a large rock facing the sea. I take a moment to admire his physique. He is a chiseled hunk of manliness. I will miss throwing my legs over his broad shoulders and watching his biceps flex as he thrusts into me.

I adjust my gown, sheer as a mist and glistening like the dew, and expose my pale pink nipples. "Odysseus."

He turns his head, his aquiline nose and short beard in profile. "My goddess?"

I move his muscled thighs apart and stand between them. "It is time for you to leave." I slip my hand under his linen loincloth, wrap my fingers around his cock and feel it swell in my hand. "You must build a boat and go home." I put my mouth on his ear and bite his earlobe, feel him expand even more. "You can build a sturdy boat, can't you?"

Odysseus pulls away and stays my slow-moving hand with his own. "Is this a trick?"

"Don't you want to go home?" I run my other hand along his jaw, recall the feel of his beard between my legs.

"I do." Odysseus swallows, looks down as my hand slides up and down his eagerness. "I miss my wife and son. But how can I build a vessel strong enough to withstand the rough s—"

I silence him with my tongue and rub my breast against his bare chest. His body tenses with pleasure as our tongues intertwine. His kisses always inflame me, and the dew of desire moistens my sex. How I will miss this man who can fuck all night and never tire!

Odysseus breaks the kiss and narrows his eyes. "Are you serious? Or is my building a boat to go home some kind of new torment?"

"You dog!" I jerk away and remove my hand from his throbbing cock. "Don't you know me by now?"

"I know you like to dominate." Odysseus grips the underside of my buttocks, his thumbs stroking and prodding the soft flesh. "I know you enjoy making me beg for your cunt."

I laugh and set a kiss on his forehead. "I swear—the earth and the sky as my witness—this is no new game." I thrust out my breasts and press his head against them. "My heart is not made of cold iron but of kindness and love for you." My fingers run through his tangle of curls. "Come." I tug on his hair. "Let's go back to my cave."

Odysseus grabs both my wrists and gives me a hard look. This sudden show of control is surprising and I try yanking away. Odysseus holds tight, his large hands squeezing more than necessary. His lips curl up, his lopsided grin an irresistible mixture of charm and mischievousness. A thrill runs up my arms and descends straight between my thighs. I look down at my hands, now constrained by the warrior king I held captive for seven years, and feel something I haven't in Zeus knows how long. I am flustered. Me! Mistress of the Isle!

"Let me go," I say. It is a command. He is used to them, having obeyed me all these years.

Odysseus loosens his grip and slides his warm hands into mine, lacing our fingers together. "It seems you already have." He stands, his cock still erect, and pulls me forward. His lips are soft and warm, his tongue circling mine with a tenderness we have not shared for some time. "I'm ravenous, my goddess."

I lift our clasped hands to my lips and scrape my teeth over his knuckles. "So am I."

We head back to my grotto home, and Odysseus takes the lead while I linger behind to admire his form.

He is divine, with broad muscled shoulders tapering to a trim waist and muscular legs that are crowned by a firm rounded ass.

Odysseus stops at the cave's mouth to cup his hand under the sweet water stream flowing between the green vines and purple blooms. Nearby, a white-throated cormorant spreads its great wings before taking flight. A falcon ruffles its feathers in seeming reply.

"Are you sure you want to leave this paradise?" My hand traces the line of his spine to his most sensitive areas, the cleft of his sweet ass. "If you stay with me I will make you immortal. Besides, your wife has aged seventeen years since last you saw her. I never age. What does Penelope have that I do not?" I draw light circles on his skin. "How can a mortal wife compare to a goddess?"

Odysseus's ass tightens and his erection parts the linen sheath around his hips. "You have no rival, my goddess. All of Penelope's graces pale beside yours." His hand skims over my breasts. "Your body, beauty, youth, and sensual appetites are beyond compare. Your nectar tastes like honey and your cunt is always as tight as a virgin's." His fingers travel downward, parting my silvery gown as two fingers dip into my warmth. "But I long to see my home."

I let out a groan of pleasure as my hips keep pace with his thrusts. "Bring me home now."

But he defies me and slows to a languid tempo.

"I have a proposition for you," he says, his cheek on mine. "I'll give you the greatest orgasm you've ever had if you help me build a boat strong enough to withstand rough waves and strong winds."

I press into his leisured thrusts, my loins heavy with wanting and my sex aching to be touched. "Since when do you think you can make a deal with a goddess?"

"Since I saw Hermes speeding away." Odysseus slips his fingers from my pink folds. "He ordered you to release me, didn't he?"

"Zeus wants you to go home." I push his hand back between my thighs.

Odysseus pulls his hand away. "Well then, I'd say that's another reason to help me build a seaworthy boat."

I lift my chin and see a newfound arrogance in Odysseus's eyes. Or perhaps I fool myself and this is the real Odysseus, the warrior king of Ithaca, the man known for his shrewd cunning. Is it possible his enchanted obedience all these years was false?

"I *will* help you build a boat," I say. "But if you fail to give me the greatest orgasm I'll conjure an unfavorable wind and hide the stars behind a blanket of clouds."

A slow smile spreads across Odysseus's sun-bronzed face. "It's a deal."

That evening he refuses to have sex.

"I demand it." I spread my thighs on the bed and flaunt my readiness.

Odysseus looks up from the table and taps the parchment in front of him. "I must design the boat, so be a helpful nymph and don't distract me."

I roll on my side and prop my head on my hand. "Do my ears deceive me or did you just give me an order?"

Odysseus crosses his arms. "If you want me to make you scream so loud they'll hear you on Mount Olympus then yes, it's an order."

"I'd rather you mount me now." It's hard to take my eyes off of his bulging biceps.

"Go to sleep, my divine Calypso." Odysseus blows me a kiss. "And *that's* an order."

I am strangely titillated by his assertive manner and marvel at the change in him, from compliant to calculating in a matter of hours.

"Fine!" I pretend annoyance, fluff the pillow, and turn away.

When dawn arises in glowing splendor, I don a gown of gossamer silver and make good on my promise to Odysseus.

"You'll need these." I hand him a two-bladed axe with a smooth olive wood haft and a polished adze.

Odysseus hefts both in his hands. "Where are the best trees?"

"Follow me." I lead my lover to the tip of the island where tall pine trees grow between alder and poplar. He goes from tree to tree, inspects each for strength, and assesses its seaworthy qualities. "Bring me an auger." Odysseus swings the axe at a large tree, his muscles rippling with the stroke. "Now!"

Again with the orders! "Later. I have other things to do." I turn around and saunter back down the path when a twig snaps behind me.

Odysseus captures me in his arms, one hand on my breast, the other between my legs. "Now," he whispers into my ear while rolling my nipple between his fingers.

"Ouch!" That's not how I like it. He knows this!

Odysseus pinches harder while his other hand parts the petals of my lust with a light touch. My pulse quickens, this rough and gentle mixture flooding my senses with lust. Harder! Softer! Pain mixes with pleasure but I don't want him to stop.

"Bring the auger immediately." Odysseus bites my earlobe. "I *command* you."

Odysseus releases me and I flee homeward, Odysseus's newfound dominance alarmingly seductive.

By the time I return with the auger, Odysseus has felled twenty trees. I sit on a tree trunk until the blue sky turns pink with dusk's glow. My admiring gaze never veers from his sweat-drenched body as he splits the trees into posts.

Odysseus puts down his tools and strides toward me. "I'll be done in a few days." He wipes his brow.

"So soon?" I smell his sweat, a delicious spice I inhale like a drug.

Odysseus nods, then lifts my chin with his forefinger. "I need more of your help."

"What do you want?"

He unties the linen from his hips. "Suck me."

"That's not part of the d—"

"It is now." Odysseus captures my head between his hands and guides me to him.

His command sends shivers of desire up my legs, and I submit by flicking my tongue over the head and sampling his saltiness.

Odysseus moans and buries his fingers in my hair. "Suck. It."

Instead, I nibble up and down the shaft, relishing this carnal ambrosia of man and sweat. His fingers knead my scalp as my tongue grazes his top ridge.

"Take all of me in your mouth," he says as my tongue swirls his length from bottom to top.

I flick off a droplet of nectar from his tip. "What do I get?" I look up at him and drop to my knees.

"The best orgasm you've ever had." Odysseus coils my hair in his fingers and tugs me forward.

"It better be." I swallow him whole and he groans. Next my mouth rides up and down his length, my tongue fluttering like a butterfly over his head while my fingers skim across the sensitive spot between his balls and ass.

"So good," he murmurs. His hand clutches my head and moves it back and forth. "So damn good. Are you wet? Do you want me to fuck you?"

I nod and speed the pace.

He's close, his legs tense with pleasure, his eyes glazed with lust. Odysseus lets out a deep moan and I move faster as he tenses again and again. But now I've had enough of being submissive—want to feel the length of him inside of me—and I pull away... I can't! My hair is wrapped too tightly around his fist.

Odysseus drops his chin and a curious smile spreads across his face. It is wicked and lustful, and for the first time I see the real Odysseus. He is powerful and aggressive and as arrogant as any god. And now it's obvious! He had been playing with me all these years, tricking me into believing I was the aggressor. All this time he had been waiting to reveal his true nature. He is no mere mortal. I suck the cock of a warrior who can snap my neck as easily as a dry twig. I stroke the balls of a king with brains as mighty as his brawn.

"Calypso," Odysseus murmurs and twists my hair, "beautiful divine nymph with no equal, your lips are paradise, your tongue my utopia."

The tighter Odysseus twists my hair, the wetter I

become. By Zeus, how I want him! Worse than ever! I take the full length of him in my mouth, press my mouth against him and draw slowly back. Twice more do I do this before I taste his cum in my mouth and hear him groan with release.

Odysseus twists my hair again, gives it a yank. "Lick off every drop."

I do as I'm ordered and hope he will pleasure me after I've completed my salty task. "My turn?"

Odysseus releases my hair, picks up his linen, and wraps it around his hips. "You didn't earn your pleasure yet, my goddess." He aims his thumb at the pile of timber behind him. "I still need your help building the boat."

I stand, and because he towers over me, lift my chin. "I never denied *you* this way."

"No?" Odysseus laughs, scoops me up, and throws me over his shoulder. "You have no idea what you've denied me all these years."

"If you fail to give me the greatest orgasm, I'll destroy your boat," I remind him from my upside down position.

Odysseus smacks my bottom and I flinch.

"You're such a naughty nymph." He smacks it again, then glides his hand over my ass, caressing the stinging skin.

I quiver with delight. The burn sets my lust on fire. How long can I endure this carnal torture?

After supper, Odysseus falls fast asleep, yet when I wake to dawn's pink radiance he is already gone. After packing a basket of his favorite foods, I hurry down the path through the forest.

Odysseus is a master shipbuilder. He's already drilled

through the planks and bolted them together with stout pins to form the hull. He has thoughtfully placed a tree stump on the ground for me to sit on; I pretend it is a gesture of kindness despite knowing it's nothing more than a way to keep a sharp eye on me.

"Come here." Odysseus beckons to me.

I rise from my tree-stump seat. "Do you need another tool?"

"The mast." Odysseus points to a thick pole lying across the hull. "Straddle it."

I throw my leg over it and Odysseus does the same behind me. With his taut stomach against me and his rigid cock pressed against the small of my back, he sets each hand on either side of my waist and rocks me back and forth.

"The mast must be secured through the coupling collar." His hands skim upward, his fingers fanned out over my supple breasts. "You'll provide the lubrication. Hold on."

I grip the mast as Odysseus continues rocking me forward while his fingers circle my nipples.

Blood rushes to my nether regions and my sex grows slippery with excitement.

"That's a good goddess." Odysseus nibbles the side of my neck.

I'm riding the mast faster and faster while Odysseus rolls and tugs at my nipples. The pole is slick, my clit engorged, and I need to—have to—come.

And then Odysseus's teeth sink into my shoulder and he shudders.

"What?" I reach behind and feel his sticky release on my ass.

Odysseus lifts my leg over the mast and pulls me off.

"No. No! I'm so close." If I can't have Odysseus, the mast will do!

His arms encircle me. "Not yet, sweet nymph."

"You are a wicked man."

"Not wicked enough." Odysseus orders me to sit near him the rest of the day, and when he catches my hand straying to my cunt to finish myself off, he binds my wrists behind my back until I promise to be obedient.

I toss and turn that night, dreams of Odysseus fucking me in wild ways leaving me more aroused than when I went to bed.

On the third day, Odysseus ties me to the mast.

"Sing to me." He loosens my robe and plants a kiss on each nipple.

Hoping my voice will entice him like a Siren song, I sing and sing until Odysseus drops to his knees and pushes my legs apart.

"Don't stop singing." He spreads my sex wide and flicks across it with his tongue.

Sweet Zeus, how can I sing when I want to moan? I arch my back, thrust my hips into his face, and lift my voice to the sky. Odysseus takes my clit in his mouth and sucks. My legs shake, my cunt throbbing for release, my song a long, melodious moan.

And then Odysseus pulls away.

"Damn you to Hades!" I shout as he walks away. "Mark my words, Odysseus, if you don't come back here right now I'll blow your boat to bits before it makes it to deep water!"

Odysseus pivots on his heel and strides back toward me.

"I give the orders now. Not you." He rams two fingers into my wetness.

I buck—so close to release—and he withdraws. "Keep singing," he says over his shoulder as he turns away.

All afternoon my songs are interrupted—any melody reduced to moans—whenever Odysseus buries his face in my sex. He teases me until my legs tremble and I plead for release. Each time he kneels before me, I struggle for control. But he knows my body too well. My pants and tremblings give me away, and he ends his torments before I climax.

Odysseus is merciless, sometimes coaxing one nipple to a hard point, other times gliding his fingers in and out of my sex. Back and forth he moves from goddess teasing—sucks and slurps and flicks—to boat building—fashioning a steering oar, driving willow strands between the planks, ballasting the boat with logs.

That night as I lie on the bed he stands over me and masturbates.

"How much do you want me?" His hand pumps up and down.

I reach out to touch. He smacks my hand away.

"Tomorrow, lover," he says and grunts his release onto my face.

On the fourth day, dawn spreads her rose-tipped fingers across the sky with a hue so glorious I shed a tear. The boat is almost finished. Today Odysseus must make good on his promise.

I complete the tasks he assigned last night. I collect all the skins for holding wine and water. I gather food as well, dried meat and fish, and fresh fruits and vegetables, enough to sustain him for his long voyage home.

The last task is bittersweet. I stack the folded fabric weaved by my own slender hands and carry it to the boat.

Odysseus unfolds one of the fabric lengths and stretches his arms wide. "Mmmm, this ought to make a good enough sail." He takes a knife and slices its length down the center.

"What are you doing?"

"Even though this fabric was woven by an immortal nymph I must test its strength." He dips it in a bucket of seawater, wrings it out, and then sits on the wide ledge at the bow. "Come here."

"Tying me up again? Has the great Odysseus already run out of ways to torture me?"

"Be a good nymph." Odysseus pats his thigh, his grin impish and his eyes dancing with mischief.

I obey. My body is his to command, to use, to tease.

Odysseus positions me over his lap. "You've been a naughty goddess for seven years." He tugs my silvery gown to my waist and smacks my ass with the wet cloth. "My lady needs disciplining."

"Ow!" I flinch as tingles of pleasure ripple through me. "I've changed my ways! I've done all you asked—showed you where the strongest trees grow, gave you an axe, and—"

Odysseus spanks me again. "Trifles!" He gently massages my ass. "I demand you do better than that." His hand smooths over my curves and into my wetness.

"How?" Four days of foreplay, of being denied, of staring at his flexing muscles glistening in the sun has left me as horny as a sex-starved satyr.

Odysseus snaps the cold wet cloth across my ass then follows it with warm caresses.

"What do you want from me?"

Odysseus doesn't answer. Instead he parts my thighs and blows his cool breath across my sex until I squirm and moan.

"Tell me, I beg of you."

"I'm sure you can think of something." He snaps the wet cloth again.

"I'll conjure a warm breeze from the island," I whimper with lust.

"Not enough." Odysseus slides his fingers over my slickness.

"I'll—"

He delivers two quick slaps.

"I'll make the night skies so clear the Great Bear and the Pleiades will be your guide."

Odysseus slips two fingers into my sex and his thumb loops around my swollen clit. "What else?"

"A following sea to speed you homeward." My legs shake, my clit throbs, and the sweet walls of my sex pulse to be fucked.

"That's more like it." Odysseus stands and I tumble to the deck.

I get on all fours, present my bare stinging ass like a gift.

Odysseus gets on his knees and wraps his hand around my waist. His cock glides over me. I wiggle my ass and push myself into him. I need him inside of me. Need to feel his hard thrusts.

"Please. I beg of you."

Odysseus slides his cock back and forth while one

hand skims up my stomach and pinches my nipple. "Who am I?"

"What?" I shift to and fro, attempt to angle my body so his cock slips in.

"Who am I?" Odysseus's voice is calm, commanding, controlled.

It's my fault. For all these years I have taught him to control his own pleasure to service mine. Now he uses this control to make me his slave.

"You're Odysseus." I jiggle my ass.

"Try again." Odysseus shifts away but his fingers continue pinching my nipple.

"You're my lover."

"Not good enough." The tip of his cock presses against my entrance for a second before pulling away.

"My king! You're my king!" I cry out.

"Yes." Odysseus enters slowly, my cunt hugging tight each glorious inch.

"Yes! My king, yes!" There's a reason I kept the man on my island for seven years. His length and girth are godlike. I buck, need it faster and harder.

"Patience, my nymph." Odysseus pulls out just as slowly, his cock rubbing against my aching clit.

"I've waited for days."

"And I've waited for years to fuck you like this." Odysseus thrusts back into me, pushing in agonizingly slowly, no matter how much I beg or grind into him.

He keeps me on the verge, the very precipice of release, until I writhe and quiver with a feverish frenzy.

"Fuck me!" I shout.

Odysseus increases his tempo the tiniest bit, raising his speed every few seconds, slowly at first, and then faster and faster and harder and harder. At last he fucks me as I like, gives me the thing I've wanted for years, but never could admit: to give in to him completely. Finally it comes—my body erupts with waves of rapture. I scream in ecstasy, grind myself deeper into him. Odysseus does not stop. His thrusts almost knock me off my knees. I peak again, spasms of joy surging through my ass and down my legs. I rest my cheek on the deck floor, my ass in the air like an offering.

Odysseus slaps my ass and I climax again.

"No more!" I whimper, my legs so weak from pleasure they wobble.

But Odysseus slaps and thrusts again and again, pain and pleasure releasing wave after wave of bliss. And then he thunders his orgasm.

My body collapses and Odysseus falls on top of me.

"Well?" He brushes my hair from my face and drops a kiss on my cheek.

My ass is stinging, my pussy bruised, and my nipples sore from his pinching.

"Best fuck ever," I say and close my weary eyes.

I wake up on the beach. The boat is in the water, Odysseus at the helm.

"Farewell, my goddess." He blows me a kiss.

I blow a different kind of kiss in return, one that creates a land breeze that pushes his vessel past the surf and into the sea.

"Farewell, my king, my love, my master." I stand on the rock shore watching Odysseus's boat get smaller and smaller until it is a speck on the horizon.

More of Odysseus's adventures and his long journey home can be found in the classic epic poems The Iliad *and* The Odyssey *by Homer. Want to read the G-rated version of Odysseus and Calypso? Check out Book V of* The Odyssey. *And no, I'm not telling you if Odysseus ever makes it home to Ithaca and his long-suffering but faithful wife Penelope.*

BY
SWORD TIP

Melanippe entered the counsel chambers, her long thick braids swinging in rhythm with her purposeful stride.

"What news, sister?" Queen Hippolyta, sitting with her mother, Otrera, looked up from the new double-sided axe they were admiring.

"The ship is indeed King Theseus's." Melanippe, dressed in wide embroidered pants and wool boots for horseback riding, removed her conical leather *kīdaris* from her head and handed it to an attendant. "I saw no soldiers on deck."

Queen Hippolyta set down the axe and leaned against her lion-skinned chair. "So it's a diplomatic mission." She rolled her eyes. "How boring."

Amazons were descendants of Ares, the god of war, their feisty natures eager for battle and conquest. Deemed the Killers of Men by those they defeated, the Amazons kowtowed to no man, not even the great hero Theseus.

"Theseus is clever," said Otrera, a stunning woman with waist-length silver hair as shiny as a blade. "I suspect this visit has another purpose."

Hippolyta raised her eyebrows. "What have you heard, Mother?"

Although Otrera had yielded her rule to her exceptional daughter years ago, her informants still stretched far and wide.

"He's looking for a wife." Otrera never minced words.

Hippolyta burst out laughing. "He looks in the wrong place."

Amazons did not marry. Ever. Neither did they take lovers, their fierce bloodline perpetuated by more efficient means.

"Do you want him greeted by warriors or a welcoming party?" asked Melanippe.

The shadow of indecision crossed Hippolyta's face. "Is Theseus worth meeting?"

Otrera shrugged. "Only if the stories about him are true. Otherwise, he's just another man with no control over his sword."

"Like the man who sired me?" Hippolyta's blue eyes glinted with amusement.

Otrera wrinkled her nose. "Such a distasteful act— fortunately it was very brief. A blink of an eye."

Hippolyta rose from the table and crossed the white marble chambers to the open door of the balcony overlooking the azure waters of the Black Sea, where Theseus's ship floated in the distance. "Tell me about Theseus." Evidence and intuition always guided her decisions.

"He killed the Minotaur and found his way out of the Labyrinth," Melanippe said. "Although Ariadne *did* help by telling him to unravel a ball of twine to find his way back out of the maze."

"What weapon did Theseus use to slay the beast?"

"He beat the Minotaur to death with his bare hands," said Otrera.

Hippolyta turned around. "Impressive. What else?"

"He convinced Hercules not to kill himself," said Melanippe.

Hippolyta wrinkled her nose. "Hercules is an arrogant brute who can't control his temper. Theseus's choice of friends leaves much to be desired." Hippolyta never let the world's opinion guide her own. She glanced at the sea again. Theseus's boat drifted in the midst of the sparkling water, as though the sun itself wished to illuminate his presence. "Tell me about Theseus's character. What sort of man is he?"

"He is loyal," said Otrera. "He stood by Hercules during his darkest hours and protected Oedipus's daughters after they fled Thebes. In fact, he took care of their unfortunate father until he died."

All three Amazons exchanged sympathetic looks. The tragedy—Oedipus gouging his eyes out after discovering he had married his own mother—was a powerful reminder to all rulers of the power of destiny.

"Loyal and compassionate. Rare traits for a man, let alone a king," said Melanippe.

"Both admirable traits," Hippolyta agreed. "Anything else?"

"He ended a hundred-year-old dictatorship, despite the elite's initial objection, to form a commonwealth," said Otrera. "Athens enjoys unprecedented prosperity now."

"A man of vision with charms enough to persuade poor and rich alike." Hippolyta tapped her finger on her lips in thought.

"I know *I* would like to meet him, " said Melanippe.

"Tell me about his weaknesses." Hippolyta's mind was not yet made up. "They might be so great that they overshadow his strengths."

"He seeks danger and thrills," said Otrera.

"That's more of a strength than a weakness." Hippolyta clasped her hands behind her back and strolled the length of the balcony and back.

Her sister and mother kept silent. They never interrupted Hippolyta while she weighed the pros and cons of a situation. After two trips across the balcony she stopped.

"The man intrigues me, even if he does think he'll find an Amazon willing to be his wife," said Hippolyta. "Send a hundred foot-soldiers in full battle gear to meet him."

"It will be done." Melanippe departed the chambers.

Hippolyta strode back into the chamber and pulled her axe from the weapons wall.

"What are you doing?" asked Otrera.

"I'm not going to sit here and wait for him." She took down her *pelta*, the light crescent-shaped shield. "I want to see Theseus's reaction when he is greeted by a hundred Amazon warriors dressed for death and dismemberment."

"Why do *you* need to be dressed for battle?"

"Because I'm joining my soldiers by hiding in plain sight."

Hippolyta stood among her warriors, each one dressed in pants, wide belt, tunic, and *kīdaris*. Some women carried a spear, others carried a bow and wore a quiver of arrows on their backs. Standing in the midst without her queenly regalia, Hippolyta observed Theseus's approach with a critical eye. She looked for signs of weakness, such as clumsiness and unease, but saw only the ramrod stance of confidence.

Wearing a laurel wreath and dressed in a straight-hemmed linen tunic, wide belt with *kibisis*, and sandals, Theseus stood tall and steady despite the small skiff's rocking in the waves as it approached shore. Though Hippolyta and her Amazons favored horses to ships, she was impressed by Theseus's sea legs.

Theseus leapt from the boat, landed solidly in foamy surf to his knees, then signaled the rowers to return to his ship. Hippolyta bit her lips, Theseus's athletic arrival prompting the smallest smile to escape.

Theseus splashed through the water and onto the beach. He was a tall man, burnished by the sun, with broad, well-developed shoulders, a narrow waist, and exceptionally muscular thighs and calves. His wavy brown hair was tied at the neck, several unruly strands blowing across his face.

"*Yassas*, hello!" Theseus smiled at the armed assemblage with the easy manner of one meeting a friend for a stroll in the garden.

Confidence was attractive, arrogance was not, and yet Hippolyta detected no excessive hubris in his demeanor. It was not until the wind subsided for a moment that Hippolyta got a good look at Theseus's face. She bit back another smile, delighted by his broad forehead, straight nose, square jaw, and full lips. Yet it was his eyes, blue as the Aegean and sparkling with adventure, that Hippolyta found most entrancing.

"Welcome, King Theseus." Orithyia, Hippolyta's general, stepped forward. "Your weapons." She motioned to two warriors.

"Of course." Theseus relinquished both his sword and the dagger from his *kibisis*. "The sword was my father's. I charge you with its safekeeping."

General Orithyia thrust out her chin. "The other as well."

"Ah, how careless of me." Theseus grinned, flashing his marble-white teeth, and removed the small knife strapped to his thigh beneath his tunic.

His genial demeanor amazed Hippolyta. Theseus appeared at ease, and even his voice, a deep, rich baritone, sounded smooth and sure.

"I am honored by this welcome. It speaks of your people's great strength."

People, not women. Hippolyta suppressed yet another smile. He was quite the unbiased diplomat, or else a shrewd liar.

"Follow me." General Orithyia walked away and the Amazon warriors fell in and flanked him on all sides.

Hippolyta, at his immediate right, could scarcely keep her eyes off of Theseus as they marched to the palace. He was a strapping man, taller than she, and with a presence so commanding she knew the stories about him must be true. Here was a man who might be worthy of her respect. Even more so because not once did he leer at the warriors' shapely buttocks swaying back and forth in front of him.

Hippolyta inhaled his scent, a blend of sea and air and male, that for some strange reason she found quite enticing. She snuck peeks at Theseus's hands. They were large and muscular, with thick fingers and clean, square-shaped nails. Hands that were more suitable for pummeling a Minotaur to death than writing treaties or caressing a lover. She imagined what such powerful hands might feel like on her body, then looked away, horrified by her lewd thoughts. Theseus was just a man! And men were...well, Amazons had no use for men.

When they entered the great chamber, the squadron moved into formation, rows of Amazons at attention in front of Hippolyta's lion-skin throne.

Theseus stood before the vacant throne while Hippolyta, standing with her squad, waited for him to grow impatient. He did not. In fact, Theseus never shifted his weight or clenched his fists.

The Amazons stood silent as statues, a show of military training that Hippolyta knew Theseus would appreciate. After a few noiseless minutes, Hippolyta issued a silent "at ease" and strode past Theseus to sit on her throne.

Theseus bent down on one knee and dropped his chin.

"Arise," said Hippolyta.

Theseus stood, his handsome face and confident stance indicating nothing less than utmost respect.

Hippolyta felt a strange heat creep into her cheeks. "To what do we owe the pleasure of your visit?"

"I had to meet the illustrious Queen Hippolyta." Theseus's bright blue eyes pierced her regal demeanor.

"You've met me. Now you may leave." Hippolyta shifted about. The man unsettled her, his gaze too penetrating for comfort.

Theseus rubbed his bearded chin. "I had hoped you

would be interested in discussing our common interests."

"What are those?" Hippolyta rested her hands on either side of the throne, her long fingers dangling over the arm in seeming disinterest.

"We are both bold leaders seeking to enrich the lives of our people, we are both skilled warriors who thirst for adventure and conquest, and we both have mutual acquaintances. Surely, a multitude of topics might warrant any number of discussions." Theseus touched his chest. "I, for one, would enjoy hearing your side of the whole Hercules girdle-stealing incident."

Hippolyta tilted her head. "Why?"

"Hercules is proud. And pride and truth are poor companions."

"Ah, so you are a seeker of truth."

"Truth, as you well know, comes in many guises."

"A philosopher king," Hippolyta teased, her dimpled smile taking Theseus by surprise. "I also seek truth." She leaned forward. "Join me for dinner and explain those adventures of yours that are beyond belief."

"I would be honored."

Their eyes locked, not as two rulers vying for dominance but as two people confessing their attraction.

Melanippe went to Theseus's side. "I'll show you to your chambers."

As Theseus was ushered from the great chamber, he looked over his shoulder to steal another glance at the Amazon queen. She was fierce and sexy. A heartbreaking combination.

Once the warriors departed, Hippolyta joined her mother on the balcony.

"Mate with him," said Otrera.

"Mother!" Hippolyta sat on the low stone wall.

"Don't tell me you didn't think about it. The man oozes sex, and he's far superior to any of the Gargareans we visit in the spring."

"He *is* well built." Hippolyta threw her legs over the wall and stared at the sea. Just thinking about the size of his muscular thighs caused a rare stirring.

"It's time you had a daughter," said Otrera after giving her daughter time to consider her suggestion.

Melanippe joined them on the balcony. "I locked Theseus in the room." She gave the key to Hippolyta. "Is dinner to be a formal affair?"

Formality meant braided hair and wearing heavy dresses from head to toe.

"No, informal attire." Hippolyta straddled the wall. "Let's see how the noble Theseus handles a roomful of breasts and legs."

All eyes were on Hippolyta as she walked to the table to join her dinner guests. Dressed in a gown made of layers of sheer fabric, she took Theseus's breath away. Her dark hair cascaded over her shoulders in soft waves, her head adorned with a slender circlet of tiny flowers. The robe-like dress offered peeks of her creamy cleavage with the slightest movement.

Theseus felt his cock swell and adjusted his tunic, much of his self-control lost when he caught sight of Hippolyta's pink areola.

"To new friends." Hippolyta raised her wine goblet.

"To new friends," replied the Amazons.

Hippolyta turned to Theseus and held his gaze

until his pupils dilated and his irises shone. Hippolyta warmed under his gaze. Eros's arrow had struck them. They both knew it. Desire coursed through their veins and heated their skin despite the cool night breeze blowing through the vaulted chamber windows.

"I hope you're hungry." Hippolyta plucked an olive from the plate and nibbled at it, her eyes admiring the curved bulk of his biceps.

"Ravenous." Theseus dropped his gaze to her bosom, which heaved beneath the gossamer layers.

She imagined his mouth on her breasts and her nipples hardened in response. No man had ever done that to her. The twice-yearly mating ritual with the Gargareans was always quick and perfunctory, devoid of seduction or caresses. Devoid of bodily pleasure but replete with the burden of procreation. Hippolyta did not think of siring a daughter when she looked at Theseus. She thought only of his body atop her, his cock inside, his tongue licking her breasts.

"Why are you here?" Hippolyta's voice was thick.

"I need a queen to help me rule Athens. I want you." Theseus set his hand over Hippolyta's.

His touch jolted her, flooding her senses with heat and desire. A warmth spread between her legs and Hippolyta felt the oddest sensation, a moist discomfort that made her want to be touched *there. Now.*

Theseus's fingers curled around her hand with the soft touch not of possession but of promise. Hippolyta stared at his hand over hers. The skin-to-skin contact felt too good to pull away from.

Hippolyta lifted her chin and met his blue eyes. "I am queen of the Amazons. I answer to no one. Your proposal offers no benefit. In fact, my acceptance reduces my present status as sole ruler. I will not be second to anyone." She squared her shoulders, her breasts thrust outward, but she did not remove her hand. "Amazons do not take orders from men."

Theseus's eyebrows knit together in dismay. "Athens is a city of great renown and Attica a land of plenty. They have no equal. Your power and authority will not be diminished in any way. In truth, it will increase."

"I have no interest in Athens." Hippolyta stretched out her arm. "These are my people. I will not forsake them. This is my land. I will not leave it to share power with another."

Theseus's eyes radiated with compassion. "You will not be persuaded?"

"No." She squirmed under his gaze, uncomfortable with his kindhearted understanding.

"Even if I have something you need?" One finger nudged between her fore and middle finger. He pulled it out. Pushed it back in. She spread those two fingers. Theseus's finger went in and out, using a light touch to rub the thin skin connecting both fingers. Hippolyta sucked in her breath, stunned and excited by the suggestive movement. Her fingers were her legs, the thin skin between, her clit.

"I . . ." She swallowed, her mouth suddenly wet, and looked down as Theseus began drawing figure eights around her knuckles.

"There must be something an Amazon queen lacks." His thumb pushed into the fleshy part at the base of her thumb.

The man was making love to her hand, each

persistent thrust obvious with meaning. Two could play this game. Hippolyta bent her thumb around his and squeezed. Theseus drew in a sharp breath, and thrust back and forth. Hippolyta squeezed tighter, her buttocks clenching to his rhythm. Sensation replaced logic; all Hippolyta felt was the thrill of his proposition and its promise of pleasure. She parted her legs and the scent of her lust wafted upwards to be inhaled by Theseus.

He leaned toward her. "Are you as hungry as I am?"

Hippolyta jerked her hand away, hid it behind her back as if it revealed her guilt, and rose from the table. "I bid you all good night," she said, addressing her guests. "Do not leave on my account. Stay and enjoy the feast."

Otrera, from her vantage point, had not seen their wanton play of fingers, but she suspected their mutual desire when Theseus stood and followed her daughter from the room.

"That will be all," said Hippolyta as two attendants opened the carved doors to her bedchamber. Theseus followed her inside.

Before the doors were shut, Theseus pushed Hippolyta against the wall. His hand slid beneath the sheer layers and moved up her thigh.

"I wanted to fuck you the moment I saw you." His lips brushed her neck while his hand moved around her hips to grab her ass.

"I—"

Theseus put his mouth over hers, his tongue eager and demanding. He tasted of wine, and as Hippolyta swirled her tongue around his, she ground her hips into his, felt his long hard cock against her silken cushion.

"You're more beautiful than any goddess." Theseus

kissed her again, his lips crushing hers, and then he hoisted her leg around his hip. "More beautiful than Aphrodite."

"And your physique must surely rival Zeus's." Hippolyta wrapped her arms around his neck as he lifted her other leg.

"Mmmm, your scent goes straight to my cock."

Hippolyta's back braced against the wall, her arms and legs around him, Theseus plunged his full length into her wetness. Hippolyta leaned her head against the wall and held tight as he rocked back and forth.

His angled entry rubbed against her clit, engorging it with a yearning that made her whimper and moan. Now she understood what drove men and lesser women mad with desire. This tension gathering in her sex was overpowering. Theseus kissed her again, his tongue moving to the rhythm of his cock. Hippolyta grabbed the hair at the back of his neck, arched her back, and willed her body to find release.

Her clit burst like a storm cloud, sheets of pleasure washing like rain over every inch of her body.

Hippolyta howled at the glory of it all, jerking her hips. "More! More!"

Her howl did him in, and Theseus lost all control. He wailed with sweet release as his cock pumped cum into the queen of the Amazons.

"Do it again!" Hippolyta pulled his hair.

Her feisty demand kept Theseus's cock rigid with desire. "As much as you want, my queen." He stepped away from the wall, and with her slick cunt still impaled on his cock, he walked across the room. He sat on the bed and leaned back. "Do as you wish."

Hippolyta, still flushed with pleasure, began riding him, her breasts bouncing in his face. Theseus pushed them together and ran his tongue back and forth over her taut nipples.

Quivers of excitement rushed through her body, her mind fixed on one glorious destination. Theseus sucked her nipple until it was as hard and shiny as the tip of a sword. Each tug swelled her clit and added girth to Theseus's cock.

Hippolyta lifted her ass and slammed into him. They grunted in unison, neither in control of the mounting tension that united their bodies into a single pulsing entity.

"Ooooooh!" Hippolyta rocked back and forth and ground her sex into him, waves of release crashing over her like the surf.

Her orgasm sent Theseus into a paroxysm of joy, his cock once again filling her sex with his cum. Hippolyta collapsed on his chest, her legs trembling, her pussy still quivering. Settling for the twice-yearly mating ritual with the brutish Gargareans would be impossible now that she had known ecstasy.

"We're not done." Theseus rolled her away and onto her back. He lifted her legs into the air and gazed at her pussy, which glistened with his salt and her honey, then lowered his head and sucked her clit.

Hippolyta clutched the covers, her ass wiggling and clenching as the tension increased. Theseus pushed one finger deep into her, found the sensitive spot at the back. She grabbed his head and moaned, felt herself gush, heard Theseus slurp it up.

Theseus's head lifted, his mouth wet, his beard coated with love's nectar. "More?"

"Do it again."

"Get on your knees."

Hippolyta rolled onto her stomach and got on her hands and knees, her buttocks raised in anticipation, the logical queen replaced by a nymph with a voracious appetite.

"What—" Hippolyta looked over her shoulder and saw that Theseus was running his tongue over the smooth curves of her ass, his finger tracing the soft flesh around her anus. A new sensation rocketed through her, unleashing a primal urge so insistent she could only gasp.

"Theseus . . ." she whimpered.

The king of Thebes rammed his cock into her and this time Hippolyta screamed at the force of the prolonged rapture. Theseus hammered into her until he growled his own release.

They collapsed on the bed in exhaustion, but Hippolyta's eyes were wide open. She had been utterly violated. Completely satisfied. No man had ever done that. No man would *ever* be able to compete with his stamina, strength, and prowess. He had ruined everything!

"Theseus . . ." she whispered. She had to tell him to leave before her resolve left her.

"Mmmm." Theseus gathered her in his arms, buried his face in the nape of her neck, and fell into an exhausted sleep.

It was past midnight when they both woke and gazed at each other in the blue moonlight illuminating the bedchamber.

"Ready for more?" Theseus set Hippolyta's hand on his cock, solid and long and ready.

"You're insatiable." She was amazed. The man was a sex god.

Theseus kissed her cheek. "I'll take that as a yes."

Hippolyta moved her hand up and down his cock as he rumbled with pleasure.

He stayed her hand. "Have I persuaded you to be my wife yet?"

Hippolyta rolled on her side, let her hand trail over the ridges of his muscled stomach to his chest. "You have an exceptionally persuasive appendage but my life is not my own. I have a responsibility to my people. An empire to build and battles to win. They would be horrified if I left for . . ."

"A man?" Theseus cupped the side of her face.

"It would be a dreadful insult to our values and way of life." Hippolyta rose from the bed and stood before the open balcony doors. "I can never be Thebes's queen and I cannot be your wife." She breathed in the scent of the night-blooming jasmine that coiled around the balcony.

Theseus joined her at the doorway and wrapped warm arms around her. "Would you leave for love?" He kissed the side of her neck.

Hippolyta shivered, not from the cool night breeze but from desire. "You confuse fucking with love."

"I confuse nothing." Theseus pressed his hard cock into her back. "I loved you the moment I saw you standing with your warriors on the beach."

"How did you know it was me?"

"You outshone all the others." Theseus sprinkled

kisses on her bare shoulder. "But it was while you walked next to me that I became intoxicated by your scent."

"I don't wear perfume."

Theseus slid his hand between her thighs. "*This* drew me like a bee to a flower. I thought of nothing else but my face between your legs." He glided his fingers into her smooth folds. "Eros shot his arrow into us both, Hippolyta. Admit it, we can't get enough of each other. Our bodies already know what your mind— because mine is already convinced—refuses to believe. When we are joined we are completely blissful." His finger snugged into her wetness. "You think too much, Hippolyta, but while this excellent trait makes you a great ruler, it prevents you from seeing the obvious. Logic should never override instinct."

"Yes, but neither should lust prevail over duty."

Theseus's left hand cupped her breast, his thumb rubbing across her nipple. "Your ass is grinding into me and your nipples lengthen to points. Listen to your body."

"No, we can only have this." Hippolyta reached her hand around and grabbed his stiff cock.

"I love you," Theseus breathed into her ear as his finger stroked her clit.

"Amazons love war." She melted into him as the pleasure gathered at her nexus.

"I want to fuck you forever." Theseus scooped her into his arms, crossed the room, and laid her on the bed.

Hippolyta spread her long legs and beckoned him with a curled finger.

Theseus chuckled. "Vying for Aphrodite's job are you?" He turned away and went to the small desk in the corner of the room. "I was wondering where it was." He picked up his sword, its finely crafted hilt and razor-sharp blade commissioned by his father, Aegeus.

"It's a beautiful weapon," said Hippolyta from the bed.

"It serves me well." Theseus spun it over his head, twirling and slashing the air to Hippolyta's amusement.

"I prefer tricks with your *other* sword." Her gaze dropped to his cock.

Theseus picked up her discarded gown from the marble floor and dangled it between his fingers. "Do you like games?" He sliced its length three times with the sword.

"War games." Hippolyta could not imagine what kind of game involved shredding her dress.

"Sex games are more fun." Theseus scooped up the torn dress and sat on the edge of the bed. "Your hands."

Hippolyta laughed and held them out as Theseus bound her wrists together. "Not much of a game."

Theseus flicked his tongue across her nipples. "Not done yet." He tied her ankles together.

Hippolyta wiggled. "I don't like being trussed up like this."

Theseus beamed from ear to ear, his blue eyes twinkling with mischief. "You will." He spread wide her downy cushion and flicked his tongue across with a teasing lightness.

Wanting more, Hippolyta tilted her pelvis toward him but Theseus lifted his head and grinned.

"Be patient, lover." He fondled each breast, then licked and sucked until each nipple was as stiff as the tip of his sword.

Hippolyta moaned and squirmed as he moved from breasts to clit and back again. His lovemaking made her forget she was a queen, made her forget the problems and responsibilities of leadership. It did, however, make her remember nature's primal urges.

"I love you," she mouthed soundlessly as Theseus kissed her navel.

Theseus watched her lips speak the words he had waited for. "This is the best part." He jammed a wad of cloth into her mouth, securing it with another looped around her head.

Hippolyta struggled, her eyes wide with panic.

"Trust me, it's better this way. You don't have to agonize over a decision or disappoint the Amazons." Theseus wound a sheet around her nakedness.

Tears sprung from Hippolyta's eyes. How long had it been since she cried? She couldn't remember. And why was she crying? Were they tears of joy? Of relief? Of sorrow?

After donning his tunic and strapping on his weapons, Theseus wiped away her tears and kissed each eyelid. "Give me a sign and our game is over."

Hippolyta remained still, her unblinking eyes staring into his. Now was the time to make a decision and she couldn't. Didn't even want to.

Theseus nodded, then scooped her up and threw her over his broad shoulders. He leapt over the balcony and landed nimbly on the ground below. He patted Hippolyta's ass, then stood still, ears and eyes in search of sentries. Finding no sign of them, he took off running through the grove.

Hippolyta had the agility to twist away from him.

She had the strength to thrust her knees into his chest. She didn't. She let Theseus kidnap her. It saved her from making an impossible decision, from having to choose between shared love and solitary leadership.

Theseus understood her dilemma just as he sensed her deepest desires. Hippolyta found comfort in this. Having the love of the greatest hero the world had ever known brought her immense satisfaction. Theseus had no equal. He was strength and intellect and compassion and daring. And sensual pleasure.

In the middle of a copse of trees at the edge of the beach, Theseus stopped and drew the sheet down over her face. "I don't want my men knowing who I've kidnapped until we are well under way."

Hippolyta nodded.

Theseus raced across the moonlit beach and splashed into the water. "Be quick about it," he told the rowers as he set Hippolyta gently down in the skiff.

Hippolyta grunted with surprise. This had been his plan all along!

"Have who you came for, King Theseus?" asked a rower.

"Even better. I kidnapped the moon and stars and sky. I kidnapped my everything."

Beneath the sheet, the last traces of Hippolyta's uncertainty melted from this declaration of love.

Once on the ship, Theseus ordered the crew to make way for home, then with Hippolyta over his shoulder he traipsed across the deck and into his cabin.

Theseus pulled the sheet from her face, untied the fabric, and pulled the gag from her mouth.

"You had this planned all along," said Hippolyta.

"Not a plan. Preparation. I had high hopes." Theseus unwound the sheet from her body.

"Is it too late to scream?" she lifted her wrists as he unknotted the silky restraint.

"You'll be screaming in a moment, I promise." Theseus freed her ankles.

Hippolyta lay back on the bed. "Finish what you started."

Theseus stripped off his clothing. "Finish? This is the beginning, my queen." He lifted her legs in the air and sunk into her misty heat. He caressed her breasts and tugged on her nipples until she writhed and moaned. He felt her pleasure mount and surge like the waves beneath them, and knew she was close.

He pulled out. "Sit on my cock."

Hippolyta sat on him.

"Like this." Theseus draped her legs over his shoulders.

Hippolyta wrapped her arms around his neck and cried out as his full length penetrated deep inside her. Theseus cupped her ass, his fingertips stroking the skin until it felt like a thousand butterflies fluttered against her loins. Their tongues battled, pushing, twirling, tasting, and sucking. Hippolyta urged him faster with her hips, but Theseus slowed down to prolong their ascent. They were one heartbeat, one purpose, one need now. Their lips separated so that they could watch the other's joy. Their rapture came together, two sharing one long cry of release.

They remained in this position, until Theseus's cock no longer jerked and spasmed, and until Hippolyta felt cum roll down her ass.

"How is it possible that I am both utterly satisfied and yet want more?" Hippolyta said.

"Because it is love."

There are different versions of this story. One has Theseus kidnapping Hippolyta; the other has her going willingly. A Shakespeare fan, I took inspiration from the first innuendo-laden scene of A Midsummer Night's Dream *when Theseus says,* "Hippolyta, I wooed thee with my sword and won thy love doing thee injuries." *Yowza! Want to read more about Theseus? Check out stories by Ovid, Plutarch, Apollodorus, and plays by Sophocles and Euripides.*

UNDER THE ARJUNA TREE

This isn't going to end well, but what can I do? I have no choice; I must obey Indra, the King of Heaven. I am an apsara, a Daughter of Joy, a celestial maiden, and a nymph of the air, forever fresh-faced and lithe, my dancing beyond compare, my seduction skills irresistible.

"Why me? There are many of us to choose from." Dressed in a towering, elegant floral-silk headdress of intricate gold, I am on my knees before him in the heavenly garden blooming with fragrant flowers.

Indra reclines on a silk pillow under a wide-leafed arjuna tree. "Menaka, you are the most beautiful apsara of all."

It is true, I am, and my face flushes with pride.

"You are the only one capable of seducing this particular man."

"Yes, Indra." I bow my head though I tremble with fear. It's no mere mortal man Indra commands me to seduce, but a powerful sage. I squeeze my eyes shut for a moment to gather my courage, and when I open them

I find Indra sitting atop a white elephant adorned with a golden collar and tasseled anklets.

"Hurry. There is no time to waste," Indra says as the majestic beast lumbers away.

I bring my hands together in *namaste* and then ride home on the next warm breeze. Back in my chambers, I bathe in sweet water, wash my hair, and prepare myself to destroy a great sage.

I am brushing my black hair to a glossy sheen when Saha, another apsara, sashays into the room. Her hips are swaying to the tragic love song she sings.

Saha takes my brush. "Who is the sage Indra wants you to seduce?"

"Vishvamitra." My eyes are shiny with tears.

Saha inhales her surprise through her teeth. "No wonder you look worried, I hear he seeks to become a *brahmarishi.*"

Seducing a man on the spiritual path to becoming a member of the highest level of seers is fraught with danger.

"It's true," I say. "Vishvamitra's spiritual strength has grown so great that Indra fears the sage will try to seize his throne."

Saha rolls her eyes. "Indra worries too much. Every time a sage completes an intricate ritual or performs a miracle, Indra believes his supremacy is in jeopardy." She drips a few drops of oil onto her hands and runs her fingers through my tresses. "Do you want me to put on your jewelry?"

My gaze travels to the tight silk dress on the bed and to the towering gold five-pointed headdress standing on the chest. "Too obvious." The gold-beaded collar, glittering bangles, and gleaming anklets are too extrava-gant for a sage like Vishvamitra. "He will take one look at me, see through my tricks, and curse me—turn me into stone." I shake my head. "No, gold and gems hold no enticement for a man with the power to curse King Harishchandra by turning him into a crane."

"Mmmm…" Saha stuck the fine-pointed brush into the kohl pot. "Then how do you plan on seducing him?"

"I will dance—it's what I do best. He must not know I am an apsara." I look up at the ceiling as Saha draws a black line across my lower eyelid.

"That's not possible, Menaka." Saha lines the upper lids. "Our beauty is far greater than mortal women. And your beauty surpasses our own! You cannot hide your beauty. Not unless you're planning on covering yourself from head to toe in a blanket."

It's true. My eyes are larger, my lips plumper and rosier, my breasts large and firm, my waist narrower and my hips wider than all the other apsaras. Even my hair is thicker and glossier, its length falling past my buttocks.

"I don't intend to hide my beauty, but I can make it less obvious and more pure." I point to the silk, gold, and jewels we adorn ourselves with.

Saha chews on her lips. "Is looking plain really necessary? I mean, think of all the sages whose penance we have broken. These gurus are all the same. We jiggle our breasts and shake our hips, and their piety disap-pears." She twirls around, her arms outstretched.

"Almost as quick as their cock appears." I spin in unison with her.

We stop, posed in the classical posture with bent

arms and legs. I laugh, my fear diminishing with her positive attitude, her encouraging words calling to mind all of our previous seductions.

"The last guru I seduced was weak, foul smelling, and ugly." Saha steps back to admire her artistry with rouge and kohl.

"I remember. You shook your breasts in front of his face and his *siddhasana* pose became Stroking Cock pose. Little good *that* pose did to bring about celibacy."

"A few twirls and one little leap was all it took before his hand dripped with ten years' worth of cum." Saha laughs.

"I like seducing the ugly ones best. They succumb to our charms with ease," I say, feeling more confident by the minute. "They are always the most arrogant, somehow believing they can achieve higher spiritual powers because they were not blessed with handsome features. As if having one blessing means you cannot have the other."

"Let's hope Vishvamitra is ugly," says Saha.

"He must be," I say. "Why else would a king who has everything—hundreds of concubines and stores of wealth—give it all up to be a *rishi*?" I select a midriff-baring *choli* and shimmering silk sari the color of coconut milk. Next I gather my hair at the nape of my neck and my tresses cascade down my back in thick waves.

"You will be back before sunset." Saha finishes weaving flowers into my hair. "And then you will tell us how quickly Vishvamitra forgot his penance for sexual pleasure."

I hope so. Whether Vishvamitra is ugly or handsome, the sage is known for his wisdom, self-control, and spiritual power—power so great Indra wants to destroy years of penance and abstinence.

Will Vishvamitra see through my tricks? Will this sari lessen my beauty and minimize the curves that drive both gods and men wild with desire? How angry will Indra be if I fail?

I smooth my sari and take a deep breath.

"Watch out for demons," says Saha, waving good-bye as I depart.

"I will," I promise, and I ride a wispy silver cloud to earth.

The air is sultry as I travel the shaded path where tiny lizards scuttle into the thick green flora, a painted grasshopper jumps out of my way, and two dragonflies zip past me. Yet, the beauty of the earth's smallest creatures is not my focus. Demons lurking behind a banyan tree or hiding between the great boughs of a peepal tree are. Demons love nothing better than kidnapping a celestial maiden. Several years ago, my friend Urvashi had a traumatic encounter with demons that resulted in serious consequences. She had been enjoying an early morning walk when two demons swooped down with claws outstretched. Urvashi tried fending off their attacks, screaming all the while. Luckily, King Pururavas, hunting nearby, heard her screams and rushed to her aid. The demons fled but Urvashi's ordeal was not over. Captivated by her beauty, King Pururavas pleaded with Urvashi to be his lover. Urvashi, feeling indebted to him, agreed on one condition: she never saw him naked. He must content himself to fuck her in the dark, under blankets, or concealing his chubby stomach with a *kurta*. The arrangement worked for a while, but then we tricked King Pururavas into revealing his nakedness to get Urvashi back.

Fortunately, neither demons, nor gods, nor man delay my trip. I reach Vishvamitra's favorite meditation spot.

The place is without beauty. The trees are scraggly, their leaves lacking vibrancy. Faded flowers droop in the heat. The birds sing off-key. Even the river is sluggish and murky.

From my hiding spot behind a tree I watch Vishvamitra meditating under an arjuna tree—or rather I see his back, which is a deep copper color and surprisingly muscular for a guru. Vishvamitra, in the lotus pose, wears a topknot, the rest of his long ebony hair flowing past his shoulder blades. He is dressed in only a *dhoti*, a loose-fitting white cloth worn between his legs and secured around the waist. Needing a better look at this impressive sage, I move, quiet as a breeze, to a closer tree.

Though I see only Vishvamitra in profile, a puff of excitement flutters my heart. He is very handsome—not old at all—with the chiseled face of masculinity, determination, and wisdom. His beard is thick and groomed, and he wears a single strand of prayer beads around his neck. He has a lean, muscular build, all sinewy limbs and perfect posture.

Handsome and spiritual! No wonder Indra fears him.

I exhale my enchantment through pursed lips. The sky becomes bluer, the sun glows with radiance, the river gurgles, its water now a sparkling azure.

Vishvamitra remains motionless, the change in surroundings either unobserved or ignored.

I step into his field of vision. One exhalation later and the flowers stand straighter, their blooms saturated with color. Each tree I walk past is infused with vitality, the boughs thickening, the leaves lush and verdant. The birds obey my soft hum and sing a melodic song. The grass, responding to my approaching footsteps, softens and lengthens. Now Vishvamitra sits on a verdant carpet. Two peacocks in iridescent display walk beside me. I wait for him to notice.

Vishvamitra blinks. Blinks again. His body remains still. Perhaps he thinks I am a beautiful hallucination.

I stretch my arms toward him, spread them wide, then raise them over my head. I sashay toward him, my body undulating to a silent rhythmic melody in my mind.

Vishvamitra squeezes his eyes shut.

I smile. This tactic *never* works. Closing your eyes does not remove the memory of our loveliness; it only enhances our curvaceous beauty. I circle around him in a slow dance. He feels my presence, senses my movements in the air's disturbance. I circle again, see the creases of eyes determined to stay closed. Another good sign.

After circling the third time, I stand in front of him and wait patiently for curiosity to get the better of him. I do not wait long. Vishvamitra slowly opens one eye. Except for the involuntary contraction of his sizable pectoral muscles, he remains motionless.

"Are you thirsty?" I offer a shy smile.

His eye shuts, and all signs of his previous meditative peacefulness vanish. The muscles in Vishvamitra's face tense with concentration. It's a good sign. He is weakening.

"It will be an honor to get water for the great sage Vishvamitra." I turn away and stroll toward the river, my rounded hips swaying, my small feet delicately stepping.

Vishvamitra watches. I feel his wide-open eyes upon me. With each step forward, my walk becomes more dance-like, my footwork more intricate, my arm movements more elaborate. Unencumbered by the tall formal gold headdress I usually wear, I am able to slowly bend backward, my arms slithering skyward as I straighten up.

I do not pause at the riverbank, but step into the cool clear water. Ankles, knees, hips, waist, breasts, shoulders, and head sink into the azure.

Vishvamitra will be leaning over, anxious, his eyes trained on the spot where I submerged. I stay under until I sense he has broken his meditative pose, is on his knees, perhaps contemplating how to save me.

I rise from the river holding a banana leaf formed into a cone. My wet silk sari clings to every curve, the milky-colored fabric transparent against my skin. Partial nudity is *always* more tantalizing.

Vishvamitra is standing, his gaze fixed on my unhurried approach. I dance slowly, not a drop of water spilling from the banana-leaf cup.

"Cool water." I offer the banana leaf with both hands.

"Thank you." Vishvamitra accepts my humble offering, his hand brushing against mine.

An odd feeling courses through me, a hot-cold sizzle that steals my breath. We stare into each other's eyes, and I am struck by the intensity of his attentions. He does not gawk at my bosom, nor do his eyes travel the length of my body and settle on the dark thatch of hair below. Rather, he looks into me, as though finding the divine within. All tenseness washes from his face, and his eyes beam with such pure goodness my own heart blooms with love.

How can this be? Heat rises in my cheeks when I realize I do not fear this powerful sage, I love him.

Vishvamitra lifts the banana-leaf cup to his lips and drinks.

I no longer want to dance because of Indra's commands. I want to dance to please Vishvamitra. The *kathak* is an elegant dance, a story told with my arms and body, my hands and fingers speaking with *mudras*, symbolic gestures. Vishvamitra is enthralled, his face beaming with pleasure. I spin about, faster and faster, his delight my own.

"Who are you?" he asks when my dancing story is done.

"I am Menaka."

"Your name is a song to my ears." His eyes rove over my curves. "Where are you from?"

"Indra's heavenly court." It's the truth, just not the whole truth.

Vishvamitra nods as though a visitation by a heavenly immortal is ordinary. "Why are you here, Menaka?"

I cannot lie. Nor can I tell the *entire* truth. The truth changed. It changed the moment we looked into each other's eyes and fell in love. "Your spiritual strength is the talk of the heavens. I had to see for myself." I inhale his maleness and flush with pleasure. "But I must make a confession."

Vishvamitra runs his eyes over my form and his breath grows labored. "I cannot imagine what such a divine woman as yourself needs to confess."

I lay his warm hand over my breast. "Do you feel my heart beating?"

"Yes." His voice is thick and his eyes dilate with desire.

I push his hand harder, feel his fingertips curve around the swell of my breast, hear his yearning exhalation.

"Menaka . . ." He sighs in surrender.

"It's as though the gods have conspired against both of us." I drop his hand and look away. "You are a great sage. This is wrong." I should be seducing him, not in love with him.

Vishvamitra cups my cheek, turning me toward him. "Love between two people is never wrong."

I close my hands in *namaste* and drop my eyes. Vishvamitra lowers his head and flicks his tongue across my fingertips.

"Oh!" I gasp, surprised and delighted.

Vishvamitra sucks gently on each pair of my *namaste* fingers, and his teeth lightly scrape over the skin. I am aquiver with desire, the warmth and wetness of his mouth flooding my feminine gate with heat.

When his mouth lifts from my littlest fingers, it is my turn. I take his hands, bring them together, and wrap my lips around each paired digit, sliding up and down their length. I suck each pair like I would his cock, imagine my tongue dancing over its girth. Vishvamitra imagines the same because his deep sighs sound like a prolonged *om*, the sacred sound of meditation.

"Menaka." He traces the curves of my lips, stares into my eyes.

"Vishvamitra." I cannot tear my gaze away from him.

We trace our lips five times—each loop causes our lips to part wider, each loop moves our heads closer.

Our lips touch but we do not kiss. Instead, we inhale the other's breath. Ten breaths we take before Vishvamitra slides his tongue inside. I meet it and we hold this tongue-touching position for longer than I can bear. My gate is as humid as a summer's day and swollen with desire. His cock presses into my stomach. His heat matches my own.

Vishvamitra is an educated man. As king he learned the art of lovemaking from the best courtesans, studied the art of Kama Sutra, and practiced Tantric intercourse. He uses this experience now to destroy the celestial maiden within me. His sexual prowess reduces me to a woman quivering with lust, impatient to feel the thrust of his cock.

His tongue circles around mine. I circle his. Our tongues entwined, Vishvamitra spreads his fingers over my neck and creeps downward until both hands rest on my breasts.

I push them forward like a gift, and then trail my fingers over his jaw and beard and downward to his well-defined pectorals. We breathe in unison, both our nipples hardening into stiff buds.

"Be patient awhile, Menaka," he says, sensing my eagerness. "Let us prolong the pleasure of our passion."

Years of penance trained Vishvamitra in the art of self-control. I never had any such training. I want his cock now!

Vishvamitra bends his head and blows through the wet fabric covering my breasts.

"Suck them," I plead and tug the *sari's* length from my shoulder.

"Not yet." His hand curls around the back of my neck and guides me to his dark brown nipples.

I purse my lips and blow cool air over one. Next, I set my mouth over it and exhale warm breath.

"Oh, Menaka." He moans and guides me to his other nipple.

I move back and forth, feel his contracting abdominal muscles, hear his pleasure growl.

I take a nip at his nipple. "You test my fortitude." He backs away, his breath heavy, then sits down and pats the grass beside him. "Lie down."

When I do he bends over me, his mouth sliding down my silk-encased belly while I pant and arch my back with wanting.

He pauses at the edge of my black curls, raises his grinning face, and lies beside me. I roll over, sprinkle kisses on copper skin, count the muscles of his concave stomach with my tongue, and lick his belly button. His *dhoti* is peaked like a tent and I want to tear it off and marvel at his cock.

Just as I grasp the corner of the *dhoti*, Vishvamitra changes position and sets a soft kiss on my ankle. The touch of his lips on my bare skin is unbearable, its exquisiteness curling my toes.

"Breathe with me," says Vishvamitra.

I match my breaths to his slow ones and wiggle as his tongue travels past my clothed shin, over my knee, and up my thigh.

"Take off my *sari*," I whisper.

"Soon." Vishvamitra places his warm mouth on my curly pillow.

I grab his topknot, push his head down. His breath seeps into every fold and crevice and I moan, my hips rocking under him.

"I cannot wait anymore!" I say.

"You must." He unwraps me, removes the silk from my body and allows me to remove his *dhoti*.

His cock is divine, thick and long and ready. I reach out for it. My hand wraps around his rigid smoothness and very slowly slides toward the base. Vishvamitra sighs even as his body tenses. With my other hand I cup his hard tight balls, brush my thumb over the tender skin. His buttocks tighten and he looks at me through glazed adoring eyes.

"I will honor the greatest sage of all." I cover the head of his cock with my mouth and he draws me forward, my hair laced through his fingers. I slow my movement despite his tensing legs and swallow his full length.

A low rumble emits from his throat, and his fingers pull my hair. He tastes of sacred energy and earthly procreation. I draw my lips back and taste the salty drops loosened from too many years of abstinence.

"The best meditation is mutual." He rolls me onto his stomach.

His cock is in my mouth, the gate of my heaven on his face. It is the congress of crow position, in its prone form.

Vishvamitra's lips surround my clit.

I stop at the ridge, only the head of his cock in my mouth.

I want to slide his cock down my throat, lick his shaft, and pump my fist until the sacred saltiness of life fills my mouth.

I don't.

We are still and let our arousal build like gathering storm clouds. Tantric sex takes control and concentration. It promises divine orgasms for those allowing arousal to take a long, meandering path. Apsaras are creatures of dance and movement. This stillness is not natural for me. It's almost unbearable. I tilt my pelvis to urge him on, but he lowers my hips with a firm hand. Every inch of skin is alive with anticipation, and yet the surge of pleasure flows to only one place.

My pleasure garden is swollen, and my pelvic muscles contract to the rhythm of our breathing. I want Vishvamitra to lick my clit, to lap at my glossy petals, to hurl me to heaven with his mouth. But then it will be over too quickly. And I don't want this sparkling feeling to end!

Tantric sex is like giving a thirsty man a drop of water at a time. Each drop tastes like honey, extra sweet and satisfying as it glides down your throat. Water guzzled never tastes as good.

The head of his cock grows bigger and harder in my mouth. I feel his arousal mount in his tensing thighs and thumping heart.

Just when I begin climbing pleasure's apex, Vishvamitra swirls his tongue around my clit. Once. Only once!

"Noooo!" I cry pulling away from his cock.

"Yes." He holds me around the waist and in one fluid movement of strength and agility sits up and sets me in his lap, my legs around his hips, his cock resting against my black ringlets.

We gaze into each other's eyes, the light of connectedness—body, spirit, and energy—glimmering with the primeval divinity found in all of us.

Vishvamitra spreads his hands under my ass and lifts, positioning me over his cock, our eyes locked and focused.

"We choose. We worship. We transcend." One inch of his cock slides into my wetness. "We love."

My moan is his, a prolonged testimony of our devotion to nature's highest joy. Vishvamitra pushes in another inch, my sacred gate tight around him. We breathe twenty long breaths together. He pushes in another inch. My velvet garden is throbbing, our unified chant now a moaning mantra. Another inch, twenty more breaths, *maithuna,* the ritual of our union awakening every sense. Inch by inch, until ten glorious inches pack my sex.

He is still, as am I, the waves we ride on this ocean of bliss swelling inside us. My sweet walls contract to the tempo of his breaths, and Vishvamitra growls his response. All sensation, all desire is crystalized into a single place. We are both teacher and student, we are both earth and sky, both primitive and divine. We are raw energy awaiting release.

I feel it in him before I am aware of my own final ascent, the point when flesh supersedes the mind, and flesh has one single purpose.

Nirvana erupts, engulfs us like a tidal wave, and we convulse with paroxysms of ecstasy. Together we sing our bliss to the heavens, the orgasm the sacred song of life and love.

Vishvamitra shifts me about, my cunt dripping with his cum, and repositions me so I face his feet. I rock into him as he rolls my nipples between his fingers, pinching and tugging them until I come again. And again.

He spreads his thighs and I lean forward, my ass near his face, and I cup his balls, still tight and full with cum. His hands slide over my body and draw circles around my anus.

"Yes. Yes." I say as he soaks his finger with my nectar and slides into my anus, while his other hand rubs my aching clit. I explode in his hand, squirt nectar into his palm, and scream to the heavens.

I am still climaxing when Vishvamitra lifts my hips, guides me to the side, and slowly shifts my leg over his head. Face to face once again, he spreads my thighs and sinks into me. This time his thrusts are rough and fast.

He shouts his orgasm—thrusts until my legs are slick with the liquor of our lusts.

When our breathing finally slows, Vishvamitra takes me in his arms as though I am a child and sprinkles my face with kisses.

"I found true joy, with you, Menaka," he says. "I beg you to be my wife."

"What about your penance? Your desire to be a great *rishi*?"

"I was a fool. Heaven is fucking the one you love. No meditation ever brought this kind of nirvana. No mediation ever made me realize that bringing my lover to nirvana was infinitely more important than my own pleasure."

Under the shade of the arjuna tree, I clutch his beard in my fist and tug him forward. "Take me to heaven again."

The story of Vishvamitra and Menaka is found in the Sanskrit epic Mahabharata. *Except for his ten-year marriage to Menaka—a lapse in his quest to attain the highest level of sage—Vishvamitra lived a long and spiritual life, the stories of his miracles and wisdom told in many Hindu legends.*

THE
WALK

I heard Mother's voice rise over the clinking of the Dongba Aspiration wind-bell outside.

"Snow Blossom!"

I rushed outside to find Mother sitting in a red lacquer chair contemplating the small pebble mosaic I designed in the middle of the courtyard.

"Yes, Mother." I wiped my hands on my apron, the crisp air of autumn morning cool on my cheek. "Would you like tea to warm your bones?"

"I do not want tea." Mother's lovely face turned ugly with deep scowl lines. "Your coming of age ceremony was months ago. When are you going? I cannot wait forever."

My finger rubbed against the edge of the apron's fabric, nervous but relieved she brought up this long-overdue question. "I do not want a man. I am happy with Bright Jade."

"*Ǎi.*" Mother rolled her eyes. "Making fireworks with Bright Jade makes no grandchildren."

I looked at the ground, trying to find the words to express feelings I did not understand. Doubt, apprehension, resentment, and frustration mushed together like a sticky rice cake.

"Well?" Mother adjusted the wide, colorful striped sash around her red jacket. "When will you go on *zou hun*?"

A walking marriage: it was the way of our people on this island of women. It's how we ensured our continued survival. The other method, sleeping outside until a south wind blew a seed into our womb never worked, although all the old aunties claimed it was how *they* became pregnant.

"I've never crossed the lake before." It was a feeble excuse. The water surrounding our island was heavier than normal water. It caused ordinary boats to sink and it was the reason men had never reached our shores, except for a shipwreck so long ago even the 130-year-old auntie could not remember.

"Wood from the trees on the island floats on the *whole* lake." Mother's eyes narrowed to slits and she pursed her lips. "Are you afraid, daughter?"

I flinched at the suggestion. "No."

"You are afraid of *something*. A man? A man's thing under his tunic?" Mother tilted her head like an owl, two eyes fixed on her prey.

"Why would I be afraid of something all women do?" I curled the end of my braid around my finger.

Mother's forefinger sprung toward me quick as a snake. "So it is not fear but rejecting ancient customs that prevents your *zou hun!*"

I blew my exasperation through my nose and gazed at the cloudless blue sky before answering. "I am not rejecting our customs. I am waiting for...spring. Yes, spring."

Mother lifted one thin eyebrow. "What? And have the women gossip behind my back that the chieftess's daughter waits on her own time before honoring her mother and our ancient ways?"

"I promise I will go in the spring." I gave her my most imploring look.

"You will go tomorrow before winter winds freeze the lake."

"Tomorrow?" I reeled backward.

"Tomorrow." Mother folded her arms and closed her eyes. The discussion was over.

"Yes, Mother." I was dragging my feet back inside the house, tears trickling down my cheeks, when I saw Bright Jade sitting cross-legged at the kitchen table, a half-crushed bowl of dried chili peppers in the center.

"Bright Jade." I plopped down next to her and buried my nose in her neck. "Mother demands I start a walking marriage tomorrow."

I loved Bright Jade. She was my heaven and earth. We were best friends and had been lovers for six months.

Bright Jade swept her long raven-colored hair over her shoulder. It was not braided, our secret signal. "That's why I'm here. I knew she was going to tell you. I heard her talking to several women the other day. Just tell her no."

I ran my fingers through Bright Jade's hair. "You want to make fireworks now? So early in the morning?"

She kissed my lips, her tongue darting inside. "I want you to have the taste of my honey in your mouth when you refuse your mother's demands." She stood up and pulled me up with her.

We kissed again, our tongues flickering back and

forth, the first spark of arousal moistening my cherry. One kiss was all it took and my mind could think of nothing but her pleasures.

Bright Jade pressed her hand against my bosom. "I'm going to suck on your nipples until they're as long as my finger." She wiggled her little finger.

Heat exploded in my garden. I had unusually long nipples. Getting them sucked brought me to orgasm. Bright Jade claimed I was lucky because I had more pleasure spots than her previous lovers.

"I know where we can go." I tugged on her hand.

We went to the stone hut next to the sheepfold. Early this morning I had cleaned and spread fresh hay.

"You must disobey your mother." Bright Jade dipped under the low doorway. "Chieftess or not you must stand up to her. Have I made a walking marriage? No. I am devoted to you." She untied her sash, tugged off her jacket, and removed her skirt, which she spread out on the hay.

"You cannot compare our mothers." I took off my clothes as well, spreading them out next to hers. "I cannot bring her shame. Her position as chieftess may be challenged." I sat down and loosened my braid.

"Your mother does not understand our love." Bright Jade set her lips on mine.

We tasted and nibbled, my throbbing clit anticipating her skillful tongue.

"Men give no pleasure." Bright Jade swept her tongue from my chin to the flat space between my small breasts. "They possess no artistry." Her mouth latched on to my breast and she swirled her tongue around my already stiff nipple.

"Suck them." I twirled her hair around my hand.

Bright Jade pulled on a nipple until I moaned, then released it with a slurp. "Men are rough and dirty and smell like pigs in mud." Bright Jade brought my head to her own breasts.

I flicked my tongue across her rigid pink tips while stroking her smooth inner thigh.

"Ooooh," Bright Jade cooed and pushed down on my head. "I woke this morning already wet for you and I had to finger myself but nothing compares to your tongue."

"You want fireworks every day," I giggled and zigzagged across her belly with my mouth.

"Stop teasing me, Snow Blossom." Bright Jade spread her pink petals.

I lowered my head and inhaled her fragrance. "Not yet." I dipped my finger into the wetness and licked it off.

Bright Jade trembled and rocked her hips forward. "Here, have more. All you want."

"I wish I could save your honey and add it to my tea." My finger dipped in again.

Bright Jade moaned and spread her petals even wider. "Stop talking and start swallowing."

I stretched out my arms and took hold of each tight pink bud, and lapped the length of her garden of delight. I lifted my head. "Like that?"

Bright Jade threw her head back and moaned.

I lapped at her again, long, slow strokes that made her pant. When her panting became louder I flicked her swollen, slick bud until she writhed and squealed. I slipped two fingers into her wetness, then drew them out and moistened the puckered hole of her backdoor.

"Ah!" she squealed. "Again! Again!"

I was busy at my task, one hand caressing her breasts, the other gliding between vagina and anus, my tongue sucking her cherry. When Bright Jade began summoning the ancient gods, I knew her fireworks were about to explode.

I pushed three fingers inside her and scratched the rough skin that catapulted her orgasm.

Bright Jade twisted my hair around her wrists. "Don't stop, Snow Blossom. Fuck me, again!"

She would let me suck her all day long if she could, but I wiggled away and spread my thighs. "My turn."

Bright Jade snaked her body over mine and thrust her tongue in my mouth. "Mmm, I taste delicious." She bit my lower lip. "Men taste bitter."

"How do you know? You've never been with a man."

"I listen to the women with children. They all say the same thing, that men taste like oversalted and sour stew."

I nipped at her small pointy chin. "It can't be that bad. If men smell so bad and taste that awful then our island would be crowded with women."

Bright Jade squeezed my breast.

"Ow!" I flinched.

"That's how a man will touch you." She squeezed again.

I swatted away her hand. "I don't want to hear any more about men. I'll tell *you* all about them when I come back from the Walk." I pushed my hips into hers.

Bright Jade's hand rested between my legs. "You don't have to Walk this year. Or next. Moon Song did not Walk until she was twenty-five."

I pulled away. "I don't want to hear about Moon Song."

"Oops." Bright Jade scrunched her face in regret.

Before Bright Jade and I had found happiness with each other, she and Moon Song had been lovers. They had broken up when Moon Song slapped Bright Jade for sticking a finger up her backdoor. Bright Jade explained that Moon Song was a boring, predictable lover, content with mouth fucking only. This made me wonder whether I had to agree to all of Bright Jade's desires to keep her love. So far I had, and I'd enjoyed them all.

"Get busy." I guided her head down.

Bright Jade stretched wide my garden. "Like a beautiful flower glistening with morning dew." She smiled, then crisscrossed my petals with a pointed tongue.

I arched my back and sighed. This was heaven. One I had never known before the devilish Bright Jade had made me smoke the sacred herb of the shamans until I was too woozy to resist her advances. By the end of the night, my nipples were chafed and my virgin lock penetrated by her persistent fingers. Since then we met almost every day.

Bright Jade lifted her chin, a shiny strand of my honey attached to her lip. "Do it."

I obeyed her command; she knew my needs better than I. My hands kneaded my own breasts, my fingers rolling and tugging at the lengthening nipples.

"You don't need me, you have yourself." Bright Jade flicked her tongue over my clit.

"I need you, I do."

"Lick them."

I stretched my neck and licked my nipples while Bright Jade flicked her tongue back and forth.

"You want a man's cock, do you?" Bright Jade thrust two fingers into me. "Like this?"

"Yes. But for babies not fucking."

Bright Jade thrust again. "You want a man's ugly little cock in your perfect cunt?" She fucked me with her fingers, her mouth wrapped around my aching clit. "You're a dirty little whore. I will tell your mother."

I groaned loudly as the pleasure rose inside me, coursing through my body, all joy radiating from the pleasure core below. My ass tingled and my hips tilted up as Bright Jade made sucking sounds. Her noisy licks and slurps sent me over the edge and I screamed, ecstasy releasing all inhibitions.

Bright Jade didn't stop; she kept eating, slurping my juices, and sending another wave of happiness through my loins and down to my toes.

I screamed again.

"Hush, little whore. You want your mother to hear you?" Bright Jade moved like a crab over me and lowered her twat over my face.

Together we brought each other to happiness again, my third scream muffled by her dripping cunt. We rolled off each other, sweaty and panting, smelling of sex, and listened to the low bleating of sheep in the fold.

Bright Jade rolled to her side, her head propped up on her hand. "Men have no stamina. One time—done."

"Nothing you've told me matters." My head rested on my hands behind my neck. "I don't care if the man's penis is as skinny as a worm or rough or smelly or quick. It is my obligation to my . . . our people." I turned my head. "If all the women on our island were like you we wouldn't be here."

Bright Jade set a piece of straw across my belly. "I don't like sharing you."

"You won't be. I need his seed not his love."

"I suppose." Bright Jade laid another straw atop my belly.

"What are you doing?"

Bright Jade added a few more straws to her design. "See? You are my star. No one else's."

I took her hand in mine. "I love you. Nothing will ever change that."

"It better not." Bright Jade stood and pulled her clothes out from under me.

I reached for my clothes, and brushed off the bits of straw. "No one—man or woman—can replace you."

Once dressed, we looked at each other and giggled. We were two proper young girls again. We kissed, mixing the tastes of each other with our tongues. Nothing tasted better.

"Tomorrow?" Bright Jade said as she ducked under the doorway.

I nodded. "I want to get this Walk over with."

"You're too dutiful." She patted my belly. "When you're too busy with your baby I will have to find another cunt to lick."

"That's too bad," I shrugged. "I was going to let you suck my milk-filled breasts."

"Oh," she laughed. "That would be nice."

I stopped when the path split in two, but Bright Jade turned toward her house and kept walking.

"I hate good-byes," she said over her shoulder.

I returned home to the whitewashed stone house with a sloping roof and upturned eaves that had belonged to a long-dead ancestor. Mother was sitting on a cushion when I opened the door. And she was waiting for me with a stern look.

"I do not like Bright Jade." Mother took a loud sip of tea. "She is too hungry for your love. Love like that flares hot but burns out. She disobeys her mother and she has no respect for the ancient ways."

I poured tea and sat across from her. "Tell me about men."

Mother shrugged. "What's to tell? They stick their cock inside, grunt once or twice, and it's over."

"How many men have you had?"

"Five, until I found a man with strong enough yang to overcome mine." Mother smiled, her straight white teeth the envy of all the women. "You were born nine months later."

I took a sip of tea. "Which way did you Walk?"

"South."

"Then I will go west."

"You are a good daughter." Mother tugged off the thick purple turban decorated with colorful wood beads and set it beside her. She unraveled her braid, fanning out her hair, which was black except for two strands of white on either side. "I will pack some food."

"How long will I be gone?"

Mother shrugged. "One day. Three weeks. That is your decision."

That night I lay in bed, my eyes fixed on the ceiling, my mind considering everything I had ever heard about the Walk. Men—young, old, married, widowed, single— were always eager to fuck us. We were exotic, with pale skin, thick long hair, strong lean limbs, and elegant noses.

The young village wives, however, were not as friendly. They refused to sell us food and worried their husbands would forgo work for pleasure, their crops left untended while they fucked us. The maidens shunned us as well. They were afraid we would steal their boyfriends' hearts. The old wives treated us much differently. They gave us food and shelter, and begged us to lie with their husbands because they were tired of servicing them. Many of the women on our island said it was less troublesome to fuck an old man. They were so excited to feel the smoothness of our young skin they would spurt their seed in the blink of an eye. I liked this plan. It meant I would not be gone more than a day or two. Relieved to have come up with a strategy, I fell asleep.

The screech of an owl woke me sometime during the night and as I drifted back to sleep a wonderful idea came to me. Why hadn't I thought of this before?

I rose before dawn, hurried into my clothes, covered myself with a thick wool cape, and ran all the way to Bright Jade's house.

I tiptoed into her house and crawled over the bed, my thighs straddling hers. "Wake up."

Her eyes flew open. "What are you doing here? Need some morning happiness before you Walk?"

"You're coming with me."

Bright Jade rubbed her eyes. "Is your brain disabled?"

"No, but yours is." I smoothed back her silky tresses and kissed her forehead. "There is no law that says two women cannot Walk together."

"No, but . . ." Bright Jade yawned.

"It will be fun, an adventure."

"Will we share a man?"

"I don't know." I leapt off the bed and ripped off the blanket. "But we will be together and both doing our duty."

Bright Jade put on her best skirt, ruffled tiers of red, orange, and white, then donned her best jacket and warm embroidered pink vest. "Perhaps, I will just watch you." She wound a red turban around her head.

"I think men like that." I tossed her the rucksack.

Bright Jade let loose a loud guffaw then clamped her hand over her mouth. Once we were certain her mother had not woken, Bright Jade stuffed a few more clothes into the rucksack.

"I can't believe I'm doing this. This is crazy." Bright Jade crept into the kitchen. "Your craziness makes me love you more." She kissed me deeply, then rummaged about for dried fish and boiled potatoes. "How long will we be gone?"

I shrugged. "As long as we want."

Bright Jade opened the front door. "Won't my mother be surprised."

The first hint of dawn was lightening the sky as we hurried down the footpath to my house.

The fire was blazing and Mother was packing a food basket when we came through the door.

Mother looked up from tying a satchel of buckwheat. "Why is *she* here?"

"Bright Jade is going with me." I stood tall, my voice confident, my eyes meeting hers.

Mother set the satchel next to the chickens' feet. "Is that so?" She gave Bright Jade her most withering stare. "Just last week your mother told me you refused to make your *zou hun*. What changed?"

Bright Jade chose her words carefully; no one wanted to anger the chieftess. "Snow Blossom's obedience to our ways made me realize how important it is to follow tradition."

Mother cocked her head and narrowed her eyes. "Did you tell your mother you were leaving?"

Bright Jade shifted on her feet. "I decided late last night." She flicked her eyes at me. "I didn't want to wake her."

"I will tell her." Mother thrust the basket of food into Bright Jade's arms.

Mother's slight was obvious, a way to remind her that my rank was superior to Bright Jade's.

"You have my gratitude." Bright Jade clutched the basket to her breast.

Mother reached under her collar and pulled out a long strand of gems, which she lifted over her head. She untied the cord and slid off a handful. "Only spend what you need." She pressed the currency into my hand.

After I tucked the gems into the inside pocket of my vest, Mother accompanied us to the shore where the lake was aglitter with the sun's first rays. Our destination lay across the large lake to where dark blue peaks rose in the distance.

A shiver ran through me, and Mother's face softened into an expression of compassion.

"Don't cross the lake after the first winter wind. It's too dangerous," Mother said.

"We won't be gone that long." I set my rucksack in the rowboat.

"Find a man with strong yang." Mother gathered her cape about her. "Look for a man with broad shoulders, strength, good teeth, thick hair, a symmetrical face, and a deep voice."

"That's a long list." I stowed the basket of food and Bright Jade's rucksack near mine.

Something resembling a smile crossed Mother's face. "Do not lie with an old man unless you have seen with your own eyes that his children have pleasing traits. A handsome noble is best. They eat well and their minds are strong." She tapped her head. "I want a beautiful intelligent granddaughter."

"Yes, Mother."

Bright Jade and I climbed into the boat, and Bright Jade picked up the oars.

"I'm glad she's not *my* mother," said Bright Jade when the little rowboat was too far from shore for Mother to hear.

We took turns rowing, our pace unhurried. The lake was calm and a light breeze blew in our direction, which we regarded as good fortune. Everywhere we looked were shades of blue. Above, the sky was brilliant cobalt. Below, the lake was a deep shade of indigo. Ahead, mountain peaks were a gray-blue.

"Which village should we choose?" asked Bright Jade as the mainland grew closer.

Villages speckled the countryside, some near the shore, a few scattered across the foothills.

I stopped rowing and let the boat bob in the water. "I don't know."

"Look." Bright Jade pointed. "Do you see the wide valley between the two tallest mountains? See the hamlet in the middle?"

The mountains on either side were steep, and the

valley between greener than the lowlands near the lake.

"It looks like the whole area is enclosed by a wall." I began rowing again. "You want to go to that village?"

"It should only take an hour to walk there."

"Why there? Why not some place closer to the lake?"

"It looks peaceful and it's closer to heaven." Bright Jade dipped her hand in the water. "If we don't find any men meeting *all* your mother's criteria, we'll go someplace else."

"We'll be gone for months!" I said and we burst out laughing.

We came ashore not far from a small fishing village and pulled the boat up the narrow rocky beach into a thicket, where we concealed it under branches. Then we trampled through the grove until we found a footpath that took us to a wide dirt road.

"More good fortune," said Bright Jade. "This road leads to the hamlet."

"Too bad it's not straight. It winds like a snake. We'll eat all our food before we get there."

We walked onward, past the rocky fields, straggly scrubs, and withered weeds. Eventually we came upon a tall boy dragging a reluctant donkey across the road.

The boy narrowed his eyes. "Who are you?"

"We come from across the lake," I said.

He looked us over from head to toe, his brow creasing with disbelief. "It takes many months to walk around the lake."

"We come from the island in the middle of the lake." I pointed to the lake, although our island was too far away to be visible.

"The middle . . ." The boy's eyes grew wide. "Are you from the Women's Kingdom?"

Bright Jade and I nodded in unison.

The boy stood tall and lifted his chin. "I'm your man."

Bride Jade gave him a hard look. "How old are you?"

"Twelve. My cock is always hard, and I have so much cum it leaks all over my bed every night. Enough for both of you."

Bright Jade and I exchanged a quick glance.

"You are too young," I said.

The boy threw back his slender shoulders, his dirty torn shirt hanging loose over his thin frame. "You don't look much older than me."

"I am a woman. You are a boy." *And too scrawny for my liking,* I thought.

Bright Jade had kinder words. "This is not our destination, but when we return home I will tell all my friends of your gracious offer."

"You will?" He smiled wide, all his teeth crooked. "My name is Pengfei. Tell them to ask for Pengfei. I will provide services all night long."

"Thank you, Pengfei," I said.

We continued on our way, the slope of the road increasing.

This time we came across an old man, his walking stick leaning against a boulder. "Pretty girls, rest a bit with me and tell me where you are going."

"We're headed up the mountain."

His crooked, toothless smile tripled the wrinkles webbed over his weathered old face. He squinted at us, then grabbed his walking stick and ruffled the hem of my skirt with it. "You pretty girls are not from here, are you? I am not so old I don't remember the distinctive style of your clothes. You are from the Women's Kingdom, eh?"

"We are."

The old man smacked his lips as though anticipating a tasty meal. "It's *zou hun* time, eh? Look no further. Here I am."

Bright Jade and I giggled.

"Don't let these wrinkles fool you. My cock is like an ox and will plow both your fields."

"Thank you, uncle, but we must decline," I said.

"Don't believe me, eh? Let me show you." The old man tugged down his pants and wagged his limp worm.

"Very impressive," said Bright Jade. "But I don't think *that thing* is hard enough to enter our tight gardens."

"It's resting, pretty girls." He stroked it. "Let me wake it up and I'll show you."

We hurried away and laughed until tears ran down our cheeks.

The sun was overhead by the time we climbed the road's steep slope and reached the entrance to the village in the valley.

"I guess they don't mind visitors." I gestured to the open gate.

The fields within the compound were far different than the ones we had just passed. These were green and well tended. Men were scattered about, harvesting, hoeing, and weeding. The air was warmer as well.

"No wonder they built a wall around this valley," I said.

The road widened and led straight to a large sprawling two-story house with several artichoke roofs. Beyond was a small village near a river.

"Lots of men here." Bright Jade nudged me.

We did not make it past the first field when a tall, strapping young man left his digging to block our way. He was shirtless and wore pants cut off at the knee. His biceps were large, his shoulders brawny, and six distinct muscles ridged across his stomach.

I glanced at Bright Jade, whose mouth hung open.

"Welcome." He wiped sweat from his brow. "What brings you this way?"

I tore my gaze from his body to look at his face. He was gorgeous! The very definition of symmetry and proportion, with a square jaw, straight nose, thick lips, and happy eyes.

"We are from the Women's Kingdom. I am Snow Blossom and this is Bright Jade." Mother never mentioned a man looking like *this*. I felt as nervous as my first time with Bright Jade. "We're on a Walk."

"*Zou hun?*" He pulled a clean cloth from his pants and wiped the sweat from his chest.

"Yes," Bright Jade and I answered at the same time.

The man looked us both up and down very slowly, even though the shape of our bodies was concealed under long full skirts and stiff jackets.

"You are both very beautiful," he said. "Like a double present."

I blushed and looked down at the ground.

When I looked back up he was waving to someone. Two more shirtless young men walked out from the field. They were equally muscular and shared the same features.

"I am Bo, the eldest," he said. "This is my brother Jian."

"Welcome." Jian's lips were not as thick as Bo's, but his eyes were larger.

"This is Qi, our little brother."

"Hello." There was nothing little about Qi. He was taller and bigger, and yet his jaw was rounder and his features not as refined as his older brothers'.

Bo jerked his thumb over his shoulder. "The master lives there. He's a very stern old man."

"My mother is a chieftess and she is also very stern. I think sternness comes with the position."

The brothers exchanged a look I did not understand.

"The master will be gone for several days," said Bo. "The big house is unoccupied."

I glanced at Bright Jade, who for some reason was suddenly shy, her eyes downcast, her cheeks flushed.

"I don't understand," I said.

Bo scratched his chin. "I thought . . . maybe we could . . . I'm not married. Of course, if you don't find me suitable…"

My cheeks bloomed with heat. "No. You're very . . . suitable. But I need to talk to Bright Jade before I . . . we decide."

Bright Jade and I crossed to the other side of the road while Bo and his brothers looked on.

"All three brothers meet Mother's qualifications," I said.

"Not all. They are poor farmers."

"You heard Bo, the master is old and stern. I doubt we will find more handsome men anywhere else."

"Bo can't take his eyes off you. You should fuck

him." Bright Jade snuck a quick peek over her shoulder. "I haven't decided which one I want. Qi's so big he might crush me."

"Have you decided?" asked Bo from across the road.

"I have decided on *you*." I walked toward Bo. "Bright Jade is still uncertain."

"I am honored." Bo smiled wide, his teeth straight and white. "Follow the road to the front door of the big house. Tell the servant, my mother, who you are and why you've come." He leaned toward me. "I don't see any reason why we can't borrow the master's bedroom while he's gone, do you?"

"As long as he won't be back today."

"He won't." Bo tugged on his pants. "I cannot woo a woman wearing dirty clothes and smelling like a sheep. I'll throw a bucket of water over myself and join you shortly."

After a moment of awkward silence, Bright Jade and I started toward the big house.

"Why does Bo think he must woo you?" Bright Jade whispered in my ear.

"I don't know. I am wooed enough by his big muscles and deep voice." I glanced over my shoulder. The three brothers still stood in the road, watching us as though afraid we might disappear. "Why aren't they married?"

"No need to. Every maiden and wife from a thousand *li* away would spread their thighs for any of them."

A servant, the cook with a grease-splattered apron, waited in the doorway as though expecting us. It was Bo's mother, her smooth skin and refined symmetry the same as her sons. I told her who we were and her face lit up, her smile revealing perfect white teeth.

"You are both as beautiful as goddesses," she said as she led us into the house. "Your clothes! Such rich colors and elegant embroidery!" She stopped before a carved, red-lacquered door. "My sons are farmers, why choose them?" Her suspicious glare reminded me of Mother's.

Was she trying to make us feel uncomfortable or did she merely seek information about the Women's Kingdom?

"They are the right age and possess worthy traits." I refused to be cowed by an old servant woman.

She crossed her arms and narrowed her eyes. "What worthy traits, *exactly?*"

I straightened my shoulders and stood a little taller. "The women on my island are all beautiful, strong, and clever because we do not lie with stupid, ugly, weak men."

"Good breeding. I knew it." The old woman nodded and pushed open the door. "Wait here."

The room was large and richly furnished with thick rugs, vibrant tapestries, carvings, and red-lacquered furniture. The master was very wealthy.

We put down our rucksacks, sat on cushions near a low tea table, and wondered aloud why our mothers did not give us more details about *zou hun*. Our quiet conversation stopped when Bo strode into the room. His long hair was neatly plaited, and he wore a red silk robe, untied and open, with straight long pants. Bo had done more than pour water over his head—he had bathed and stolen the master's clothes.

My heart did a somersault when he sat next to me.

"How does this Walking Marriage business work?" Bo's easy demeanor lessened my nervousness.

"We find a man we like and lie with him," I said just as Jian and Qi, also bathed and wearing the master's clothes, entered the room.

"If we don't like him we find another." Bright Jade scooted over to make room for Jian and Qi.

Bo rubbed his chin. "Are you virgins?"

Bright Jade and I giggled, which caused Bo to clear his throat.

"Are you best friends?" asked Jian.

"The best," said Bright Jade, and she bit her lips.

Qi leaned toward us. "You are more than friends. *I* think you are lovers."

Bright Jade and I shared a quick glance. Was it so obvious?

Bo, sitting behind me, touched my turban. "May I?"

I nodded, my nervousness turning to excitement.

Bo lifted off my turban and my braid tumbled down. With deft fingers he freed my hair, his light touch sending shivers of pleasure down my spine. Without asking, he untied the sash and unhooked the frog closure at my neck. My jacket fell open, my pert breasts on display. Bright Jade's eyes flashed with anger.

Bo removed my jacket and kissed my neck. "Bright Jade is jealous." His hands covered my breasts. "Bright Jade, show me how you kiss Snow Blossom. I want to do it right. I want Snow Blossom to like me."

Bright Jade removed her turban. Then Qi loosened her hair while Jian took off her sash and jacket.

Jian, in the middle of us, leaned back so Bright Jade and I could share a quick kiss.

"Show me how you *really* kiss," said Bo, kissing the nape of my neck and stroking my hard pink buds.

I was already wet, my clit throbbing. Bo's caresses and watching Qi feel Bright Jade's breasts filled me with shameful new desires. I enjoyed watching the men feel Bright Jade *and* I wanted all of their hands on me *and* I wanted Bright Jade to watch. Did Bright Jade feel the same?

I got my answer. Bright Jade thrust her eager tongue into my mouth with a soft moan. To my surprise another mouth joined ours, an insistent tongue wedging between. It was Jian's. The three-way kiss made me tremble.

Bo's hand slipped under my skirt. "You're so wet." He slid his finger between my petals.

I turned my head and we kissed for the first time. His mouth was warm, his lips soft as pillows. I opened my eyes when I heard Bright Jade moan *really* loudly. Qi was sucking on one of her tits and Jian on the other. Lucky girl!

Bo helped me out of my skirt and removed his clothes. His cock was as big as a cucumber!

"Show me how you and Bright Jade make fireworks," he said.

With Qi and Jian still sucking her tits, Bright Jade spread her thighs. I got on my knees and buried my tongue into her wetness. Bo's hands held my ass, his cock gliding back and forth against my garden.

"I'm going to fuck you now, Snow Blossom." Bo pushed, pushed again, and I cried out into Bright Jade's cunt as his length entered me.

This was nothing like Bright Jade's two slim fingers! He filled me completely.

I lifted my head, Bright Jade's honey on my face, and

she scooted away, Jian taking her place. My lips encircled his cock while Bo fucked me from behind. The tension mounted quickly—much too quickly—and my fireworks erupted amidst everyone's moaning and panting.

Bo pulled out and joined Jian, and now I had two cocks to suck. Jian cried out and cum squirted out into my mouth. Bo laughed, slapped his ass, and shifted position so now I was sitting on Bo's face. His tongue slurped my clit and his finger pushed into my anus. My cry of ecstasy was cut short by Qi's cock—smelling and tasting like Bright Jade's sweet cunt—pushing into my mouth. I came again and again, ripples of pleasure surging through my body.

I fucked them all. Once, twice, I lost count. One time their cocks filled all my orifices at the same time. It was while Bo and Qi sucked my nipples into long hard points and Jian and Bright Jade gorged on my dripping cunt with their fingers and tongues that I screamed, the uncontrollable bliss convulsing my body and lifting my soul to the sky.

I sucked three cocks and tasted all their balls, and my tits were slick from four mouths. I had never known such wild joy, the feel of so many hands and tongues on my body—an ecstasy beyond compare.

My pussy was sore and my mouth tasting of everyone's cum by the time we collapsed with exhaustion. Bright Jade slept between Qi and Jian, her face serene with contentment. I lay in Bo's arms, a tear running down my cheek.

Bo wiped it away. "What's wrong, Snow Blossom?"

"How can I return to the island and be content with only Bright Jade after this?"

"You don't have to go back right now." Bo spread his fingers over my flat belly. "Don't leave until there's a baby inside."

"How can there not be? My thighs are sticky with buckets of cum."

Bo kissed the nape of my neck, and then rolled on top of me. "You make me so horny, Snow Blossom. I've never met a woman like you." He slid his cock inside of me and I sighed with pleasure. "I have a confession to make."

"You are already married?" That would break my heart.

Bo smiled. "No, we are all unwed. But I was less than truthful. We are the master's sons, his heirs. And though our father is stern, he taught us the value of working and the importance of respecting the land, which is why we often work the fields. Much to father's dismay, my brothers and I have not found worthy women—the wealthy maidens we know are all frail and timid and boring. Great fortune smiled upon us with your visit! Father will be pleased, even if all three of us must share you both." His thrusts were unhurried and loving. "Stay awhile."

Bright Jade and I stayed through the winter. Each day we fucked and sucked on one another. Each day we found ourselves more in love with the brothers. When the master returned he approved of the arrangement, especially when we told him we raised only the female babies.

When the lake thawed, Bright Jade and I rowed back to the island, our big bellies celebrated with much fanfare.

Bright Jade and I visited Bo, Jian, and Qi regularly. Though our Walking Marriage was unconventional, it quenched our desires for uninhibited sensuality.

We were both fruitful, and by the time I became chieftess I had three boys and three girls. Bright Jade had four boys and two girls. All our children were strong, beautiful, and clever.

I loved all three brothers, Bo a little more than the rest, but Bright Jade most of all.

The Women's Kingdom, also known as Asian Amazons, is a mythical tribe of women who inhabited an inaccessible island near Tibet. The earliest reference to the Women's Kingdom is found in Huainanzi, *an essay collection from the second century BC. Hui-shen authored another narrative about the Women's Kingdom in 507 AD. Strangely enough, the myth is not far from the truth. The Mosuo, an ethnic group located near the Tibetan border, is a matriarchal society where sexual unions are unrestricted and women dominate the household.*

WEB
OF LIES

The long black hair cascading over her shoulder was more alluring than the beautiful waterfall she sat near. Her face was slim and delicate except for large eyes. She was the ideal beauty in all ways, even her white skin, which was softer than an emperor's pampered firstborn son.

Chiyo drew up the bottom of her sky-blue silk kimono and stretched her long, shapely legs, arching her tiny feet like a dancer. She was hungry. Ravenous, really. But she bided her time because her sort did not reach four hundred years of age without patience and cleverness. And since Chiyo planned on living a thousand more, she chose her nourishment carefully.

Beyond the grove of flowering pink cherry trees, a galloping horse approached. The beat of hooves upon the ground sent vibrations into Chiyo's sensitive body. The horse stopped and the air shifted, a subtle quiver signaling a man's approach. Chiyo scurried behind the leafy thicket surrounding the waterfall, which spilled over a series of moss-covered rocks and slick boulders.

A samurai emerged into the clearing, which was lush with ferns and pink with a carpet of blossoms. He traipsed to the riverbank in his *ō-yoroi* armor complete with helmet, armored sleeves, greaves, scaled breast-plate, and the wide, striped *kusazuri* skirt of a caval-ryman. It was a nobleman's armor, made with the finest metal and strongest leather. He removed his helmet, his hair in a neat topknot, and knelt down to drink the cool water from cupped hands.

A bird darted from a maple tree and the samurai's hand flew to the hilt of his sword.

"Good thing, you're quicker than me, little bird," he laughed. "I'm so hungry I might have swallowed you whole."

Chiyo smiled. She was well acquainted with a hunger so voracious you ate what you should not.

The samurai stood under the cherry tree whose long weeping boughs draped over the narrow river to skim the surface. He was ruggedly handsome, favored with the strong nose and the full lips of masculinity, his eyes bright with intelligence. As he pulled off his sandals, Chiyo crept soundlessly forward for a better look. The clearing was secluded and serene, the perfect place to take a nap or an impromptu dip.

Not fooled by a handsome face, Chiyo's interest piqued when he began unlacing his armor. Unlacing the six parts was a tedious process and gave Chiyo time to study the colorful design painted on the armor that identified him as a member of a great clan. Underneath he wore a plain tan silk kimono of finest quality.

Chiyo sucked in her breath with delight when he shed his kimono. His chest was wide, his well-developed pectorals flexing as he folded the kimono and set it on a nearby rock. Chiyo held her breath as he unwound his loincloth, the cut below his waist a *V*-shaped arrow to his cock, then exhaled her excitement when she saw its size.

How long had it been since she had sucked on a warrior's cock and swallowed his cum? Years? The sour saltiness of farmers and merchants never satisfied. Samurai cum was far superior, its essence rich with ferocity and domination. Chiyo's mouth filled with the liquid of wanting as she remembered the taste of another samurai long ago.

Her hand went under her kimono to the moist whorls between her legs. Her hunger came with a price, a lust that made her physically vulnerable and sexually frustrated. She found the sensitive pink root that ached when hungry and rubbed it back and forth. Her eyes never left the samurai's virile physique. It took only a moment, her orgasm a blossom of release that made her whole body shudder. Unfortunately, it would only be a brief respite from the nagging throb that would continue until she had him.

The samurai pulled out his topknot, his black hair tumbling past his shoulders, and entered the river. He dove below, then shot out like a jumping fish, an arc of water spewing from his mouth. He swam under the waterfall, the cascade showering his body, and again dove back into the churning water below. When he emerged a second time he shook his head like a wet dog and laughed. The unrestrained laughter of a happy man prickled her skin but did not change her course of action. He was the one. Or would soon be.

The samurai threw back his head, immersing his hair, and smoothed it back from his forehead as he walked up the riverbank. He looked like a god as the water droplets clinging to him sparkled in the sun.

Chiyo's lustful throb began anew. The man was divine! Though eager to meet him, she waited until the samurai put on his kimono, which clung to his skin and accentuated his muscular build.

Chiyo patted her hair to make certain not a lock was out of place, then, nimble as a spider, darted behind a maple tree near the footpath.

The samurai turned his head at the faint rustle. "Hello?"

"Oh!" Chiyo's dainty hand touched her breast. "Pardon the intrusion. I didn't know anyone was here." Chiyo clutched the short neck of her *biwa*, her four-stringed lute made of mulberry.

The samurai swallowed, his good manners forgotten he was so dazzled by Chiyo's beauty. "Forgive me for trespassing." He bowed, suddenly feeling foolish in his wet kimono and untidy hair. He tore his eyes away from the petite maiden and looked at his armor heaped on the ground. "I was just leaving."

Chiyo dropped to her knees, several cherry blossom petals floating past to join the carpet of pink around her. She stood the *biwa* in her lap and drew the triangular plectrum across the strings.

The samurai let his *kusazuri* slip from his hands, delighted by the clear sounds of those few notes. He paused to listen.

Encouraged by his interest, Chiyo played a short melody. "Are you a samurai?"

"Yes, from the Fujiwara clan." The samurai left his armor to sit near Chiyo. "You play beautifully, but I have never heard that song before."

Chiyo bit her lip and dropped her gaze. "I compose my own songs."

"Would you play another of your songs for me?"

Chiyo lifted her gaze and smiled coyly. "I will compose a song just for you."

The samurai's eyebrows lifted with delight. "My own song?"

Chiyo nodded, fluttered the plectrum up and down the strings and began singing. The lyrics told a tale of valor and strength and skill, and yet the melody was full of erotic vibrations that made the samurai think of a naked woman stretching her body like a cat in the sun. His cock stiffened.

"It's the most wonderful song I have ever heard," said the samurai. "What is your name?"

"Chiyo," she answered, and blushed.

"I am Takeshi."

A tiny spider fell from the branch draped overhead and landed on Takeshi's hand. He set his hand on the ground and waited for the spider to scurry away. Chiyo was moved by his regard for nature. Other men would have crushed it between their fingers or flicked it away.

"Do you want to hear another song, Takeshi?"

Takeshi had an important mission to complete, and being alone with this maiden was improper, yet he could not seem to leave. Was the grove enchanted? Was the maiden a *kami*, a spirit sent to keep him from his mission? He didn't think so.

"I would like that," he said.

Chiyo sang another song, and this one caused Takeshi to imagine disrobing the maiden and lifting her legs in the air while he fucked her. He shifted his body to conceal his rigid length, ashamed the maiden might see his undisciplined lust. His cock began to throb, the melody making him think of her silky pink wetness.

Takeshi felt a tickle at his ankle and saw a tiny spider spinning a web around his ankles. It was nature's way of telling him to stay a bit longer.

Chiyo stared into his eyes as she sang the last note of the song, holding his gaze for longer than was proper. Takeshi found her captivating, with flawless pale skin, lips like cherries, and brown eyes promising a thousand pleasures.

Chiyo touched his hand, her fingers light as a web. "Tell me about yourself, Takeshi."

Takeshi was a man of action, not words. Nonetheless he found himself spilling his heart to her. He talked about his father, his mother, his clan, his love of reading about his great-grandfather's fire-inspired battle strategies. Chiyo stroked his hair while he confessed his dreams and divulged his greatest weakness, his search for perfect love. Her touch was magical, all Takeshi's worries carried away by her soft voice and featherlight hands. He felt wonderful, her presence a cocoon of serenity. Each breath he took filled his lungs with happiness. *This* was perfect love.

Chiyo brushed her fingers across his cheek and he was so overcome with adoration that he took her slim little wrist and touched his lips to it. It was wrong, too forward, and he let go.

"I am sorry, Chiyo. I was overcome by your perfection."

"Do not apologize for doing what you had to." Chiyo pressed two fingers to his lips before she leaned in to kiss him.

She tasted like cherries and her breath was as fragrant as a blossoming garden. Takeshi wanted more. Much more. His tongue sought hers and she responded with a sigh. Chiyo climbed into his lap and wrapped her arms around his neck. She inhaled the scent of his raw masculinity and savored the feel of his eager tongue. Kissing him was more delicious than a sweet red bean cake. A kiss that increased her hunger for his other flavors.

"I love you," Takeshi said. "I will ask your father for your hand in marriage."

"You want to make me your bride?" Her eyes lit up.

"You are my perfect love, Chiyo." Takeshi nibbled her neck.

Chiyo could not wait one second longer—she untied the *obi* belted around his kimono and skimmed her hands across his chest. Next she pushed the silk away to draw circles around his hard brown nipples.

Takeshi moaned, his hunger as great as hers. Chiyo bent toward him and fluttered her eyelashes across his nipples. Takeshi groaned, all self-control slipping away. When her tongue flicked across his chest, he scooped up a handful of cherry blossom petals and scattered them over her.

The feel of the petals against her cheek sent new shoots of pleasure through her, made her clit engorge with wanting. Her mouth moved downward, past the petals, and she ran her lips back and forth over the ridges of his muscled stomach.

Takeshi could not stop the dream, could only marvel

at the sensual talent of his perfect woman. He was paralyzed by pleasure, her lips and tongue his only thought.

Chiyo continued slowly downward despite his moans and her *real* hunger. Takeshi put his hand on her head, his throbbing cock aching for release.

"Chiyo!" Takeshi threw back his head as her tongue trailed leisurely up his length. He wanted to shove his cock in her mouth, make her suck hard. He didn't, as he was too ensnared by her appetite for carnal pleasures. When he looked down at her again she was gazing at him, adoration shining in her eyes.

Chiyo took delight in his waterfall-fresh genitals, the musk of his virility untainted by sweat. She flicked her tongue across the slit, teasing out a tiny salt pearl of cum. The droplet was enough to send prickles of pleasure throughout her body. She cupped and stroked his balls, pleased when Takeshi's legs tensed with mounting excitement.

Chiyo's attentions increased, her tongue moving faster until it lapped and slurped. The moment she felt his ascension commence she slowed her pace. Takeshi moaned her name—it was the delirious chant of a lover succumbing to sheer sensation. Chiyo swallowed him whole, then eased his huge cock in and out of her throat past her tight lips. She felt every ridge, every morsel of his skin. His scent shifted, an animal heat emitting through his pores. It increased Chiyo's appetite. Her hunger for his elixir became a craving she *had* to satisfy.

Takeshi's lust spiked, his body aflame with a single yearning. "Chiyo." His fingers dug into her hair and his groans became yelps.

Takeshi cried out in ecstasy. His body bucked and

twitched, and yet Chiyo kept sucking, her fingers applying soft pressure to his balls. She wanted every drop.

Takeshi held her head as she sucked and swallowed, devouring his cum like she was parched.

Except Chiyo's thirst was not yet quenched. She lifted her head and licked the taste of heaven from her lips.

"That was amazing." Takeshi gave her a lopsided grin, his lids heavy, and fell asleep.

Chiyo curled next to him and felt the beginnings of his cum take hold. Already her hands looked smoother, her lungs held more air, and her vision sharpened. Cum: The perfect food. And this was only the first course.

When Takeshi awoke from his nap, he gazed at Chiyo and found her more beautiful than before. "I have business at the village." He brushed a tiny white spider from her hair. "When I return we will go to your father." He detangled himself from her long slender limbs and put on his armor, which Chiyo helped him lace together.

"I will be back in the morning," he said.

"I'll be waiting."

They kissed deeply, and with a regretful look he walked into the grove of trees.

Despite his nap, Takeshi felt sluggish, his feet dragging, his limbs heavy as he mounted his horse. He did not question his weariness as he rode, his thoughts too preoccupied with the perfect maiden of erotic sensuality whose body he planned to enjoy for a lifetime. When he arrived at the village, Takeshi delivered the letter to the clan leader.

The clan leader read it and nodded. "Perfect. All is in order. I will sign it immediately." He looked at Takeshi with a worried crease across his brow. "Did you stop anywhere along the way?"

"Yes, a small waterfall west of here."

The clan leader and advisors exchanged troubled glances.

"Is there a problem?" Takeshi stood straighter. He was not intimidated by these wrinkled old samurais.

"There is a cobweb on your hair," said the clan leader.

Takeshi brushed it off. "The perils of sitting under a tree."

The clan leader folded his arms. "Did you meet anyone there?"

Takeshi's eyes widened. "A young maiden."

The old samurais grunted with displeasure.

"Do not go there again," said the clan leader. "That was not a maiden, that was a *Jorōgumo*. She lures young men to their deaths by changing her form into that of a beautiful woman."

"She sucks them dry," said the old samurai advisor. "Sucks their life force from their bodies so she stays young and lovely."

Takeshi was polite. He did not laugh at these old men's tales. "Thank you for the warning."

Takeshi enjoyed the clan leader's hospitality for the rest of the day and even met his unmarried daughter. She was pretty enough. Nonetheless Takeshi was unmoved, his heart already loyal to Chiyo, his perfect woman.

After a breakfast of steamed rice, miso soup, pickled plums, and fish, Takeshi bid the clan leader farewell.

"Do not return to the waterfall," said the clan leader as Takeshi mounted his horse.

Takeshi assured him he would not. As he galloped away, he suspected the reason for the clan leader's foolish tale about the *Jorōgumo*. It was a way to keep the beautiful girl for his son.

Chiyo was waiting for Takeshi when he arrived.

"I was afraid you wouldn't come back." Chiyo threw her arms around his neck, her nails scraping his skin, and kissed him. "Father is eager to meet you. He says it's important I marry before the clan leader steals me for his son."

I knew it, thought Takeshi as he held her perfectly shaped face in his rough hands. "There is no time to waste."

Chiyo stepped away and sat under the cherry blossom tree, a single teardrop on her pale cheek. "Once you state your intentions father will not let us be alone." She stretched out her arms, drawing Takeshi to her side. "There will be nowhere to hide, no place to taste your lips . . ."

They kissed, their tongues grazing along teeth, thrusting and curling around each other. Lust overcame good sense, and Takeshi slid his hand over her body, his need mounting when he discovered she was not wearing all the layers beneath her kimono, that only her tightly wrapped *obi* prevented him from seeing her naked.

He plucked at the *obi*, frantic to unwind it, Chiyo's sighs of pleasure driving him mad with desire.

Chiyo flung back both sides of the kimono, her white slender body aglow against the pink silk.

"Perfection." Takeshi touched her pert breast, its pale pink areola perfectly round, her rosy nipple stiff with need.

Chiyo arched her back into his hand and cooed. "Don't stop, Chiyo. I am yours."

Takeshi was unable to stop—everything about her, from her skin to her scent to her soft voice, destroyed his self-control. He removed his kimono and fell upon her. His hands stoked her body, and his mouth covered her breasts. Chiyo cooed beneath him, her own hands running along his back and grabbing his ass. She dragged her nails over his shoulders and down his back, leaving a thin red line. Lust pooled inside her, concentrated in the warmth at the junction of her legs. She raked her nails over his back again, continued downward and over his firm ass. Takeshi returned the pleasure by scraping his teeth over her nipples. The sting deepened Chiyo's hunger and made her clit ache even more.

"Takeshi," she whispered. "My almost husband, I want—I need to have your cock in my mouth again."

Takeshi groaned, rolled on his back, and spread his legs. "I am yours."

His cock, the size of Chiyo's forearm, made her squeal with pleasure. She rested her mouth over the head while she stroked his inner thigh, and Takeshi emitted short puffs of pleasure.

"Suck me, Chiyo." He nudged her head down.

Chiyo lapped at his balls instead, holding them in her mouth while she stroked the skin beyond.

Takeshi let out a long cry of joy and his ass lifted off the ground.

Eager to taste his cum again, Chiyo wrapped her fingers around his girth and slid up and down. Her tongue worked vigorously around his head. Swirl. Flick. Suck. Swirl. Flick. Suck.

Takeshi's thighs tensed and relaxed, his paradise close. Chiyo went faster, her tempo matching her own clit's rhythm. Swirl. Flick. Suck. Swirl-flick-suck. Takeshi flew to heaven on the wings of ecstasy, his pelvis bucking against her mouth as Chiyo sucked and slurped every delicious drop of his salty elixir. Each swallow made her hornier. It was the result of virile cum, and Takeshi's was especially potent.

Too ravenous to detect subtle nuances yesterday, Chiyo notice the flavorful tang of his cum today.

Takeshi rolled on top of her, his cock still rigid. "Let me pleasure you."

Chiyo wrapped her thighs around him. "Fuck me, Takeshi. Take me to paradise." As horny as she was during similar moments, no man had ever made her climax. Maybe Takeshi could.

"You took the edge off my lust, so now I will fuck you until you beg me to stop." Takeshi thrust inside her wetness.

Chiyo whimpered as her small body strained to stretch around his size. She felt whole, complete, and filled to the brim with his love. Takeshi moved slowly, angling his withdrawal so it rubbed against her engorged clit.

Takeshi's skin was hot against Chiyo's, his heated steady strokes inflaming her. She gave herself over to the sensations sizzling at her core and closed her mouth over his and inhaled his essence. She was so lost to the feeling of his fucking she forgot to control the web she was spinning around them, the cocoon that would keep him trapped until she sucked every drop of life from him.

Takeshi had felt the faint tickle as the first strands wrapped around his ankles, but thought nothing of it until he saw thousands of tiny spiders suspended from the branches overhead. The old samurais had spoken the truth. Takeshi's dream bride, the perfect woman, was a cold-hearted *Jorōgumo* who would suck his life dry. What a fool he had been to believe such a beautiful maiden might gorge on his cum with such passion.

The venom Chiyo had infused into his neck with her nails coursed through Takeshi's body. He didn't care. He wanted to remain at this pleasure plateau forever, to feel her lips sucking his mouth, to slip his cock back and forth in her silky walls, to orgasm and orgasm until he died.

Chiyo spun her web around his legs and past his waist. The strands were light as a feather yet strong as iron, allowing only the movements of his thrusting pelvis. Each time she sighed or moaned the web thickened.

Takeshi slowed his pace, not to delay his orgasm but to prolong their fucking and take her to paradise.

Chiyo felt the air's vibration above as hundreds of spiders swung to the rhythm of her sweet agony. Chiyo crested the waterfall of bliss with such force that she cried out as she tumbled over the precipice, her body writhing, her limbs jerking, her skin quivering with relief.

Takeshi fell with her into the churning pool of orgasm, but he was ready. Just as the web covered his shoulders his true spirit emerged and a row of spiky scales arose from his spine.

The cocoon ripped open, Chiyo's lethal love strands

shredded by his razor-sharp ridged back. Takeshi pushed Chiyo off and leapt away from the tree where spiders shot strands at him.

"My name is not Takeshi," he said. "It is Tatsuo, Dragon Man. I am a dragon not a bug, my beautiful *Jorōgumo*." He shook his head and scattered the few spiders that had managed to alight on his head.

Tatsuo stretched his neck and lifted his arms to the air. His limbs thickened, turned emerald colored, and his skin hardened into iridescent scales. Two horns sprung from his head and long sharp teeth sprung from his dragon mouth. He reared up, his rear claws piercing the ground, and puffed out a cloud of fire that turned all the spiders to ash. Then he bounded into the grove.

Chiyo sat up, sated and surprised, her pussy dripping with his cum. "Damn."

Stories about the Japanese shape-shifting Jorōgumo—*aka, ensnaring bride or whore spider—date back to ancient times. Fortunately, you can find more modern versions about this devious slut in many manga stories.*

THE
KISS

The sky is plowed with somber billows of gray. A few rays of sun wink through the thinnest clouds, casting, for a moment, warm light on a stone castle or sleeping hound or thatched hut. The sun plays no favorites, its life-giving splendor a capricious gift to poor, young, old, rich, healthy, and sick. The same can be said for rain and wind. Nature is an unpredictable and volatile goddess. Heed her well. For I am she.

I am the streams, rivers, and lakes. I am the rocks and mountains. My divine breath nourishes the smallest weed and the greatest tree. My heartbeat sustains the cattle, goats, and wild beasts. My eyesight is enhanced by high-soaring birds. I am the Auld Wyfe of Thunder. I am the Cailleach.

I have a great task today: The land needs a new king, and so I tread down the dirt-packed path toward the lake, my staff steadying my hitched gait. My hip is sore and a sharp pain bites at my heels. Whereas humans grumble at these aches, I smile. They are reminders of a long life blessed with journeys and strength. At the lake's edge I bend over, both gnarled dark hands resting atop my staff, and look at my reflection.

Mo chreach! Good heavens! I turn my face from side to side. Creases upon creases! Across my forehead and chin, around my eyes and chapped thin lips. The brown spots and ugly splotches look like mud splatter. I touch my hair, white as new-fallen snow, and stoop even lower. Bright blue eyes stare back. Ah, there I am, beneath this wrinkled skin and hunched body.

"I can find one worthy man. I always do," I say to my watery reflection.

A cold wind blows across the lake and I draw my faded plaid wool cloak close around me, then turn toward the path leading to the nearest village.

I plod forward, dead leaves and grass crunching underfoot, no flora slowing my pace, because I have no time to admire Nature's gifts. As I near the village my stomach grumbles. What I need is a bowl of parsnip and onion stew, or a bit of fried trout, or a cup of barley porridge to revive my failing strength. The wooden trestle takes me over the ditch and into the village. A few women sit in front of their homes, round windowless structures of straw and mud-daub walls and heather-thatched conical roofs. Except for the crude painting of a chicken and a mug of mead at the entry, the tavern looks like all the other structures. Lured by the aroma, I go inside and sit on a rickety stool near enough to the center fire to bask in its warmth.

"If you don't have any money you best be leaving," says the tired-faced proprietor in dirty tunic and worn *bracae*.

I pull a coin from under my gray wool dress. "I'll

take whatever's in the pot."

The proprietor squints at me—I'm used to this, my voice is ever youthful—and walks over to inspect the coin. "A bit old to be traveling the countryside by yourself." He plucks the coin from my fingers.

"Age is a happy privilege."

"That it is." He ladles stew into a wooden bowl. "Where are you from?"

"Everywhere."

"Everywhere?" He sets down a steaming bowl and wood spoon before staring into my clear blue eyes and, as with most, finds in their crystalline depths a preternatural truth. "I'd not believe you except for the look in your eye."

I stir the soup, inhaling the aroma of fennel, parsnips, and onions. "What look is that?"

"Like you've seen the world and had many adventures."

"You saw all that in my eyes?" I blow steam across the first spoonful.

"The tongue is a deceiver, but eyes never lie." The proprietor crosses the room, plops down on a stool, and begins plucking a scrawny chicken.

I savor each spoonful of stew, the taste calling to mind another tavern keeper many years ago. I was on the same mission, finding a worthy sovereign, and had stopped to eat at a tavern much like this. That inn, however, was crowded with men. All brutish, vulgar, and drunk. Except for one. A tall, lanky young man with honey-colored hair and a pure heart. A few months later he became my third husband—or was he the fifth—I've had so many husbands I don't remember. Anyway, Arden was one of my favorites. The man made love for hours! And not during the early years of our marriage when I was a young lass with smooth skin, round hips, bouncy breasts, and a tight twat. No, Arden was a rare lover: a sensual man who sucked on my tits and gorged on my clit until he died at ninety years old. Not a day passed during our seventy-year marriage that Arden did not take me in his arms each night and stroke my body until I shook with ecstasy.

Arden was a man of the soil, coaxing great yields from tiny plots and growing vegetables of exceptional size, and these talents extended into the bedroom. Arden loved fucking me with parsnips and carrots, which he insisted I make a stew of the next day. Sometimes as he slid his cock between my breasts, I fucked myself with a large parsnip. Other times he fucked me with two or three carrots clenched in his fist. *Mo chreach*, I would come so hard, I'd squirt my bliss out my cunny. "Rain on me," he would say while I licked the turnip like it was his cock, and his own cock thrust into my cunny. And rain I did. My cry of ecstasy loud as thunder before I gushed with pleasure. Arden loved his vegetables as much as he loved honey. He would coat my tits and ass with honey and lick for hours. His honey-ass licking always made me orgasm, and before he had a chance to lick it clean I would shout "Fuck me, fuck me," so loud the sheep started bleating. When the children were grown and gone, we ate our supper off each other's body. He'd tickle my nipples with parsley and brush a sorrel leaf over my clit and—

"Any ale to go with that?"

I start, lost in the memories of happy times and sexual longing, and find the innkeeper standing over me.

I tug out another coin. "Tell me about the men in these parts."

"Looking for a new husband?" He lifts a bushy eyebrow.

I guffaw despite his accurate question. "I'm looking for a man of honor."

The proprietor sets down the ale. "Well, most seem honorable enough until they're drunk on mead." He scratches his straggly beard. "Around here, the young ones think they know everything—can't give them any advice. The older ones work hard taking care of their wives and bairns. A couple months back, though, a young man stopped in for some supper, said he was from the north and had come to visit his uncle—the laird of these parts." The innkeeper pulls a stool near him and takes a seat. "The inn was busy that day so I didn't have time to talk to him, but he made an impression just the same."

"Why is that?"

"He spoke like he was educated and..." The innkeeper tugs on his beard in thought. "Well, calm and sure, like he was used to having people listen and respect him. But that's not why I remember him. It was how he stopped a raging argument that was one fist from a brawl."

My ears perk up. "How did he do that?"

"About five villagers—good but ornery men—were arguing over the pike fishing, something about the best way to catch them, when all five pull out their knives."

"Over fish?"

"The best way to catch a pike is a fair argument in

these parts. So, this lad, calm and cool, steps between them and asks a few questions. A few minutes later, their knives are sheathed and they're laughing."

"Just like that?"

"Just like that. Before you know it, the fishermen are buying each other rounds and joking with the lad like they're old friends."

"Some folks have a way about them," I say.

The proprietor stands. "Don't know if the lad is honorable, or even which gods he prays to, but his easy way with those clansmen was impressive."

"Some of the most evil men I know have hundreds of friends." I drink deeply from the mug of ale, and taste the added henbane, which increased the brew's potency.

"Aye, isn't that the truth."

I finish the ale, wipe my lips with the back of my hand. "Thank you, sir. Best stew I've had in a long time."

"Not staying the night?"

"No, I best be going. I've got a long way to go." This wee village doesn't have the kind of man I am looking for.

I pass a few women along the street, but not one offers a greeting. This irritates me. I am the Cailleach! I taught mankind how to thresh using a holly stick and hazel wood. Ignorant fools. Their eyes see only a hobbling woman leaning on her walking stick. Their minds are blind to my true self. What words or help they would offer if they knew this aspen stick is a *slachdan*, one thump on the ground making soil unfertile or the shoreline rock-strewn. They do not see the goddess within.

My fingers tighten around the *slachdan* when a young wife, assuming I've come to beg, hurries inside her home. I am glad to cross over the trestle, removing the mud from my shoes with my *slachdan*. No sense carrying the village's discourtesy with me to the next place.

Nearby, a hooded crow caws and lifts off the fence post, his white body and black wings framed against the blue sky as he soars skyward. I follow his flight and see twenty miles into the distance, where a large village nestles against a hill.

My mind wanders as I walk. To earlier times and other husbands. I've had many. So many I lose count. The crow swoops down, alighting on a boulder ahead, the urgency of its caw reminding me of Maccus, husband number three—or was it four? Maccus was one of my favorite husbands. He was a big man with a huge cock, his lust so urgent he took me whenever and wherever the mood struck him. The crow's caw also reminds me of his rhythm. Caw-caw...caw. Maccus would swoop down on me like a crow and take me. Against a tree. On the ground. Anywhere. It was always a delightful surprise, his cock hard and eager as he lifted my skirt and rammed into me. Two thrusts later I would be wet, his eager hands groping my breasts. His impatience excited me beyond measure—he was so overcome with lust for me he couldn't control himself! During our wedding feast, I slipped away to pee and Maccus followed me. The sound of my water tinkling on the ground made his cock stand forth and he pushed me against the tree, lifted my dress, and thrust homeward. I wrapped my legs around him and enjoyed the ride as he ram-ram...rammed into me. No fondling, no caresses, just raw passion between husband and wife.

"You're as tight as my fist." Maccus's fingers dug into the soft flesh of my ass. "And slippery as a fish. Finally, I found a woman who likes to be fucked good and hard."

When we returned to the feast, my back was bruised, my pussy sore, and cum ran down my leg. Maccus's attacks never stopped, and my cunny got wet just anticipating them. Once, during the eve of Samhain, I was stirring a pot of stew over the hearth when Maccus sat at my feet, threw my skirt over his head, and supped on my clit.

"Keep stirring." He slipped two fingers into my wet slit.

It was difficult to stand, let alone stir soup, when my legs shook with pleasure. I ended up beating the wooden ladle against the stone hearth as my excitement mounted, snapping it in half as I crested, my body jerking and trembling as the pressure broke over me and coursed through my limbs.

Maccus scooted out from under my skirt, licked his lips, and pulled down his bracae. He bent me over and fucked me from behind until I came again.

He pulled out then, and set my hand on his cock, warm and slick from my cunny. "Stir my pot, Cailli."

I finished him with my hand, his cum spilling into the stew. On Samhain, we got so excited eating our special stew, we put aside our bowls and fucked right there on the table. One of the legs snapped in two mid-thrust, but that didn't stop us. My ass slid down the tilted tabletop, Maccus's deep thrusts and the wobbly table shaking my cunny into a precarious bliss.

The years passed and Maccus remained horny as

ever. I'd be bent over picking blueberries, my ass wiggling, and this would incite his lust so much he'd take me right there. He demanded I feed him the sweet berries while he ram-ram . . . rammed into me. I never bathed alone. Each attempt resulted in my legs wrapped around his hips, his cock plunging inside, my cunny sluiced with cum and lake water. While we sat at the table at our youngest's wedding feast, he slipped his hand under my skirt and rubbed my clit. A coughing fit covered my orgasm, normal enough for a seventy-year-old woman.

"Fuck me, Cailli." Maccus licked his finger. "The taste and smell of you is making my cock ache."

So while family and friends supped on salmon, I was on my hands and knees, Maccus rubbing my ass through the skirt as he drove into me.

"Still tight as my fist and slippery as a fish," he said.

"Granny, what are you looking for?"

I turned my head, saw my eldest granddaughter, a redheaded lass just seven years old, walking down the path toward us.

Though the brambles offered some concealment, Maccus arranged my skirt but didn't pull out. "Granny lost her ring. I'm helping her look for it. Don't worry yourself and get back to the party."

We waited until we no longer heard the twigs snapping under her feet, then Maccus smacked my ass hard and sunk deep into me. The thrill of almost getting caught and Maccus's impatient thrusting ripened my clit. Each of his thrusts ratcheted me nearer to bliss. We orgasmed together, his grunts and my moans united in ecstasy. Afterward, he adjusted his bracae, helped me up, my knees creaking with the effort, and dusted away the bits of leaf crushed into my skirt at the knees. We returned, two old folk, wrinkled and hobbling, no one the wiser.

I am so lost in the past, my clit aching with the memory of good fucking, that I am surprised when a large stone house appears around the bend. Sitting on a stool by the door, a ruddy-cheeked young man with thick, curly red hair and eyes blue as the loch sharpens his blade with a whetstone. He leaps to his feet when he sees me struggling up the steep path.

He slips his arm around my thick waist. "Lean on me, granny." His smile is warm and bright as summer. "Why don't you rest a bit at the top?" He's a strapping youth, strong limbed with muscles like granite.

"I suppose I should." I let him help me to the stool, my knees creaking as I sit.

"Some ale or mead for you, granny?" His gaze rests briefly on my *slachdan*, giving a quick squint at the letters carved into it.

"Aren't you a kind lad. Some mead would be nice," I say impressed by this handsome young man's hospitality. "My name is Cailli. What's yours?"

"Judoc," he says before disappearing inside.

Moments later he returns with mead and a plaid blanket, which he drapes carefully over my shoulder. "Don't want to catch a chill when the sun dips behind the hill, do we?" He sits on the ground in front of me. "Where are you going?"

"I'll know when I get there." I sip on the honey-sweet mead.

"*How* will you know?"

Judoc's refusal to be satisfied with my vagueness reveals his intelligence, which makes me wonder if this is the lad the tavern keeper told me about.

"I've been on this journey before. My heart will tell me when I have found honor and valor."

"How often do you find those?" Judoc's eyebrows lift with another probing question.

"I've found them before, and I will again." I move my head from right to left. "Where are your wife and bairns?"

"I'm not married. Haven't found the right woman yet."

"Picky are you?" I poke his leg with my *slachdan*.

Judoc chuckles. "Discriminating. How many miserable marriages have you seen?"

"Too many."

Judoc tilts his head, his loch-blue eyes bright with intelligence. "Were you fortunate enough to have a happy marriage?"

"Indeed, I was." All seven of my marriages were happy but I can't tell him that.

"What's the secret?"

I lean forward, resting my chin on both hands on top of the *slachdan*. "Do you *really* want to know or are you just humoring an old woman?"

"I've inherited my uncle's lands and the lassies are flocking to me like seagulls over a boat full of fish. They wiggle their asses, bat their eyes, and brush their bosoms against my arm. With so many choices, how can I find the woman who will be a helpmate and not a hindrance to my aspirations?"

Ah, so this *is* the lad the tavern keeper spoke of. "What *are* your aspirations?"

"Helping my tenants prosper. Settling old disputes with angry lairds." He thrust out his arm. "Unifying this land."

"Worthy goals." I draw the blanket around me. "I will reveal my secret to a happy marriage but it's *my* secret, others may have different secrets."

Judoc glanced at the sun dipping below the hill. "I'll make you a deal: Tell me your secrets and I will share my supper and give you a warm bed to spend the night."

"Deal."

Judoc helped me from the stool and into the house. It is a fine three-room home with carved furniture and braided rugs.

"This was my uncle's home. A few months ago I came to visit, only to find him dying with fever. Since he had no sons he bequeathed me all his property. He was a clever man; he understood people as well as he understood numbers and letters."

I sit down on a chair near the hearth. "And your father?"

"Also a great man. A laird north of here." Judoc stirred a pot hanging over the hearth. "The gods have given me an opportunity I cannot refuse: A bond to both north and south. A bond I will use to unite the warring clans."

Judoc is the one! The new sovereign I have been searching for.

Judoc sets a bowl of stew before me. "Now tell me the secret of a happy marriage. What kind of lady will help me unite our land?"

"Two things." I slurp the broth from the spoon. "First, a sense of humor. Second..." I mush the parsnip between my teeth and swallow. "A lady who loves fucking you."

Judoc spits out his mead, laughing so hard, tears spring from his eyes. "Granny—"

"Cailli," I remind him.

"That was the last thing I expected from your wise lips."

I laugh with him. "Why? Great fucking binds you together when times are tough and makes the easy times feel like paradise." I lift my gnarled finger in the air. "You *must* pleasure her. Find out what she likes. Help her discover her sexuality."

Judoc's eyes widen.

"Teach her how to suck your cock. Lick her cunny until she screams and bucks with pleasure. Make sure her pleasure comes first. Her juices will slicken your ride and her fervor will throb against your cock and increase your pleasure."

Judoc gulps down the rest of his mead.

"Suck on her tits and stroke the skin around her anus and have her do the same to you. Pleasure knows no bounds. Explore them well, every nook and cranny of each other's bodies. Let her inhale the scent of your balls. Rub your cock between her breasts and rain your cum on her. Fuck hard and fuck often."

Judoc shifts in his chair, and I can see his cock is stiff.

I sit back and smile.

Judoc stands and walks to the hearth for a refill. "No wonder you have a glint in your eye. You've had years of good loving. How long since your husband died?"

"Ten years." Since the last one. "We had sex the

morning he died. Oh, he was a horny old goat. Twice a day and sometimes three if he finished his chores early."

Judoc returns to the chair, his face flushed from the heat of both hearth and loin. "I need a woman like you, Cailli."

I open my arms. "Here I am."

Judoc laughs. "If only you were younger or I were older . . ." He gobbles down his stew. I forgot how much a young man can eat. When the bowl is empty, he points to the bedroom. "Would you prefer my bed or a cot by the fire?"

"I'd prefer a kiss."

"My pleasure. I can't remember when I've had a more enlightening conversation." Judoc sets a soft kiss on my wrinkled forehead.

That won't do at all.

"I'll lie by the fire," I say. "My bones need the warmth."

Judoc lays a thick mat near the hearth, piling it high with blankets. He bids me good night and lies on the big carved bed in the other room.

Walking all day tires me out, so I fall asleep quickly. Sometime during the night the fire goes out and I begin to shiver. Judoc must hear my chattering teeth because he gets up and rekindles the flame. My skin is old and thin, and I shiver despite the warmth.

"I'm sorry I let the fire go out, gran—Cailli. I'm a poor host." Judoc lies down behind me. His body heat warms my bones better than any fire. "You're freezing." He hugs me until I stop shaking.

I snuggle into him, the fragrant smoke mixing with the scent of his maleness.

"If I had a woman like you, I would be happy," he says into my white hair.

Despite my stiff neck, I turn my head. "You'll find the right woman."

Judoc touches his lips to mine. It's a kiss of goodness and heartfelt respect, of admiration and adoration. It's the right kind of kiss.

It happens quickly. My brittle bones strengthen. My hair changes from white to deep auburn. My skin smooths and tightens. Every wrinkle vanishes. My stomach firms and plumps, and my ass grows round and succulent as a blueberry. My breasts swell and lift, and my breath sweetens.

Judoc jumps up and stares at me, his mouth agape. "Who are you?"

I pull my dress off, the firelight casting a golden glow over my young naked body, and enjoy the heat of his stare.

"Are you an enchantress?" Judoc's gaze wanders the length of my body.

"I am the Cailleach, daughter of the little sun. Your righteous kiss turned me back into a young maiden again." I roll on my side so he can better admire the dip of my waist and curve of my hip.

Judoc's mouth hangs open. "*The* Cailleach? The ageless goddess of winter?"

"Yes, and the Mother of Mountains and Maker of Kings." I bite my lip and smile.

Judoc kneels before me, his head shaking in amazement. "My kiss transformed you? Just like that?"

"Just like that." Now is not the time to tell Judoc I have chosen him to be the next great sovereign. He is too besotted, my beauty and nakedness inflaming his lust.

Judoc stretches out his hand to trace the contours of my body. "Your skin is as smooth as butter." His eyes shine with desire. "I want you, Cailli."

"You may have me." I thrust out my breasts.

Judoc gives me a tender grin. "I want *you*, but not just your beautiful body for one short night. I want the sassy spirit that captured my attention the moment you came to my door." Judoc tugs on my nipple. "Would you ever consider wedding a man like me?"

I stroke his face, rough with stubble. "You'll have to prove yourself."

He bends over and kisses my forehead, then my eyelids, nose, cheeks, and chin. "Cailli, Cailli." He brushes his mouth across mine, parts my lips with his tongue, and rolls me onto my back.

He tastes of ale and vigor, and I savor his prodding tongue with my own. He is bold as his lips, teeth, and tongue explore my mouth. He bites my lips and I yelp with delight. The satisfying sting sends a tingle straight to my cunny. I nibble back and he groans, his hand finding my bosom and its ripe nipples. Judoc lowers his head and sucks hard on each one, each fervent tug engorging my clit. His hand caresses my belly, skims over my hips to grab a fair handful of ass. I gasp at his confidence as his hand slides between my cheeks to feel my cunny from behind. I drape my leg over him as his fingers glide over my wetness and bring it to my anus. I arch my back and moan and he does it again, two fingers rubbing against my clit then back up to encircle my anus. My cunny throbs and my sphincter pulses tighter with each pass.

Judoc gives each nipple a quick bite before laying me on my back and pushing my thighs apart. "I know you'll like this." He spreads me wide and sticks out his tongue.

I gasp! His tongue is long! Longer than I've ever seen before. He curls the sides inward and I giggle.

"Fuck me with that tongue!" I say.

"Not yet." Judoc laps his tongue across my cunny while I writhe under him. Tremors of anticipation gather at my engorged valley, building as he loops his tongue around my clit.

I grab a fistful of his red curls and spread my thighs wide, and when I feel his tongue enter my sex, I cry out with delight. I am molten beneath him, my nether parts throbbing, my mind fixed on release. And then, as the pleasure pushes outward, he shoves his finger into my anus. Finger and tongue thrust in unison as I scream my pleasure to the sky. It is waves crashing against the cliffs. A flock of birds lifting up all at once, the air tumultuous with their flight. My toes curl as bliss thrashes over my body.

Judoc scrambles atop me, lifts both legs over one broad shoulder and plows into me.

"You're so fucking tight!" he gasps. "I can't hold back—I can't. . . ." He slows down and looks at me, takes measured deep breaths, controls himself. "I'm going to fuck you often and hard, Cailli. Just like you like it."

Judoc brings me to orgasm three more times before he loses control and hammers against me without restraint. He rumbles his orgasm as one hand tugs my hair.

Sweating and sticky and smelling like my pussy, he lowers himself beside me. "Am I worthy?"

"Never had a man double fuck me with tongue and finger." I smooth his curls back from his forehead. "You might just be my new favorite."

The morning dawns cool and clear when Judoc kisses me awake. "Will you marry me?"

I wrinkle my nose and giggle. "Only if you do it again."

And we do. Again and again.

Years pass, and Judoc unites the clans, bringing prosperity and peace to the land. I give him six sons and four daughters. My happiness is revealed through the seasons with fine weather, fertile land and animals, and plentiful fish and fowl. Judoc lives to be ninety-nine years old, and our marriage is full of laughter and love and good sex. And before I know it I am old, once again the Auld Wyfe of Thunder.

I am the Cailleach. Heed me well.

Stories about the Celtic Goddess of Ireland, Scotland, and England date back to before Christianity. The ninth-century poem, "The Old Woman of Beare" is a favorite. The Cailleach, also known as the Queen of Winter and the Veiled One, is credited with forming the rocky cliffs, mountains, and megaliths.

OF TOLLS
AND TITHES

"Oh my." Janet looked out the window, surprised to see dark clouds obscuring the September sun. "I must get home. Father will be worried and it looks like it's going to rain."

Cheek to cheek, Janet and her best friend, Brianna, gazed skyward at the gathering storm.

"Stay here tonight." Brianna nudged Janet. "We can ask Nora about . . ." She burst into a fit of giggles.

Sex. It had been the topic of discussion all afternoon, the two virgins of marriageable age whispering about the mysteries of men and what to expect.

"Nora? The cook? Oh my. She's so old," said Janet, sniffing the air.

It smelled like rain.

"*You* ask Nora." Janet picked up her green mantle, draped the long wool fabric around her shoulders, and adjusted it to cover her head.

Brianna blanched. "She'd tell Father, and then he'll lock me in my room until my wedding day. No, *you* must ask her."

Janet smiled. "Next visit." She tapped a kiss on Brianna's cheek. "I have to hurry. My father will lock *me* in a room if I'm not home before dark."

Brianna opened the front door. "Maybe you can catch a ride home on a farmer's wagon."

"Father doesn't like me taking rides from his tenants. They'll expect a reward. I'll take a shortcut," said Janet.

Brianna pursed her lips and narrowed her eyes. "Don't go through the forest. It's too dangerous. Tam Lin will stop you and make you pay a toll for crossing."

Janet laughed, her scattered freckles dancing on her cheeks. "I'm not afraid of a faerie no one has ever seen before." She tucked a disobedient lock of golden hair behind her ear.

Brianna's fingers dug into her arm. "My grandmother met him and had to pay the ultimate price."

Janet was a kindhearted girl; she did not want to tell Brianna that Tam Lin was a story invented by young women as a way to justify lost virginity. What better way to explain the lack of blood on the nuptial sheet than a faerie stealing your virginity because of a shortcut through the woods?

"Okay, I won't go that way." Janet's stomach twisted at the lie, but she didn't want to offend her friend. In truth, she was more fearful of her father's anger than an imaginary faerie.

"Promise?"

"Promise." Janet hugged Brianna just as the first drop of rain hit her freckled button nose.

Janet hurried away, hitching up her kirtle and breaking into a run at the edge of the village. As the crow flies, her house was not far, just beyond the large grove of alder, ash, birch, and oak. But because the town folk believed it was inhabited by fae, no road had been cut through it, the only way to the lord's manor a wide dirt road around the woods. Janet's father, Lord Grady, having read philosophy at the University of Oxford, did not believe in fae. Yet he never scoffed at the villagers' belief, although he did remind his daughter that the woods were fine places for poachers and thieves to hide.

Another drop splashed on Janet's rosy cheek. It wouldn't be long before the clouds opened up and poured down.

Janet lifted her face to the sky and felt a third drop. The rain would feel good on this hot September day. She was about to round the bend when she heard angry shouting. She stopped, inching forward until she saw the cause of the fracas. Two of her father's tenants were yelling at each other, one farmer pointing at his overturned cart of asparagus, carrots, and peas. The second farmer, his own cart filled with broad beans and cucumbers, pointed to his donkey's lifted hind leg.

Worse yet, a rowdy group of big-boned farm boys carrying sickles and hoes were coming from the other direction. Janet knew trouble when she saw it. Although her intended shortcut was farther down the road—a dogleg through the edge of the woods—she changed her mind to avoid the men, and stepped into the woods just as the first scatterings of raindrops fell to the ground.

If she walked fast enough she would make it home before dark, the trees providing some shelter from the rain. Soon enough, Janet spied a footpath that seemed to meander in the right direction.

The early evening storm clouds emitted an eerie light, all grays and dull greens under a drab plum-colored sky. The raindrops plop-plop-plopped, loud splats on the leafy canopy that rolled off and splashed to the ground. It sounded like twice the rainfall.

Janet lifted her foot and checked the underside of her soft leather shoes. They were still dry. She swallowed her uneasiness as the tall trees closed in around her, their gnarled limbs reaching out overhead like woodland specters. Only the twittering birds eased her foreboding.

Up ahead was a small clearing with a covered stone well draped by a tangle of roses and honeysuckle over its roof. The clearing was bright and vivid with green ferns and pink petals. The sweet fragrance of both flowers drew Janet like a bee. Moss hugged the stone well in a checkerboard pattern, and an old wooden bucket sat on the ledge. Nearby, a steed the color of milk munched on some grass. Surely, the horse belonged to someone.

"Anybody here?" Janet stepped into the clearing, glad to leave the forest's dark gloom despite the light rain.

The horse looked up, shook its head, then walked into the woods.

Assuming the horse had wandered away from his owner and she was alone, Janet took a moment to pick a few roses growing near the well for Ethne, the old cook who was like a mother to her. Janet took hold of a thick vine and snapped off a long stemmed rose in full bloom.

"Mmmm." Janet inhaled its sweetness and reached out for another.

"You're destroying my home."

Janet spun on her heels and found a shirtless man

leaning against a tree, large muscular biceps crossed over a hard, hairless chest.

She thrust out the flowers, surprise making her forget that it was her father who owned the Carterhaugh woods and fields. "I'm sorry."

The man tucked his chestnut-colored hair behind his ears. Janet gasped.

His ears were large and pointed. His pale skin without blemish. And his hair had an unnatural sheen. Janet blushed. The green cloth tied around his hips was scandalously low and stopped too high above his thighs. The faerie was practically naked!

He pushed himself off the tree and circled about her. "How dare you steal from me?"

The faerie was tall, the top of Janet's head well below his broad shoulders.

Janet straightened her spine. "Steal? These woods belong to my father, Lord Grady."

The faerie rolled his eyes. "The Queen of Faeries owns these woods. Lord Grady is merely a temporary *mortal* caretaker."

Janet chewed on her lip in thought, then wiggled the roses at him. "I *said* I was sorry. Here, take the flowers, and I'll be on my way."

"You have a toll to pay first." The faerie gently pushed back the mantle over her head. He sighed with pleasure as he spread his fingers into the nape of her neck, releasing the coiled blonde tresses. "Your hair is like spun gold." He combed his fingers through it, his touch sending shivers of pleasure through Janet. "I could get lost in its waves and"—he wrapped a tendril around his finger and pulled Janet close—"curls."

Blood pounded in Janet's ears and her mouth watered as though she were hungry. "Are you Tam Lin?"

The faerie bent down. "At your service." His warm breath tickled her ear.

A squeak sprung unbidden from Janet's lips.

Tam Lin's finger wandered over her cheeks and the bridge of her nose. "Did you know your freckles match the pattern of the stars overhead?"

Janet's eyes grew wide, his voice and touch so enthralling that all her fears vanished. "How do you know? The sky is overcast." At that moment, several raindrops fell on her face.

Tam Lin lifted a droplet to his finger and tasted. "Delicious." He flicked off the others with his tongue.

His intimate touch sent thrilling quivers through Janet's limbs, and a strange warmth gathered below, a pleasing tug in her nethers she had never felt before. "I best be going." She took a step backward, tripped over a tree root, and fell on her bum.

Instead of helping her up, Tam Lin sat beside her. "The woods are a dangerous place for pretty girls." He placed his hand on her bare ankle.

"I *really* must be going." Janet made no move to get up. The feel of his fingers stroking her ankle stirred her nethers even more.

"As soon as you pay the toll." He slid off one shoe and held her wee bare foot in his large hand.

"I don't have any money," she said as he slid off the other shoe. "Or jewelry."

Tam Lin lifted her foot to his mouth and whisked a kiss across the underside that rocketed a hot tingle up her leg.

Janet sucked in the damp air. "I can get it for you. Father will pay you."

Tam Lin shook his head, then wrapped his lips around her big toe and sucked.

"Oh my!" said Janet. His sucking stiffened her nipples!

Tam Lin slowly drew her toe past his lips. "The toll is gold, jewels or..."

"My toes?" Maybe the myth was wrong and Tam Lin just had a toe fetish.

"Your maidenhead." Tam Lin snaked his hand up her kirtle and caressed her inner thigh.

"*Oh* my!" Janet exhaled, the heated tug in her nethers now quite uncomfortable. She crossed her legs and scooted away on her bum. "Father will pay you *double* the amount."

"The Faerie Queen demands the toll be paid immediately." Tam Lin crawled forward and caught the hem of her kirtle. He drew himself over her, pushing her down until her head rested upon a pillow of velvet moss. "Faerie Queen's rules, not mine. I'm only her captive and a member of her elfin knights." His index finger traced the edge of her flower-stitched bodice.

Janet breathed hard, her eyes trained on his hand. Was it only an hour ago that she and Brianna had discussed *this*? "The Faerie Queen kidnapped you?"

"Aye, many years ago I was on a hunting trip with Lord Roxburgh, my grandfather, when something—the Faerie Queen no doubt—spooked my horse and sent him rearing. I lost my balance and fell off right into the Faerie Queen's arms and into faerie land. But enough about me." Tam Lin brushed his hand across her bodice and Janet's breasts heaved beneath. "A man could feast on your bosom for hours." Tam Lin gave them a gentle squeeze. "But a faerie could suckle for a lifetime." He pulled the neckline over her shoulders and shimmied the kirtle over her lovely heavy breasts, grinning when he saw the large mauve areolas and pointed pink nipples.

"Oh my!" said Janet as two fat raindrops dripped down and ran between her cleavage.

A breast in each hand, Tam Lin lowered his head and flicked his tongue up the tiny rivulet. The touch of his tongue moistened her cunny.

"*Oh* my!" Janet arched her back and thrust her bosom forward.

Tam Lin massaged her breasts, his mouth wandering over her creamy skin and his tongue licking her nipples. Janet couldn't protest—didn't want to protest. The sensations rendered her incapable of anything but most unladylike sounds.

Tam Lin kissed upward. He nuzzled her neck before tracing her lips with his thumb. "What's your name, my bonny blonde lass?"

"Janet," she panted. The feel of his hand as he caressed her breasts made her breathless with desire.

"May I kiss you, Janet?" His breath was fresh as the forest after a rainfall, with a hint of rosemary.

"Oh yes, please."

He ran his thumb over her lips until she parted them. Then he teased the soft underside of her lower lip. Her tongue flicked over his. The lass was ripe and ready, hungry to be deflowered.

"Taste me, Janet." He stuck his thumb inside, her mouth warm, her tongue looping around him.

When Janet began to suck on his thumb, he withdrew it and set his mouth over hers. Her tongue was eager, probing and demanding. Janet wrapped her arms around him and smashed their lips together. She drew her breath from his, plundering his mouth, ravenous for the taste of him.

Tam Lin drew his hands downward, pausing only to circle her nipples, before he pushed the kirtle to her ankles. Janet quickly kicked it off. He caressed her smooth ass and drifted over the golden thatch of curls.

Janet's eyes flew open and she pushed him away. "Not—"

Tam Lin kissed her nose, then rolled off her, smiling at the frightened but horny virgin sprawled atop the mossy bed.

Janet bit her lip—her frightened look was so appealing that Tam Lin felt a stab to his heart.

"I'll be gentle." Tam Lin picked up the discarded flowers, plucked off a petal and, using its tip, traced a slow line from her forehead to the mound of golden curls. Janet cooed, her thighs separating. Tam Lin plucked another petal and set it on Janet's lips. "Eat."

Janet sucked in the petal and chewed, surprised by its sweet taste.

Tam Lin flicked the bloom across her breasts, her thighs parting even more, then he fluttered the flower downward, flickering it over her golden thatch until her back arched.

Janet's nethers throbbed with a wondrous but annoying sensation, like an itch needing to be scratched. "I'm afraid."

Tam Lin spread her thighs, inhaled her fragrance,

and his cock swelled even larger. "Afraid of your own body? Nonsense." He pulled her to a sitting position, spread her wide. "You're like a flower."

Janet looked down. "Oh MY." It *was* a flower. With pink petals and small nub. "But where does *it* go?"

Tam Lin untied the cloth about his waist, revealing his cock that was twice as long as her foot and thick as a maypole.

"*Oh my!* How will that ever fit inside me?"

"Quite well." Tam Lin took her hand and guided it to him. "Ah…" he sighed as her hand closed around it.

Janet squeezed his cock, gasping when she felt its hardness and squealing with delight when his skin moved beneath her as she pumped. She stopped when Tam Lin groaned.

"Am I hurting you?"

"Best kind of hurt, Janet." He wiped a raindrop from her lash. "Go ahead, indulge your curiosity."

Janet felt the smooth head, walked her fingers down his shaft to his balls. She gave a soft squeeze, astonished by its softness, then brushed the sparse hair back and forth.

Tam Lin lifted her hand away. "Now it's time to explore yourself, lassie." He spread her wide again, his breath growing ragged as he watched Janet touch herself.

"Oh my," she said upon discovering the thrill of rubbing the little nub. "Oh-oh my."

Tam Lin joined her exploration and dipped his finger into her. "My cock goes here." He lifted his finger to her mouth so she could taste. As she licked, his cock jerked, and he hoped he wouldn't spill his seed too soon.

Janet continued to rub her clit. She couldn't stop, the pulsing throb a pleasure she never wanted to end. And yet she knew instinctually this road ended someplace wonderful.

The rain fell more quickly, Janet's coos grew louder, and Tam Lin knew it was time. He climbed between her legs. "Are you ready, wee lass?"

"Oh yes," Janet groaned.

Janet grabbed his ass as Tam Lin glided his cock back and forth against her clit, Janet's *oh-mys* warming his heart and hardening his cock. When her *oh-oh-ohs* reached a fevered pitch, he slid into her wet wonderland.

Tam Lin took her maidenhead at the same moment Janet climaxed. The bursting pleasure, accompanied by her packed cunny, catapulted her into faerie land. The world twirled around her and the air exploded in colors.

"*Oh my-my-my!*" Janet cried into the storm, the rain falling fast and hard.

She wrapped her legs around his hips as Tam Lin plowed into her, each thrust extending her bliss. They moved as one, their skin rain slick and hot. Tam Lin ground into her, her rapture speeding his own. Faster and faster he thrust. His tempo matched the only thing he heard, Janet's sweet *oh-mys*. He came with a howl and his cock squirted into her fleshly furrow.

Tam Lin arched his back as the final squirt sunk into her. "Oh my."

Janet laughed and opened her mouth to catch the rain. Her hair was soaked, her clothes wet, and her cunt sore, but she had never felt so wonderful. Sex was better than galloping across a field. Better than hot tea on a cold day. Better than eating warm blueberry pie fresh from the oven.

Tam Lin rolled off her, his cock still hard. "The toll is paid. Best fuck I ever had." He gestured to his horse. "Get dressed, my sweet Janet. My steed will take you to the edge of the forest."

Janet stood, her legs wobbly, and struggled to pull the wet kirtle over her body. She stood there, hands on hips, the fabric clinging to every curve. "Is that it then?"

Tam Lin looked away, his heart aching. "I'm sorry, lass." He wanted to fuck her again. Wanted to wrap her in his arms and confess his love. Wanted to tell her that never in a hundred years of taking maidenheads had his heart ever hurt for a girl's leaving except for today.

After putting on her shoes, Janet snatched the flowers. "I'll be taking these."

Heavy hearted and with his cock still eager for more, Tam Lin watched her mount his steed and disappear into the woods.

It wasn't until Janet saw her house through the trees and pouring rain that the shame of her actions crushed down on her.

"Tam Lin seduced me," she said to herself as she slid off the horse. She gave two quick pats on the horse's hindquarters and it turned away back to its faerie owner.

Janet hitched up her kirtle and ran the rest of the way home. Maybe it was a dream. She knew better. Tam Lin's seed stuck to her thighs.

"Dear child," said Ethne throwing a thick blanket over her shoulders the moment Janet ran through the front door. "Take your clothes off before you catch a fever. I'll bring you a pot of tea."

Janet's tears loosened as she bounded upstairs to her

room, only stopping when Ethne brought in a gleaming silver platter of biscuits and a steaming pot of tea. It wasn't until Ethne closed the door behind her and Janet lifted the teacup to her lips that she realized fucking Tam Lin was the most horrible, tragic, wonderful, exciting event of her life. She wanted to tell Brianna how amazing fucking felt, how it was nothing like they thought, how the old women were wrong about it all, how it felt to have your tits sucked and your nethers fondled, how incredible to feel a man's cock deep inside you. But she couldn't dare tell Brianna. Or anyone. Why, she was a fallen woman now and would have to pretend to be a virgin when she got married.

Weeks passed and Janet grew unwell. Ethne blamed it on her getting caught in the rain. Her father said it more likely she had caught sickness from someone in the village.

It was mid-October, the first chill in the air, when Janet sat with twenty-four ladies playing chess. Her stomach lurched and she leapt from her chair and vomited lunch into a nearby bucket.

"Still ill, child?" asked a gray-haired widow.

Janet put her hand to her belly. "Usually I'm only sick in the morning."

Twenty-four heads looked up from their chessboards, their eyes flickering back and forth amongst one another with a knowing look.

"You look a bit fuller at the bust, Lady Janet," said another. "Has Lord Grady's best knight stolen your goodies?"

The ladies' collective inhalations sucked the air from the room in anticipation of Janet's answer.

Janet's face turned beet red. "I did not lie with Sir Darach."

The knight was a womanizer with a penchant for drink and brawls.

The ladies saw shame on Janet's face and believed otherwise, especially when she did not deny her loss of virginity.

Janet excused herself and fled to her room. Pregnant! She was ruined! No man would marry her now. And her father—well, she didn't know what he'd do when he found out.

Janet set her hand on her flat belly. "The toll was too high. Not only did I fall in love with a faerie I can never marry, he sired a half-fae bastard."

That night after supper, Lord Grady summoned his daughter to his study. "Did he rape you or take you willingly?" He looked over the brim of his whiskey glass.

"I . . . I . . ." Janet clenched her dress, her hand shaking.

Lord Grady set down the cup with a loud thump. "Tell me, child. Did Sir Darach rape or seduce you?"

"I . . ."

"Janet, the man's been eyeing you a while. Tell me he raped you and I'll run a sword through his gut and save your honor."

"It's not his." Her voice squeaked like a mouse.

"Whose is it? Another lord? His son? Not some poor stable boy, I hope."

Janet blinked back her tears. "Oh Father, it's Tam Lin's."

Lord Grady threw back the whiskey and poured more. He studied her face—the obedient girl had never lied to him before—and found no evidence of deceit.

"The faerie in the woods that the villagers believe in? *That* Tam Lin?"

Janet ran to her father and threw herself at his knees. "I swear to you Father, it was him."

"What did he look like?"

Janet described Tam Lin's flawless skin, chestnut hair, and honey-smooth voice. She left out his chiseled physique, full lips, and enormous cock.

"Well, I'll be damned. You described him perfectly." Lord Grady lifted Janet's chin. "What am I to do with a half-fae bastard child?" He shook his head. "I waited too long to marry you off. It's partly my fault. Leave me be, daughter, I need to figure out how to take care of this mess."

Janet ran from the room and straight into Sir Darach, who had been listening at the door.

"I'll marry you, Janet." He took hold of her elbow. "After you give birth, I'll take the fae babe into the woods for the Faerie Queen."

"Ohhhh my." Janet jerked her arm away and ran to the scullery where she found Ethne slamming dough on the wooden table.

"I wondered when you'd come." Ethne folded the dough in half, pressed down hard, then smacked it on the table again.

"You know how to get rid of it?"

"Aye, but best do it soon, tomorrow if possible." Ethne folded and smacked, then told Janet where to find the plant that would expel the cursed half-fae child from her womb.

Though she spent the night weeping, Janet crept out of the manor early next morning before she lost her nerve. The pale purple flower she needed grew in abundance at the edge of the woods and Janet picked a large bouquet, her tears falling fast as she thought of the love she felt for Tam Lin and his unborn babe.

"I've no choice." Janet set her hand on her belly. "I'll be miserable if I marry Sir Darach and mortified for abandoning my newborn to the Faerie Queen. But if I keep you, I couldn't bear Father's humiliation and the shame I would bring upon him." She patted her belly. "You're cursed, anyway. A misshapen babe belonging to neither world."

"Cursed?" Tam Lin jumped down from the tree at the edge of the woods. "Janet, why do you want to kill the bonny babe created from our love?"

"Love?" Janet entered the woods. "It was a toll I had to pay."

Tam Lin took her hand and walked with her deeper into the woods. "Janet, I've thought of nothing but you since we met, and I confess, your *oh-mys* quite stole my heart." He lifted her hand and set his lips upon it. "A baby! *Our* baby. And just when I was ready to die."

"What do you mean?"

"Every seven years the Faerie Queen must pay a tithe to the devil. Usually it's a human captive or a faerie that has fallen out of favor with the queen. This time I know it's me—she's angry that I fell in love with you—so on the only night when the veil between our worlds is whisper thin she'll give my dead body to the devil."

"No." Janet dropped the pale purple flowers. "There must be some way to save you and break the curse."

Tam Lin sat down on the ground. "The Faerie Queen

is powerful and her magic too strong for a young lady like yourself."

Janet sat beside him and drew her fingers over his muscled biceps. "My strength comes from the strongest muscle of all, the heart." She clasped his hand to her bosom. "Tell me how to save you."

Tam Lin smiled at Janet. Her courage swelled his heart with love and admiration. "On the eve of Halloween, precisely at midnight, the faerie folk will gallop past Miles Cross."

"I know the place well."

"Hide in the bushes until both the black and brown horse pass. When the white steed passes, pull the rider off and hold him tight."

Janet's eyes widened.

"It will be me, Janet."

"How will I know?"

"I'll have a glove on my right hand but not on my left. My hat will be cocked above my brow and my hair will be hanging down. Hold me tight and don't be afraid when the Faerie Queen changes my form into a snake, a bear, a lion, and a red-hot iron. I'm in there, I promise, so hold tight. When I turn into a burning piece of coal throw me into the well."

"And then?" asked Janet chewing her lip all the while.

Tam Lin exhaled. "The spell will be broken."

"I can do that," said Janet with more confidence than she felt. She rested her head in Tam Lin's lap while he stroked her hair. "Tell me about faerie land."

Tam Lin told her everything, even confessing about his days as a mortal when he was an arrogant and insolent young knight. The hours passed quickly as the two lovers shared their hearts, their hopes for the future and that of their babe.

"Bring a green mantle," said Tam Lin after giving her a long lusty kiss. "It must be green."

The week passed quickly, and on the eve of Halloween, Janet crept out of the manor, ran to Miles Cross, and hid in the tall weeds by the stone well. At midnight, she heard the thunder of hooves.

Janet laid her hand on her belly. "For the sake of my true love and baby, I will not be afraid."

Through the reeds, Janet watched the faerie folk approach. The black horse passed. The second was brown. The third was a rider on a white steed with a gloveless left hand and flowing brown hair. Tam Lin! Janet sprung forward and grabbed the rider's ankle.

Tam Lin toppled from the horse and Janet wrapped her arms around him. For a second their eyes met. Then Tam Lin's eyes turned red, the irises narrowing and elongating into vertical black slits. Strong black scales wrapped around her and an adder's tongue flicked out. It was the Faerie Queen's curse. Janet held tight and closed her eyes. Suddenly Janet's arms felt as though they were being spread apart. When she opened her eyes the snake was gone and she found herself staring into the amber eyes of a large brown bear. He opened his mouth wide and bellowed, his four long incisors closing in on her. Janet screamed and tilted her neck away. Abruptly, the bear's fur changed, the thick rough coat turning into a plush pelt. The pupils morphed into a predatory yellow, with eyes rimmed in black. A lion opened its cavernous mouth and roared.

"I love you, Tam Lin," she shouted to the beast.

Quick as a lightning flash, the lion was gone. A red-hot poker was now clutched to her breast. Luckily, her thick wool mantle and layered kirtle protected her from getting burned. The fire-hot poker disappeared in her arms and a small burning piece of coal appeared. The final change! Janet held it tight in her gloved hand as she raced to the nearby well and tossed it in. The coal sizzled and floated for a moment before sinking under the water.

"Oh no!" cried Janet peering into the well. "Tam Lin, where are you?"

Tam Lin burst out of the water gasping for air. He took a deep breath and then touched the top of his ears.

"I'm human again! You did it, Janet. The spell is broken." He climbed naked out of the well and let Janet drape her green mantle around him.

"You wretched scoundrel!" screamed the Faerie Queen, flying out of the woods. Her lips were curled into a snarl, her eyes two dark slits, her face misshapen with rage. "You fell in love? I should have turned your heart to stone or blinded you!"

"Be gone, Queen of Faeries," said Tam Lin. "I've been in your service for too long."

"Arrggh!" The Faerie Queen flew around them twice before soaring back into the woods.

Tam Lin took Janet in his arms and kissed her, a human kiss that was rough and demanding, yet needy with love. Janet raked her hands through his hair, the faerie silkiness replaced by coarser locks. They devoured each other with their mouths, tasting, licking, probing, nibbling, and pausing only to declare their love.

Janet brushed her hand against Tam Lin's bare chest,

his human skin more exciting than the faerie smoothness.

"You're different and yet still the same." Janet traced
her finger down the pleasure trail of his stomach. "Oh
my, *that* hasn't changed at all."

His cock was still twice as long as her foot and thick
as a maypole. She clutched his cock and stroked its
length until he groaned.

"I haven't thanked you properly." Tam Lin scooped
her up and carried her to the well, where he sat her on
the wide ledge. He hiked up her kirtle, knelt down between her legs, and buried his head in her pussy.

"Oooh mmmmy," said Janet as his tongue swiveled
around her nub.

He ate well, slurping her honey, and flicked his
tongue across her pink bud until her legs quivered. Janet grabbed hold of his hair as the throbbing pleasure
mounted. He took long, languid strokes up and down
her cunny, drawing out the rising tension coursing
through her nethers.

Janet arched her back, held his hair tight, spread her
legs wider, and let out a long moan that sounded *nothing*
like *oh-my*. Tam Lin stroked her creamy inner thighs as
he slowed even more. This time Janet squealed loudly to
the sky. Slow lick by slow lick, he climbed the stairway
to her heaven, until her writhing groans signaled the
beginning of the end. He put his lips around her clit and
sucked, and Janet screamed and bucked against him,
smashing his face into her. Tam Lin pushed two fingers
into her and she howled with joy, her orgasm coming in
great waves.

Tam Lin stood up and his cock slid in to her sopping-wet joy. Janet climaxed again as he entered, his length and girth filling her beyond capacity. Tam Lin hoisted her legs over his shoulders and plunged deep, her ass lifting off the well with each fevered thrust. Again her pleasure mounted, tightening around him, her walls pulsing to his rhythm. Tam Lin pushed deeper and deeper, slower and slower, until his mind was gone and his ravenous cock took over. Together they crested the heights, their dual pleasure a single cry of ecstasy.

He stayed inside but lowered her legs around his waist. "I'll be fucking you like that for the rest of our lives."

"Oh my," said Janet.

The legendary romantic ballad of Tam Lin comes from Scotland. The first known printed version is found in 1549 in The Complaynt of Scotland, *a collection of folk legends, bible stories, and political tales published during the time of Mary, Queen of Scots.*

DIPLOMATIC
NECESSITIES

The landscape shimmers with the intense heat, hill upon hill of desert sands shifting and blurring beneath a cloudless sapphire sky. My caravan, loaded with gifts and goods, plods onward toward Israel, to Jerusalem, and to the wise king whose shrewd letter has bid me to pay him homage. I, Bilqīs, Queen of Sheba, ruler of over fifty thousand people, agreed to King Solomon's summons in hopes of negotiating a trade deal benefiting both our nations.

Above me, the *howdah's* awning shades me from the searing sun. Below, the saddle cushions my ride atop the camel's swaying gait. No queen has ever taken this six-month long and fifteen-hundred-mile journey over such parched and hostile terrain. My camels are loaded down with gold, precious gems, rare wood, myrrh, and the most valuable commodity of all, frankincense. The caravan takes a timeworn trade route, over *wadi*, dry riverbeds, and following the Red Sea north until we cross the Jordan River.

My *serdar* assures me we are near. He is an intelligent general whose courage, tenacity, and humanity I admire and value.

Duvsha, my servant and treasured friend, rides with me. She knows when I need conversation and when I require silence.

"Do you think King Solomon is as wise as everyone says?" asks Duvsha.

"Perhaps," I say, although I have my doubts.

"What about the gossip that he controls jinn and makes them sit behind his throne to do his bidding?"

"*That* I would like to see." I wonder if King Solomon knows my parentage. "Although I'm more interested in how he built such a powerful and prosperous nation."

"All this," says Duvsha, indicating with a sweeping gesture the long line of camels ahead of and behind us. "Because of a hoopoe."

The bird—tan except for its white-and-black-striped wings and spiky-plumed crown—had flown all the way to Jerusalem just to tell King Solomon about my beauty and wealth. Or so he claimed in his letter. More likely, traveling merchants told King Solomon of my prosperous nation in a far off land.

"One small bird will be responsible for great changes," I say.

When we enter Jerusalem a few days later, our large caravan causes every inhabitant to leave their mud brick dwellings to watch our procession. They know wealth and power when they see it, and all but the most feeble follow us to the palace. But it's not the people I study from behind the beaded, tasseled, and gold-threaded drapes of the *howdah*. My gaze is fixed on the enormous stone structure looming like a mountain over the city. Solomon's Temple. I am alone today, Duvsha riding with other handmaids, and have no one to share my amazement with.

"Magnificent," I say aloud, unable to contain my awe.

The palace is huge, its walls made of large axe-cut stones that rise three stories tall and are capped by a flat cedar roof. Slim rows of windows are squared, uniform, and in a logical arrangement. I have never see its like. My Temple of Almaqah, with its thirty-foot bull-and-ibex frieze, is grand but nothing like this.

I arrive at the palace and steady myself as the much-decorated camel lowers to its knees. I make a final adjustment to my head covering to make sure the long strands of jewels are draped becomingly and cover my face. King Solomon must be the first to see me.

"My queen, are you ready?" my *serdar* whispers from the other side of the drapery.

"I am."

Solomon's welcoming party issues a collective gasp when the drapery parts. I take Duvsha's outstretched hand and place my foot on the first wide step of the palace. The other handmaids take their positions around me and together we slowly ascend the steps and pass the hordes of dignitaries, inhabitants, and guards flanking our way. The crowd ripples with whispered conjectures, my appearance and magnificent entourage piquing their curiosity. Ordinarily, I would not submit myself to walking amongst a crowd—preferring to be carried in my royal litter by slaves—but not today. A more submissive entrance is required.

The palace's interior is much grander than the outside. Each wall is cedar-lined, and the vast chambers are adorned with stone statues and friezes depicting all types of beasts, trees, and cherubim.

As we enter a dazzling gold-painted reception hall, my gaze sweeps back and forth beneath the veil. My head never moves—it's best not to appear *too* impressed.

King Solomon waits on the other side of a shallow, crystal-blue pond. How odd I must cross over it. Perhaps it is some ritual ablution that must be performed before meeting him.

I study the king. He is a handsome man, tall and robust, with a thick dark beard. His eyes are deep set and glimmer with knowing and pride. His nose is well shaped and strong, and, I suspect, flares when angry.

I lift my long red skirt, displaying my shapely, sugar-waxed calves, and hear one hundred gasps. I'm glad they can't see my eyes roll. I know the gossip. Some of Solomon's advisors claim I am a demon with hairy legs and cloven feet. This is a test, and I passed. I step into the glistening pond, surprised to discover it is not water but countless tiny crystals.

I cross this crystal pond alone, leaving my attendants on their knees behind me. At the other side I kneel down, my head to the floor.

"Welcome to Jerusalem. Arise," says King Solomon with a deep smoky voice that seems to nestle at the base of my neck.

I rise and lift the veil. I am beautiful. This is not vanity or conceit but a fact based on many experiences and opinions. Even before I was queen, men were enamored by my appearance, envious women sneered, and babies cooed. Although beauty is a benefit for a woman, it is a disadvantage for a queen. Beauty is not equated with intelligent leadership, but with carnal desires. Beauty is like a thick mist—it hides a woman's other traits, good or bad. What a mistake mankind makes when they value beauty over all else.

Today, however, I will use my beauty to my advantage, and have even applied makeup to enhance my features. My amber eyes are lined with black kohl, the lids shimmering purple and dusted with crushed amethyst. My lips are reddened with berries, my brows groomed and shaped to enhance my almond-shaped eyes. Between my brows and to the bridge of my nose hang multiple strands of rubies and other gems.

I look into the eyes of the king and find him staring, agape and transfixed.

"It is a privilege, King Solomon," I say. "And an honor to be summoned to your palace."

His mouth opens but no words come out.

I smile then, revealing my straight teeth, polished white with crushed pumice and vinegar. "Your palace is magnificent."

"I find it pleasing." Solomon finds his voice. "I've prepared a feast in your honor."

Our eyes meet, the flecks of russet in his dark brown eyes holding me captive. In them I see truth, wisdom, and righteousness. And desire. His gaze drops to my lips, then travels downward as though he could see beneath my mantle and tunic.

I stifle a laugh. We are two powerful, wealthy rulers and yet we act like shy servants. An odd sensation quivers between us like an archer's bow. Or rather it feels like a sling—the kind shepherds use to launch rocks at their prey—spinning faster and faster, the rock in the leather pouch awaiting its explosive release. I look at Solomon and see the man, not the king. He looks at me in the same way. Imperial obligations and artifices dissipate like the first drop of rain in the desert. We are man and woman with desires that smolder beneath our opulent clothes and jeweled crowns.

I am not prepared for this, had not expected he would exude such raw masculinity. The man practically smoldered.

"Once again," I incline my head. "I am honored by your hospitality."

Solomon smiles, not the practiced, formal smile of a ruler but a genuine smile that crinkles the corner of his eyes. It's a wide, endearing grin that warms my heart and heats my loins.

"This way," Solomon says escorting me through the chambers. "After the meal, you will be shown to your quarters."

Following a good distance behind, our retinue of dignitaries and attendants are unusually silent. They prefer eavesdropping to idle chatter.

"Your palace is beyond compare," I whisper, mindful of a hundred curious ears.

"As is your beauty." Solomon steps so close our mantles brush together. "I must confess, I am already smitten."

I arch an eyebrow. "So soon? Such swift emotion explains the thousand wives and concubines you keep."

Solomon winces as though he had stepped on a sharp rock. "Diplomatic necessities. Nothing more."

"You must have a broader definition of diplomacy than we."

Solomon laughs, its deep tones like a caress at the back of my neck.

"How does the Queen of Sheba define it?" His sideways glance contains the perfect blend of humor and respect.

"The art of making people feel respected and valued." I struggle to stay serious. His charm quite sweeps me away. "Of finding satisfying ways to mend relationships, and establishing amity and partnerships."

"I achieved all this by acquiring wives and concubines. How do you? Are you married?"

"You know I am not."

"Does the high priestess of Almaqah foreswear men?"

I have had men. I keep several for my pleasure, each one chosen not only for his muscular physique and untiring persistence but for his inability to sire children. My child, when and if I decide to have one, will be the progeny of a great ruler.

I am not the chaste woman I present to my people—it's a necessary lie—a diplomatic necessity to appear beyond the desires of the flesh. I look into Solomon's eyes. What would he think if he knew I have had a man sucking on each tit, one eating my cunt, and one's cock down my throat at the same time? What would he think if he knew I was often like a bitch in heat, my cunt so aromatic that my men claim they can smell my desires from their chambers? What would he think if he knew I could take two cocks inside me and fuck for hours?

"What do *you* think?" I answer cagily.

Solomon's head dips down to my ear. "I think you like to fuck." He straightens up and sniffs the air. "I smell cunt."

My eyes widen. It's true. I'm wet, my mind already wondering what he looks like naked, what his skin tastes like, and how large his cock is. "You're a very naughty king. Why, the smell could be coming from your own harem."

"I've been called many things—a prophet, a magician, a sinner, an exorcist, a tyrant—but *never* naughty. Do you like naughty men?"

"Only those willing to negotiate a favorable trade agreement."

Solomon inclined his head. "Ah, so the Queen of Sheba is a shrewd negotiator as well as a beautiful diplomat."

"Call me Bilqīs," I say as we enter the vast hall where row upon row of low tables are heaped with food.

There is fish, chickpeas, lamb, almonds, olives, bread, honey-dipped pastries, and herbed *labneh.*

"My friends call me Sol." He sits on a tasseled pillow.

"You have friends?"

Solomon laughs again. "As many as you." He indicates the pillow next to him. The table provides us with the ability to have a private conversation as well as an elevated view of the chambers.

"Friendship is a luxury." I watch as our retinues take their seats according to their ranks. "I have many trusted advisors and faithful handmaids, yet consider only Duvsha my friend."

"What is your definition of a friend?"

I press my hand to my heart. "Friendship is felt, not defined."

"Like love."

I lift one shoulder and smile coyly.

After my plate is heaped with food and my goblet full of wine, Solomon turns to me, his expression one of respectful curiosity. "Tell me about your parents and how you came to be the Queen of Sheba."

"My mother's name was Ismenie. She was a good jinni—"

Although Solomon's eyebrows lift with surprise, he refrains from commenting. He demonstrates an impressive amount of self-control considering I just admitted to being a daughter of fire and smoke.

"She fell in love with the king's advisor," I say. "They had a torrid affair for months. Her beauty and exotic lovemaking caused him to neglect his duties."

"Exotic lovemaking?"

"It is the way of female jinn." I pluck an olive from a golden bowl. "Jinn know the secrets to making a man...." I slurp in an olive and smile.

Solomon is spellbound, his eyes focused on my mouth, his quick exhalation audible when I lick my lips.

"A man . . ." he encourages me to continue.

"Experience a pleasure so extraordinary they . . ." I pause again, select another olive.

"They . . ."

"Are taken from this earthly world and into one of exquisite decadence and desperate sensuality."

Solomon swallows. "And does a half jinni possess the same . . . skill?"

"It is a quality, an essence, part of a jinn's magic.

Not a learned skill." I take a sip of wine. "When I was born, my mother decided I should grow up in the desert, away from the evils of court. When I was much older, I learned from a passing caravan that the new king was a wicked greedy man who killed for pleasure and demanded exorbitant taxes. My people were being crushed by his vicious rule."

Solomon grimaces at such senseless leadership.

"I snuck into the palace one night—"

"How?"

"Like this." I show him my most seductive smile. "And I slipped into his chamber, disrobing before he had a chance to protest. Perhaps he thought I was a temple prostitute sent as a gift by an advisor."

"My advisors never send gifts like that," he grinned.

"One look at my naked body was all it took. I stretched out my arms and he came to me without hesitation. After stroking and sucking my breasts, he threw me over his shoulders and flung me onto the bed. I spread my thighs so he could see my readiness."

Solomon leans on the table, his chin resting on his cupped hand.

"I took wine from the nearby table and spilled it over my body. 'Drink,' I said and he lowered his head."

"Did this evil king marry you? Is this how you became queen?"

"Indeed not. That night he ate at my pleasure gate, my loud moans so exuberant he was lost in pleasure. I held my hand tight against his head, and he did not see me take the dagger at his bedside and plunge it into his back." I point to the spot on my lower back. "Not the quickest death but my best option at the time."

Solomon inhales and stares. "Beautiful *and* deadly." He pours more wine into my golden goblet. "Then what?"

"I chopped off his head—easy enough with the sword he kept in his room. I took his head, dripping with blood, to the great chambers and proclaimed myself queen."

Solomon studies my face as though reading a text, facial muscles shifting under his skin in thought. "You're fearless and violent and sexy and . . ." He leans close. "I don't remember my cock ever becoming so hard just *listening* to a woman."

"I imagine you don't *ever* listen to women." One corner of my mouth curls up.

"Just their sighs and moans. But you are..." He exhales and grins. "Unique." He turns away and claps his hands. "The gifts," he calls to the crowd.

The gifts I brought King Solomon are carried in. Coffers of gold, precious jewels, and strands of rare gems. Large chests of spices, myrrh, and frankincense. Crates of the finest linen, woven thin as a mist, and vibrant with colors. Boxes filled with pelts from wild beasts. Large sacks of brilliant-hued plumage from exotic birds.

Solomon is impressed; I see it in his eyes.

"The goods," he says next.

My bookkeeper steps forward and reads from a lengthy list the quantity of merchandise I have to trade. Of course, Solomon's own auditors will evaluate and confirm the products over the next few weeks.

"We *will* discuss a trade agreement," Solomon says afterward. "There is only one problem."

"What is that?"

"You have brought *things*. I have another trade in mind that involves *services*." He looks at me from under thick dark brows.

"I will *never* relinquish my masseuse." I cross my arms in mock indignation.

Solomon laughs again, its hearty sound penetrating into the nape of my neck, my body delighted by the soothing timbre and depth of his voice. I've never found a man's voice so compelling.

After a public exchanging of riddles—a favorite pastime of his that I had prepared for—and watching a troupe of talented dancers, Solomon shows me to my quarters. It is a grand building not far from his palace with all the necessary appointments and refinements required for a queen with a large retinue.

"You will join me later for light refreshments?" he asks. "We can discuss *trade*."

His emphasis on *trade* does not go unnoticed by Duvsha, who presses her lips to suppress a giggle.

"Yes," I say. "We can *begin* the negotiation process."

Disappointment flashes across his face. "I find lengthy negotiations tedious." He turns and walks through the door.

"He's gorgeous!" says Duvsha when he is out of hearing. "His eyes! That smile!" She fans herself with her hand.

"My cunt's been wet all day," I say as Duvsha removes my jeweled headpiece.

"Should I summon your men?"

I'm tempted. I need a cock. Maybe two. Except there are spies here, I am certain of it. I wouldn't be surprised if one hid in a hollow wall and watched through a tiny hole.

"No. I only need a quick release." My negotiation skills will be impaired if I'm so horny I can't think straight.

"Of course, my queen." Duvsha finishes undressing me and then instructs my handmaids to fill the tub.

Behind the drapes, while I recline in the water with my thighs spread, Duvsha's fingers manipulate my clit. Her skilled fingers and my fantasies about fucking Solomon have me climaxing in less than a minute.

"Again?" she asks.

"Yes." I throw my head back as she continues to rub the engorged knot at my center. This climax takes a little longer to build, my walls throbbing for lack of a cock. Duvsha, sensing this, uses a carved wooden penis to fuck me as her fingers glide over my clit. One-two-three thrusts is all it takes for my body to shake with release.

The orgasms take the edge off. I am now confident in the control I must have when I see Solomon again.

That evening, ten armed guards arrive and escort me to Solomon's palace.

He dismisses all but two of the guards. "In light of your fondness for chopping off kings' heads, I'm sure you won't mind." Solomon's lips curl into an impish smile.

"Not at all." For a moment I am disappointed, but then I bite back a grin. Having witnesses will be fun. "Though I must warn you that I am far less cautious."

Solomon's forehead furrows briefly as he tries to interpret my meaning. "Ah." His brows shoot up at my suggestive innuendo. "Unbridled spontaneity does have its merits." He clears his throat.

The guards follow closely behind us as Solomon shows me to his lavishly appointed personal chamber where a table is set with wine, fruit, and tartlets stuffed with delicacies.

We talk of many things: the difficulties of leadership, our troubles with greedy merchants, and the headache of squabbling advisors. We do not discuss a trade agreement, instead doing something far more important; discovering our similarities regarding policies and ambitions. We both despise prejudice and have little tolerance for those seeking to profit from others' misfortunes. Dispensing fair justice, we agree, is not easy, the truth usually hiding beneath a tangle of lies and half-truths.

Solomon stands by the narrow window that looks out over Jerusalem. "I've never met a woman with a mind as sharp as a man's."

I rise from the table and join Solomon, the two bored-looking guards now snapping back to attention. "Intellect is not a trait exclusive to men. I've met too many stupid ones."

"Maybe we should also discuss a trade of advisors?" Solomon smiles. "A few of your intelligent women for some of my senseless men?" He touches the edge of my sheer red veil and tugs.

"Never," I laugh as the veils slips off and my unbound hair is revealed.

"Lovely," he says, pleased by the thick black waves that fall to my waist. "There is a matter we still need to discuss that has nothing to do with trade." He lifts the veil to his nose, inhales, then drapes it around his neck.

"Some matters are best left unspoken." I look up at him, my eyes conveying the heat of my yearnings.

Solomon shrugs off his purple mantle and pulls the blue tunic over his head, his naked body now fully exposed. He is strong and fit, his muscles thick and sinewy, curving and bulging like a warrior's, not a king's grown soft from idle luxury. Black curls cover his chest, short spirals I want to run my fingers through. A downy line runs down his taut stomach and into the thick thatch that has been trimmed short and shaved into the shape of an upside down pyramid. His cock is long and rigid, and slants slightly left.

"I never rush negotiations." I slowly pull my veil from his neck, wrap it around his slim hips, and tie a knot at the side. I flick my gaze at the two wide-eyed guards standing nearby. Their riveted concentration adds a thrilling edge to my mounting lust.

"Usually I prefer the customary bartering, but your method is clearly superior."

I lift a long strand of small ruby beads from my neck and hang it on his cock.

"Put on as many as you like. My cock will hold them all," says Solomon.

"You only need one strand." I loop the strand over, careful not to touch his cock, which jerks and twitches with eagerness.

I look up, find him enthralled, then loop it over again. I do this again and again, tugging each loop so it tightens at his base. His cock swells and he breathes heavily. A moment later Solomon's cock is wrapped in smooth ruby beads, only the head peeking out. I do all this without touching him.

His eyes are glazed with lust and wonder when my hand wraps around his bejeweled cock and pulls.

"Oh god," he moans as hundreds of beads roll and spin over his length and tighten around his base.

I tug again, his cock twitching and expanding. A few more strokes and the strand breaks, his engorged cock snapping the thread. Ruby beads bounce on the floor, scattering everywhere.

"Ohhh!" he groans and cum shoots out.

I am ready, cupping my hand under him to catch every creamy drop. He pants as I walk to the table and add his cum to my wineglass.

"You're fully clothed. Didn't even touch me," he says. "You *are* part jinn." He touches my shoulder. "I must have you, Bilqīs."

"Not yet." I stir the wine, sit down, and gesture to the chair opposite.

"At least let me look upon you." He gestures to his hard cock. "I want more. I *need* more."

The guards look like they need more as well. One's tunic is peaked like a tent at his crotch. The other already has a telltale wet spot.

I shrug the fabric of my dress over my shoulders and bare my breasts. Solomon is transfixed. My golden-brown breasts are generous, the areolas dark and large, my nipples thick and rigid. "You are too impatient."

I sip the wine, and he sinks into the chair, exhaling his arousal.

"Delicious." I take another sip and lick my lips.

"You're a tease."

I lift one shoulder, then trace a circle around my nipples. Solomon's breath becomes heavy again as I stroke myself and sip the cum-infused wine. He wraps his hand around his cock and masturbates.

"I beg of you, Bilqīs," he groans. "Let me fuck you."

"Not yet." I tug on my nipple, moan, and drink more wine. The thrill of having three men's attention makes it difficult to restrain my throbbing clit.

"Let me. . . ." He reaches out, but I lean away and study the way he pleasures himself. He strokes himself slowly, twisting his wrist, drawing out his ascent. His eyes never leave me and, every time I drink my cum-infused wine, he moans.

With a long groan, Solomon orgasms again, his pelvis thrusting forward. He catches his own cum, depositing it into the goblet I hold out.

"Even better," I say after finishing the wine and smacking my lips. "Negotiations have commenced."

Solomon is defeated, his dreamy eyes and satisfied grin evidence of my charms.

"I hope they never end," he says.

I bid him good night and am escorted back to my room by the guards—the eight who waited outside the chamber and the two glazed-eyed witnesses.

We spend the next day together. He gives me a tour of his palace and regales me with tales of his youth. He shows me his most precious possession—or rather I see the door of a sealed room called the Holy of Holies, which houses a large gold-plated chest of rare wood containing the ten sacred commands of his god. His god, the only one he prays to, intrigues me, and the remainder of the day is spent learning more about him. That night, Solomon summons me to his quarters but I feign tiredness.

He calls me to his side every day for a week. He is as wise as he is interesting, and I find it increasingly difficult not to succumb to his charms.

On the sixth night, he summons me again, this time sweetening the plea with a gilded litter waiting to convey me to his chambers. I cannot refuse, especially since the path from my door to the litter is strewn with rose petals. This fragrant trail continues all the way to his chambers.

"Welcome." He shows me inside, where a multitude of petals cover the floor and a hundred flower-filled vases fill the room.

"Did you cut every flower in Israel?" I sit at a table laden with food.

"The whole world," he laughs and lifts the conical clay lid. "I had my favorite dishes prepared for you."

"Where are your servants?" I ask, looking about.

"I dismissed them." He lifts a bit of lamb to my mouth. "Try it."

I let him feed me. "It's spicy, yet delicious."

"Here, try this."

Each dish is a spicy taste of vegetable, fruit, fish, and meat. Solomon feeds me each bite, relishing my enjoyment of his favorite dishes. We talk and eat and laugh, the hours passing quickly.

"I cannot wait any longer, Bilqīs," says Solomon. "I've been having wet dreams in my sleep like a young man, I want you so bad."

I rise from the table. "Not yet."

Solomon stands. "Stay the night. I promise I won't try anything."

"I don't believe you."

Solomon blows his exasperation through his nose. "If you promise not to take anything of mine, I promise not to seduce you."

"Take anything?" I flinch, insulted by his insinuation. "You don't trust me? Take me home."

"You will have to walk back to your quarters alone. In the dark. Without a lantern to guide your way."

"Then light one and summon your guards."

Solomon rubs his chin. "There's no more oil and the guards are gone."

"Fine," I say, shaking my head at his attempt to keep me here. "I will stay the night. And if I take anything you are free to touch me."

A wide grin on his face, he leads me to his bedchamber. Solomon's bed is large, sumptuous, and scattered with more rose petals.

"My clothes stay on." I lay my head down on the soft pillow, the wine and food making me more weary than I realized. Solomon extinguishes every light but one, a small lantern on the other side of the room.

"Good night," says Solomon lying next to me.

I close my eyes and fall into a dreamless sleep.

It's dark when I awaken, my mouth dry as the desert, my tongue on fire from the spicy meal. I sit up and pour water from a pitcher beside the bed. It quenches my thirst but does little to cool the heat in my mouth.

Solomon's hand snakes around my waist.

"What are you doing?"

"Our deal. You took something of mine." He tugs my tunic down past my shoulder and sets a light kiss on my back.

"Water?" My mouth drops open with surprise.

"A deal is a deal." He nuzzles my neck.

It was a trick. A well-played and cunning trick. Had it been anyone else, the ruse would have angered me, but instead I am pleased. Our teasing dance had gone on long enough.

"I always honor my agreements," I say, delighting in the feel of his tongue trailing up my neck.

He pushes my tunic farther down and cups each breast, his thumb brushing back and forth across my nipples. "Smoother and softer than I imagined," he breaths into my ear.

The deep timbre of his voice seeps inside and races down my spine, lodging in my tailbone and stirring my desires. I lean back into him and turn my cheek. He softly kisses my parted lips. Solomon is slow and thoughtful; the impatient king replaced by a deliberate lover. His tongue grazes over my lips, teases them open, and glides inside. He is a skilled kisser, unhurried and assertive, a man used to compliant wives and concubines.

I am not those women.

I push back. My tongue demands more. He grips my breasts tighter as our tongues wrestle, our mouths hungry to taste and nibble.

Solomon pulls back, his breath coming hard. "I've met my match," he says, sticking his thumb in my mouth.

I suck hard, swiveling my tongue around it, and scraping my teeth across the tip. I pull it out slowly and shift about so we are face-to-face.

"Are you thirsty?" he asks pinching my breast. "The tang of our spicy meal still lingers."

"You have a remedy?" My nails rake through the thick curly tangle spread across his wide chest.

"Of course." Solomon pulls me into his lap and presses his mouth to mine, our deep, hungry kisses more urgent. "Better than water," he murmurs cradling me in his arms and rising from the bed.

Still locked in the kiss, Solomon carries me through several chambers. He stops in a small bathing chamber aglow with three small lanterns. He sets me on my feet and pushes down my tunic.

"You're hairless!" His eyes widen with delight.

"Only men should have beards." I tug on his own.

He groans his approval then takes my hand and brings me to the edge of the large tub that is sunk into the floor. He dips in a ladle and brings it to my lips. "Milk."

I drink. It is warm, sweet, and delicately spiced. "It's delicious."

"Milk, honey, and cardamom." He lifts the ladle to his lips, then presses his mouth to mine, dribbling the milk into my mouth. "Hungry?" He dips the ladle back into the bath.

"Ravenous."

Solomon pours the sweet milk over my breasts. He licks it off, his tongue tip following the rivulets while I purr with pleasure, my delta wet with the waters of rising lust.

Solomon again scoops me up, this time stepping into the milk bath and laying me down upon a wide shallow step. I am partially submerged, not deep enough to cover my ears. Solomon dips the ladle into the pool and pours more milk over my body.

"Not as ravenous as I." His mouth lowers and he licks. Across my shoulders, down my breasts, and over my belly.

He slurps milk from my navel, and pours again, the

milk running into the deep channel of my delta, which is already heated and pulsing. Solomon splays me with thumb and forefinger, then draws another ladle and pours, the milk cascading like a waterfall to fill my womanly estuary.

"Milky cunt. My new favorite dish." He lowers his head and licks my milky sweetness.

He spreads my thighs, the milk sloshing about my anus and stimulating every inch of my soaked bottom. His hands glide upward to my breasts, where he pinches and pulls the rigid nipples. I am a river of pleasure, awash with the tides of desire, fixed only by the ebb and flow of his touch. His tongue slurps as he splashes milk on me, its cool wetness and his warm mouth intensifying my rise. I lift my legs high in the air. The rivulets of milk run down my legs and into his meal.

"I have a better way," Solomon says.

He stands, steps down into the milky pool that comes to his knees, and picks me up. He turns me upside down and arranges my dripping thighs over his shoulders so that I'm facing outward, my head almost touching the pool. I am at his mercy hanging this way, my breasts dripping with milk, while he drags his tongue over my clit. I reach behind me, and my arms strain around his hips as I spread wide his asscheeks.

My head grows light and it feels like I am suspended, spinning in space, my cunt a whirlpool sucking me inward. I am at Solomon's mercy and he uses it to his advantage. Supping on my clit, he bends his knees and lowers my head into the milk bath. I hold my breath—both sensations are so intense that I writhe in his arms.

He rises back up and I inhale and then squeal with a

deluge of tremors that flood my body. I am lost, torrents of rapture exploding over me like a breaking dam. He holds tight, his face sinking deep, stretching my orgasm until I whimper.

Solomon lifts his head, his beard forming two points that drip with my sweet froth. He eases me down and into the milk bath before sitting down himself. I scramble on top of him, impaling myself upon his length, and ride him up and down. Palming the back of my head, he draws me close. Our tongues do their own kind of mouth fucking as we buck against each other.

"I like this milk bath." I scratch his chest and my nails leave a thin red trail under his curls.

Solomon groans. "You're like a wild lion summoning my inner beast." Lifting my ass, he pulls slowly out, and turns me around. "I want to see that golden-brown ass in action."

I straddle him, ride him backward, my shimmying ass lifting and sinking. Solomon moans, the splashing milk cooling our burning loins. I know how to ride a man, how to clench his cock, how to submerge him into that primal eddy. Solomon's moans deepen and his legs tighten with pleasure. I slow the pace, draw out my rise and descent, and twist my hips while squeezing my cunt around his cock. But the sound of his groans acts like a cloudburst that rains pleasure and washes away all self-control. It sweeps me to the edge and hurls me over into the source of all life.

Solomon lifts my ass high. "Not yet. Get on your knees." It is a command.

Legs shaking with orgasmic surges, I do as he demands, my hands and knees on the low wide step. He stands behind me, dribbles milk down my ass, and glides into me. The servile position is my favorite, so contrary to my everyday life. My ass tingles as he caresses milk around my anus and plunges back into me, slamming harder each time I cry out.

"Harder. Harder!" I cry as he drives into me.

Solomon smacks my ass hard, the sting an explosion of pleasure that once again catapults me into a rapturous abyss. My body erupts. I shove my ass back to feel the whole of his cock. Growling, he sinks deep. He smacks my ass again, then grabs each cheek, kneading and pushing his cock into me, ringing out his pleasure until he sighs with relieved satisfaction.

Solomon pulls out and sinks into the depths of the milk bath. "Come here, Queen of Sheba, and tell King Solomon how you want me to fuck you next."

I slide into the bath, slither into his lap, and whisper a decadent fantasy.

His laugh is deep and robust, the sound echoing in the chamber. "Now that's a diplomatic necessity I will eagerly indulge in."

And he does. Time and time again we engage in countless wanton indulgences.

I stay with Solomon for three years. I decline his repeated offers of marriage but this does not affect our diplomatic or carnal relationship. He understands I have a nation to rule.

I leave Jerusalem with many valuables: wealth, wisdom, a new devotion to Solomon's god. And Solomon's unborn child.

There are five versions of King Solomon's and the Queen of Sheba's famous meeting: Christian, Islamic, Jewish, Coptic, and Ethiopian. Each portrays the enigmatic Bilqīs, or Makada as she is also known, a bit differently. The Kebra Nagast, *written in an ancient Semitic dialect, provides the most complete story of the enigmatic Queen of Sheba.*

RIVER RUNNER

Nova poked her head around the doorway of the stone and adobe home. Her best friend Yoki looked up from her basket weaving. Yoki's name meant *rain,* and like the rain, hair cascaded down her back like rippling water. It's what made her squash-blossom hairstyle so much bigger and fuller than that of the other unmarried maidens of the village—she had lots more hair to wrap around the *U*-shaped styling wand.

"Come with me, Yoki." Nova set down her basket.

"Why?"

"I was collecting yucca when the most beautiful flute music drifted by on a breeze."

Yoki put down the half-completed basket and laughed. "You're just like your name, always chasing butterflies...and imaginary music."

Nova pulled Yoki to her feet. "Come *on.*"

They descended the ladder to the ground. The pueblo was quiet today. Every able-bodied boy and man was hunting antelope, leaving the women and children to do their daily chores without them.

"Where are all the mothers?" asked Nova as they walked past the other homes.

Great-grandmother, wrapped in a blanket because she was always cold, stopped in the middle of her storytelling to three girls. "They're all at Muna's. Discussing the best marriage prospects for you both."

Yoki and Nova looked at each other. So it had begun!

"Where are you going?" asked great-grandmother.

"I heard flute music," said Nova.

Great-grandmother lifted her sparse gray brows. "Describe the music."

"Beautiful and lively. It made me want to dance."

Great-grandmother's face creased into a web of wrinkles when she smiled. "I haven't seen or heard Kokopelli since I was your age."

The three young girls sitting nearby jumped to their feet. "Kokopelli?"

They took off running, climbing up the ladders to their homes as nimbly as scurrying lizards.

Yoki and Nova laughed. Girls who had not gone through the corn-grinding ceremony of puberty were frightened by this mischievous god. And for good reason. Besides being able to summon the rain, Kokopelli carried corn, beads, shells, turquoise, blankets, and seeds from every plant in the world on his back. That's not what frightened young girls though. Kokopelli also carried unborn babies. Those girls were much too young for that womanly gift!

"Go." Great-grandmother flicked her long gray hair away. "See if it's him."

Yoki and Nova dashed across the mesa.

"Where were you when you heard him?" asked Yoki when they reached the narrow steps carved into the plateau.

Nova pointed into the distance. "See the yucca there? Beyond that hill."

They raced down the steps. They knew every step, each indentation and groove of every stone. At the bottom, Nova took the lead, running north, skirting the scrub, and avoiding a rattler coiled in the shadow of a large rock. She sprinted to the place where the yucca clustered together like a pack of coyotes.

"I was here." Nova pressed her lips together and listened intently. "There. Did you hear it?"

Yoki grinned. "I hear it." She grabbed Nova's hand. "It's as beautiful as you said."

The melody was light as air, brilliant and clear, a lyrical poetic prayer to the earth and sky that captured the maidens' hearts.

"Is that him?" Yoki shielded her eyes against the sun's glare.

A lone figure emerged from the shadow of a high plateau a mile away.

"It must be. The music is getting louder."

"We should make cornmeal muffins for him," said Yoki.

"Us? No, Takala should. She's been married four years and has no baby. Come on, we need to tell her!" Nova waved to the figure in the distance before they spun about and raced back home.

"Do you think his cock is as big as they say?" Nova skipped up the steps.

"Bigger!" laughed Yoki.

"Do you think he knows the men have gone hunting?"

"Why don't you ask Kokopelli when he comes?"

The girls burst into a fit of giggles. Once at the top, they raced across the mesa and climbed the ladder to Muna's home.

Breathing hard, Yoki and Nova entered the room crowded with wives, young and old.

"Kokopelli is coming!" said Nova.

Twenty heads swiveled toward Takala. The shy wife buried her face in her hands.

"Go, Takala."

"Make cornmeal muffins for him."

"This is a good day."

"Your prayers have been answered."

The wives offered kind words and encouragement to the childless Takala, who reluctantly stood and plodded back to her own home. The wives followed her out, spreading the word to grandfathers too frail to join the hunt and to the grandmothers sleeping in the sun.

Kokopelli was coming! There was so much to do. Food to make. Hair to style. Best dresses to put on.

Soon, everyone heard Kokopelli's flute, his joyful song rising to the top of the mesa.

"Take hold of Kokopelli's staff and pray for a long life," said a grandmother to her married daughter.

"Which staff is that? The one of wood or the one of flesh?"

"Both of them." Grandmother made two fists and jerked them up and down.

The wives and grandmothers laughed. The music grew louder and louder, and everyone held their breath.

Kokopelli danced into their pueblo. He wore a too-short breechcloth around his waist and deerskin moccasins. His forehead was tied with a colorful cotton belt and atop his head was a crest of spiky plumes. He wore his hair in a *hömsoma*, tied in a black cloth at the nape of his neck. He was handsome and athletic, with graceful sinewy limbs that swayed to the rhythm of his melody.

The women sat down while he played, his music so enchanting they felt as if they had all been struck with a bit of love madness, *tuskyaptawi*. Kokopelli sang a song about being fruitful whatever you do, whether it is weaving baskets, stringing beads, shaping pottery, sowing seeds, or making babies. *Plant your time and you will succeed*, he sang.

The wives brought him fresh *piki* bread, roasted dove, bean soup, and prickly pear. Takala, her head lowered, shuffled her shy feet across the mesa and offered Kokopelli a corn cake.

Kokopelli gobbled it down and pronounced it delicious. Takala blushed, but when Kokopelli pushed away his breechcloth to uncover his cock, her hand flew to her mouth.

Yoki's and Nova's jaws dropped. Kokopelli's cock was huge, and as long as a gourd. Kokopelli lifted his flute to his mouth and played a suggestive tune just for Takala. He moved close to her, brushing her shoulder with his and making seductive eyes at the shy wife. He whispered in her ear.

"What do you think he's saying?" Nova asked Yoki.

"Sit on my gourd." Yoki buried her face in Nova's neck to muffle her laughter.

Kokopelli took Takala's hand and together they went to Takala's home. He set down his flute and Takala lay on the bed, squeezed shut her eyes, and turned away her head.

Kokopelli crouched down and laid his hand on her flat belly. "This energy is good." His hand moved to her head. "But this energy is blocked."

Takala grimaced.

"Do you always do that?" asked Kokopelli.

"Do what?"

"Make that face when your husband is close to you."

"Just get it over with." Takala wished Kokopelli would stop talking and just *do* it.

"I'm not surprised you have no babies. Bad energy." Kokopelli stroked Takala's cheek. "Tell me how it is with him."

"He puts it in and it is done."

Kokopelli rubbed his chin. "Is he young?"

Takala nodded. "We are a good match. We are both shy."

"A shy man and wife do not make good lovers." Kokopelli kissed Takala's forehead. "I'll help you but you must make me a promise."

"Anything."

"Do everything I say and don't make that face again."

"I'll try."

Kokopelli slid Takala's *manta* off her shoulder, pulling it over her young ripe breasts to her waist. Embarrassed, Takala looked away.

"Look at what I'm doing." Kokopelli removed his feathered headdress, plucked off one feather, and swept it back and forth over Takala's breasts until her nipples hardened. Next he lifted his palms and set them gently across each breast.

Takala drew a sharp breath of surprise and her eyes widened as her nipples stretched like flowers toward the sun into Kokopelli's palms. He slowly rotated his hands, rubbing the tips of her nipples. Takala gasped. She had been impatient for Kokopelli to fuck her, but now she thought only of the wonderful feeling knotting inside her.

"Do you like that?" asked Kokopelli, despite knowing she did.

"Oh," sighed Takala, wondering if this was what people felt when they had love madness.

Kokopelli bent his head and kissed the top of her full, soft breast. He cupped both breasts in his hands, and inched his way down until his lips kissed her nipple. Takala took a deep breath and stared at the knot of hair on the back of his neck. Kokopelli was kissing her breasts!

Kokopelli took a nipple in his mouth and sucked, and Takala's ass lifted off the blanket.

"You suckle like a baby." Takala set her hand on his burnished shoulder.

Kokopelli lifted his head. "If you want a baby, your husband must suckle like one." He moved to the other nipple.

Kokopelli's tugs and licks stirred a strange feeling in Takala's *löwa*. It felt like the first few steps of a dance, her feet not yet in rhythm to the beat.

Kokopelli untied the cloth belt and pulled Takala's *manta* over her hips and down her shapely, strong legs.

"You're beautiful, Takala. I must pray to your *löwa*."
He lowered his head and kissed her knees, one hand
massaging her breast, the other drawing zigzags across
her thighs. Takala's breath was ragged. Her legs tensed
with both pleasure and anxiety.

Kokopelli lifted his head and uncoiled the string securing his *hömsoma*. Unbound, his glossy hair fell over
his shoulders and down his back like a cascade of black
water. He shook it and laughed, then gathered it in his
hands and dragged the ends over her thighs. Takala's
tension left her body and her thighs parted like a blossoming flower.

Kokopelli offered his ponytail to Takala. "Take hold
of my hair. Pull when you feel the energy of the world
inside you."

Takala did not know what that meant but made a
fist around his hair anyway. Kokopelli lowered his face
between her thighs. She was moist and smelled of woman. He danced his tongue over her, the rhythm like the
thumping feet of a Butterfly dance.

Takala tugged his hair. She felt the earth's pull on
her *löwa*, felt the sun's warmth on her skin, and the
wind's gusts on her heart. She tugged again.

Kokopelli's tongue danced fast and deep. Takala kept
tugging. When Kokopelli felt Takala's buttocks join in
the rhythm, he knew she was close. He lifted his face,
glistening with her dew, spread her thighs, and settled
himself between her legs.

Kokopelli's cock was enormous. Bigger than any
human's. But he pushed his way into Takala's slippery
löwa. Takala whooped and grabbed Kokopelli's firm
ass. Like the river after a storm, her body was swept

away in an eddy of pleasure. The strong current pounded her body and soaked into her skin and soul. Kokopelli kept thrusting. The shy wife needed more than just one lovemaking lesson.

"Get on all fours," said Kokopelli.

Takala remembered her promise to do anything he asked and got on her hands and knees. Kokopelli took her from behind, his gourd-length cock thrusting into the shy wife who wasn't so shy any longer. With one hand on her hip and the other clasping her two long ponytails like a rein, he rode her hard. Takala sang fertility's song, a long joyful croon that Yoki and Nova heard as they crouched next to her door outside.

Kokopelli sang his own song and sowed his seed deep inside her.

Afterward, he asked Takala to fix his hair. She wrapped its length and tied it tight.

"When your husband comes home you will show him what I did."

"I will, and I'll tell him to plant his time *here*." Takala pointed to the sticky slick entrance to her *löwa*.

Kokopelli emerged from the home, ate the prepared food, then told more stories and played the flute until late into the night. He left the pueblo after playing a tune that made everyone so sleepy they went to bed.

But Kokopelli wasn't done yet. He had seen the lusty-eyed looks of Yoki and Nova. The maidens were eager to experience the pleasures of marriage.

The next morning, Yoki bounced into Nova's home.

"It's hair-washing day," said Yoki.

Since their mothers had told them to expect visits of eligible men from other pueblos, the maidens kept a schedule. The pretense for these visits was trading. Yoki and Nova knew better. It was a way to meet single men from different clans. So far, they had met several they liked. Clean, shiny hair styled into a squash blossom was *very* important.

Nova took the yucca soap and grass brush, and followed Yoki down the ladder. They talked about Kokopelli's visit as they crossed the mesa, descended the steps, and walked the wide path to the river.

"Looks like Kokopelli is bringing rain." Nova pointed to a distant mesa where a gray cloud mass stretched wide and heavy in the sky.

"I wonder if he is also bringing Takala a baby?" Yoki took off her moccasins and pulled her *manta* over her head.

"We'll know soon enough."

They untied each other's squash-blossom hair, two black waterfalls falling to their waists.

"Do you think Kokopelli is handsome?" Nova walked into the river.

"Handsome enough to *do business* with." Yoki burst out laughing. *Doing business* was grandfather's phrase for fucking. As if trading turquoise for shells gave the same pleasure!

"No wonder the adults are so happy on trading days." Nova splashed Yoki.

They played in the water, splashing and diving, and whipping their hair about. Kokopelli was watching them from behind a vertical ledge of red rock upstream. It was time for some fun.

"What's that?" Nova pointed to an object drifting toward them. Against the current!

Yoki stopped her splashing and narrowed her eyes. "No. It can't be."

The object floated between the two girls, spun about, and veered toward Yoki. She grabbed it and lifted it out of the water.

"It's Kokopelli's cock!" said Yoki.

It was! And though the maidens had never touched a cock before they knew the shape and size of Kokopelli's. He had made sure everyone saw his when he was dancing.

Yoki and Nova looked down river. There was no sign of Kokopelli.

Yoki stroked the smooth skin of Kokopelli's cock. Her fingers followed the length and fondled the soft skin at the tip. She pushed back the foreskin, examined the shiny head, and tapped the tiny hole at the top. "We need to know how to make our future husbands happy."

Kokopelli's cock leapt from her hand and dove into the water. Yoki and Nova squealed and their eyes searched the river's depths.

"There it is!" Yoki pointed behind Nova.

Kokopelli's cock circled her three times and disappeared under the water.

"Find the cock! I want the cock!" said Nova.

"Oh!" Yoki's arms flew from the water. "Oh, Nova. It's trying to get *in* me!"

Kokopelli's cock pushed. A virgin *löwa* was a tight squeeze, but once in it was glorious.

Yoki smacked her hands on the water. "It's too big. It won't—" She yelped.

"What happened?" asked Nova.

"It's in!" Yoki reached for Nova. "Help me, his cock

is lifting me off my feet. Oh—" Her feet slipped on a slick rock and she fell back, Kokopelli's cock still thrusting.

Nova lifted Yoki under her arms. "I have you."

Yoki's head rested on Nova's chest. "Oh, oh, oh." Yoki's slim brown legs spread wide and floated upward. "It feels so good. I just wish Kokopelli had sent his hands down river as well."

"Use your own."

Yoki massaged her own breasts, stroked her nipples, already firm from the cool water. Her back against Nova, Yoki closed her eyes and let the sensation of Kokopelli's cock and her own hands swirl around her. She felt like a blossoming flower, like a hawk soaring on a breeze, like a beating drum. All at the same time!

"What does it feel like?" Nova felt her friend's body tense and relax, shiver, then tense and relax again. Yoki's heavy breathing made Nova horny.

"Like the path to happiness." Yoki's hand slid over her belly to her throbbing *löwa* and stroked the nub.

Surprised and delighted that Yoki's *löwa* was slippery with pleasure, Kokopelli slowed his thrusting cock. He had a lesson to teach. Humans were too eager to race down the path of happiness. Sauntering along the path delivered a more fulfilling experience.

Kokopelli snuck a peek around the rock ledge. It was all going to plan. Was there anything better than fucking two virgins on a sunny day? Kokopelli lifted his gaze to the sky and sent a silent message of thanks to the gathering clouds. The clouds rumbled an answer.

Yoki panted, her body succumbing to the fleshly demand of her *löwa*. Her back arched and lifted skyward and out of the water. Her nub ignited, embers of bliss sparkling over her limbs. Her soul flared outward to dance with Earth Mother, Sky Father, the Sun, Moon, and all the kachinas. She hissed her rapture while her legs thrashed. And then her body sunk heavy into Nova's arms, her trip to the sky and back complete.

Kokopelli's cock hauled itself out of Yoki's snug *löwa* and dove deep underwater.

"Is he leaving?" Nova was confused. She wanted Kokopelli's cock inside of her, except she was afraid.

Yoki detangled herself from Nova's arms. "I hope not. It's your turn."

"I don't know." Nova chewed on her lip.

"There he is!"

Kokopelli's cock leapt from the river like a fish, then made a wide circle around the girls. Even from his hiding spot upriver, Kokopelli sensed Nova's anxiety. Nova would be a challenge. A fertility god, he knew how important it was for every maiden to enjoy baby making. He employed an old trick.

Nova stretched out her hand as Kokopelli's cock drifted away. "Don't go!"

That's all Kokopelli needed to hear. His cock spun about and veered straight for her. His cock circled Nova four times before flying from the water and into her arms.

Nova gripped it with both hands, felt it swell and stiffen even more. She pushed back the foreskin and rubbed her palm over it. Kokopelli's cock jerked and trembled.

"Taste it," said Yoki.

Nova licked the tip. It tasted like the river with a hint of salt. "You try it."

Yoki licked the head. "It's so smooth." She swirled her tongue around the head.

Nova licked the length and together the girls wound their tongues around Kokopelli's cock.

Beyond the bend, Kokopelli gripped the rock, his breath ragged as a runner after a race. "Those maidens will certainly make their husbands happy," he thought.

"Look," Nova pointed to the creamy bead leaking from the tip. She licked it off. "Salty and . . ." She squeezed the tip and more seeped out. "The taste reminds me of the smell of the shells we trade for."

Yoki wrapped her lips around the tip and sucked hard. "You're right. Do all men taste the same?"

Kokopelli braced himself against the wall. Took measured breaths. It was taking all his willpower not to spill his seed. Two maidens licking his cock challenged even his self-control. He wanted his seed inside their sweet snug *löwas*, not their mouths.

Kokopelli's cock squirmed away and plunged into the river.

"Did we make him angry?" asked Nova.

"I hope not." Yoki looked into the water's depths.

Kokopelli's cock bumped Nova's calf.

"It's him." Nova looked down.

Kokopelli's cock nudged her thigh, nudged higher, and higher. He pushed until he wedged himself between Nova's closed legs.

"What do I do?" Nova stared down, unable to move. She was torn between fear and desire. A man's cock inside was what made you a real woman, *not* a squash-blossom hairstyle.

"Let him in," said Yoki, and she moved behind Nova. "I've got you."

Nova leaned against her friend as Kokopelli's cock

wedged between her soft thighs. With its head tilted upward, the cock bumped against the entrance of her *löwa*, which was thicker and tighter than a skin stretched across a drum.

"Relax. It's fun," said Yoki.

Nova yelped. Kokopelli's cock broke Nova's seal and struggled to push itself inside Nova. Once all the way in, Kokopelli pulled halfway out, thrust in again, softening her *löwa* with each thrust. Nova closed her eyes and surrendered to Kokopelli's cock. Her anxious *löwa* grew misty with desire as Kokopelli's cock glided effortlessly in and out. A strange, wonderful energy gathered at her *löwa*'s entrance. Her feet tapped the river bottom to the beat of her awakened spirit while her long moan soared skyward. Nova's skin tingled like it was being brushed by a grass broom. Nova spread her legs, let them float on the water and submitted to the energy that was Kokopelli's thrusting cock. She was water and sky and earth, her weightless body afloat on a pleasure cloud. Then Nova jerked and twitched in fleshly release.

"We're ready for a husband now," said Yoki when she felt her friend return to earth.

"Mmm." Nova sighed and stared at the gray sky as the first raindrops fell on her lashes.

Yoki looked around. "Where is Kokopelli's cock?"

His cock had already headed upstream. It glided under the water, sluggish and exhausted. At least for today.

Nine months later three babies were born to two happy brides and a no-longer-barren wife. Kokopelli lifted his flute to his mouth when he heard the news and danced into the next pueblo.

Kokopelli is a trickster and a fertility god of some southwestern Native American tribal cultures. There are probably as many stories about him as there are images of his iconic form on ancient petroglyphs. Over the centuries, his oversized phallus has become less pronounced. On today's images it's gone completely, covered by a kilt, probably so as not to offend our more modern sensibilities.

RIDING
THE MARE

"Help me! Someone, please help!"

Not far away, an old woman picking wild berries heard the shout. She cocked her ear and stopped to listen. A long, loud wail followed a few moments later. The old woman slung her basket over her arm and followed the cry deep into the forest.

She found a maiden sitting on the ground, her skirt making a wide circle over the leaves and pine needles. Suspicious it might be a thief's trick—although the old woman had nothing of value—she crept forward, her soft leather shoes making no sound, and peered around the trunk of a big old oak tree.

The maiden was fair-skinned and beautiful, with brown doe-eyes and full lips. A pure white veil covered the maiden's hair and her striped cylindrical headpiece was threaded with gold and embellished with coins, one row strung across her forehead. The silver beads hanging beneath her chin matched a multi-strand necklace, and her red dress was richly embroidered and belted with sheer layers of multicolored silk. This Armenian maiden was no commoner.

The old woman stepped from behind the tree. "Are you lost?"

The maiden's head lifted. "You found me!" She bounced up, nimble as a cat. "I was getting worried."

"Where is your home, child?" The old woman shifted the basket of berries into the crook of her arm.

The maiden swung her head from left to right, and exhaled her exasperation. "I have no idea."

"You don't know where you live?" asked the old woman, thinking the maiden was daft.

The maiden raised her eyebrows as if insulted by the question. "I *live* in the palace. I just don't know which direction that is." The maiden squared her shoulders. "I am Princess Nazani."

A princess! *The* princess? What good fortune! The old woman curtsied. "How did you come to be lost?"

Princess Nazani lowered her eyes. "It's all my fault. My parents and I were arguing—they want me to marry a horribly ugly prince—and I became so angry I ran and ran and ran…" She lifted her gaze and shrugged. "I've been wandering for *hours* but nothing looks familiar."

"You're a good way from the palace, at least a half-day's journey on foot. You best come home with me before it gets dark. We don't want to meet any hungry bears along the way."

Princess Nazani looked around as if expecting the beast to leap out at any moment. "Father says there are leopards too."

"Not in these parts. Unless it's lost too." The old woman beckoned her forward. "Come along, I don't live far."

As they walked, the old woman was delighted to discover that the princess was a curious, intelligent girl. She asked lots of questions, from where to find the best blackberries to what the old woman liked best about her village.

When they came to the edge of the forest, the old woman pointed to a house built of volcanic rock. Nearby, a tall lean figure with three trout strung over a shoulder emerged from the copse of fruit trees and waved.

"Is that your son?" asked the princess.

It was a common mistake. Folks often mistook the old woman's daughter for a boy. Garin was a tall girl with broad shoulders, a square jaw, and a strong nose. She often dressed as a man, like today, claiming trousers and a shirt with an *arkhaluk* was better for completing her daily chores. She also preferred fishing and hunting to sewing and cooking. Despite the old woman's attempts at matchmaking, Garin insisted she would never marry.

"That's Garin." The old woman did not correct the princess's assumption.

"Mother!" Garin waved. "Looks like you found more than berries."

"This is Princess Nazani," said the old woman, approaching the house. "She was lost in the forest."

Garin's mouth dropped open. A princess? She glanced down at her worn dirty trousers, suddenly aware of her manlike appearance. She could not remember ever being so flustered. "Welcome to our humble home," she said, her voice too loud and overly formal as she held open the door.

Princess Nazani blushed and lowered her eyes. Garin's handsome face made her unexpectedly bashful.

"She thinks you're my son," whispered the old woman as she passed under the low door frame.

A wonderful fluttering filled Garin's belly. Garin pulled at her collar, her body suddenly too warm. She couldn't tear her eyes away from the princess. Neither could the honest and forthright Garin tell the princess that she was a girl.

She's gorgeous. And she's blushing at me. At me! My body is cursed. I should be a man. I feel like a man. Now I understand what the men mean when they talk about seeing a woman they want to fuck.

Not for the first time, Garin wondered why she was born in a woman's body. It was a secret feeling she had never told anyone. How could she possibly explain that a man's heart beat inside her woman's body? People would think she was crazy. Better for them to think her fondness for wearing pants and men's activities was a character flaw or peculiarity.

If the princess thinks I'm a man, then I'll play the man.

Garin put the trout on the table and sat in the big chair by the fire. "Can Mother get you something? Water? Some bread?"

The old woman was about to scold her daughter for not helping, then snapped her mouth shut. Mother and daughter looked at one another, a silent agreement to keep up the ruse passing between them.

"Water, thank you." Princess Nazani batted her thick black eyelashes at Garin.

While the old woman fetched the water, Garin and Princess Nazani tried looking everywhere but at each other. It didn't work. Their gazes met so often they flushed pink and shifted uncomfortably in their chairs.

"Well, what should we talk about?" asked Garin, having no idea how to flirt, let alone with a princess.

"Well," Princess Nazani said coyly, "you can ask me questions."

"Ah . . ." Garin did not know what kinds of questions were proper to ask a princess.

Happily, Princess Nazani was a talkative girl who found royal protocol very tedious and both asked and answered her own questions. Age: sixteen. Interests: riding, hawking, and rug weaving—but only when it rained. Favorite flower: gladiolus.

"And that's why I ran from the palace," said Princess Nazani, finishing the story about how she came to be lost in the forest. "How could I marry a man with both an ugly face *and* a mean-spirited personality?"

"I know I couldn't," said Garin truthfully.

Princess Nazani giggled. "Of course not." She glanced at the old woman busy in the kitchen. "Do you have a sweetheart?"

Garin shook her head.

"Whyever not? You're *very* handsome."

The old woman threw her daughter a stern look that she pretended not to see. Those stern looks became questioning ones during supper.

The princess didn't notice, as she was too enamored by Garin. Not once was Garin anything but supportive and understanding when Nazani talked about the problems of being a princess.

By the end of supper, Garin and Nazani were chatting like old friends.

I should tell her I'm a girl just three years older than

she. Oh, Mother is giving me that look again. I'll tell Nazani tomorrow. Right now I just want to sit and listen to her talk and imagine her naked.

"*I'll* show the princess to her room." The old woman stood.

Princess Nazani flashed Garin a bright smile. "I'm overwhelmed by your hospitality. I wish . . ." She bit her lip and fluttered her eyelashes, hoping they spoke what she could not.

Garin understood and it made her man's heart lurch. Their wish was *almost* the same. Nazani wished Garin were a prince, and Garin wished she were a man.

Later that night, Garin rapped softly on Nazani's door, determined to tell the princess the truth.

Clad in Garin's own white chemise, Nazani opened the door, her dark hair falling in thick waves to her waist. "It's you," she smiled.

Once again, Garin was struck by her beauty, imagining what it would be like to run her fingers through Nazani's tresses.

"I will take you back to the palace tomorrow." Garin tried not stare at Nazani's large upturned breasts through the thin cotton.

"So soon?" Nazani pushed her plump lips into a pout.

Garin swallowed, felt her body warm with desire. "I'm sure the king and queen are frantic with worry."

"Oh, I *know* they are." Nazani dragged her teeth over her lower lip. "Can I ask a favor? It's a rather big one."

Garin nodded. She would do anything for the princess.

"Will you kiss me?"

Garin's eyes widened. "You're a princess."

Nazani put her hands on her hips and the sheer fabric of her chemise stretched across her breasts to reveal her hard pink nipples. "That's right. And as I am your princess you must do as I ask." She tilted her face upward.

Garin leaned down and kissed her. It was quick and closed mouthed, yet Garin had never felt anything so wonderful.

Eyes glinting with mischief, Nazani snatched Garin's hand and yanked her into the room.

"I want a *real* kiss." She closed the door. "The kind my maid gives to the stable boy."

Garin couldn't tell Nazani the truth now. Not when the only thing she wanted was to kiss her again. Garin wrapped her arms around Nazani and pressed her lips to Nazani's, this time prying open Nazani's mouth with her tongue.

Nazani's tongue was just as eager, and together they tasted and explored.

Tell her!

Garin tried pulling away. Nazani's demanding lips and tongue wouldn't have it. The princess crushed their mouths tight.

I feel like a real man with Nazani.

Garin's hands roamed over Nazani's narrow waist and full hips, rising again to feel her breasts—so much larger than Garin's. She groaned. Their hips ground against each other, their mouths melded together.

Nazani pushed close, her arms tight around Garin. The thrill of this handsome man's hands on her body made her feel deliciously improper and *very* horny.

A knock on the door startled them apart.

"Everything all right in there?" asked the old woman. "Do you need anything, Princess?"

"I'm fine," Nazani answered without opening the door. "I'll see you in the morning."

Garin and Nazani stood motionless until the old woman's footsteps faded away.

"Garin," Nazani stroked Garin's cheek. "You're as hairless as a woman."

Garin rubbed her chin. "I'll never have a beard." *That's the truth, at least.*

"Good, I don't like them." Nazani's hands snaked around the back of Garin's neck. "You're nothing at all like those dreadful princes coming to ask my father for my hand in marriage. They're always so superior, so subtly patronizing whenever I tell them my views on things. Not like you. You like me for me."

"I like every part of you," said Garin. "Your smile, your eyes, your spirit." Garin's gaze rested on Nazani's breasts. "Everything."

"I like everything about you too." Nazani stood on her tiptoes and whispered into Garin's ear. "Especially how you make my body feel all tingly and wonderful."

"Mine too." Garin softly kissed her lips, pulled Nazani's hands away, and stepped back. "I should go."

Tell her! Tell her NOW!

Nazani's finger dragged across Garin's lips. "That's probably a good idea. I don't want to do something we shouldn't." Her eyes slid sideways. "Or rather do *more* of what we shouldn't have done in the first place."

There's no chance of that. I don't have the right parts.

Garin grinned. "I was just obeying my princess." She kissed Nazani's hand and left the room, careful of the squeaky door.

The old woman was in the hall, leaning against the wall, arms crossed. "What were you doing in there?"

Garin strode into the main room and flopped down on the chair near the fire. "I love her, Mother."

"Life has not been kind to you, Garin. You finally found love and it's all wrong." The old woman sat next to her daughter and stroked her back. "I could not ask for a better daughter, and yet sometimes I have felt that you're more like a son. You remind me so much of your father, your untiring strength, your courage, your honesty, your preference for clever girls."

"I'm cursed." Garin blinked back tears. "My own body fights with my mind." Garin grabbed her mother's hand. "Tell me the truth, Mother. Did a gypsy curse you while I was in your womb?"

"No, that would have explained your problem." The old woman tapped her chin in thought. "There's a woman in a nearby village who says her son is more coquettish than any girl. Maybe that's who you're meant for."

Garin scowled. "I want to make love to a woman not a man."

"I don't know what to tell you, child, but I know it must be a miserable thing not to fit into the skin given to you." The old woman patted her daughter's back. "Go to bed and stay away from the princess. There's nothing you can offer her—even if you *were* a man."

The next morning the old woman burst into the house waving a crinkled announcement. "Come quick.

Look! I was leaving town when I saw the king's messenger nailing this to a tree. It's a reward for the safe return of the princess."

"Did you tell him I was here?" Princess Nazani's lips pouted with disappointment.

"Of course," said the old woman. "He is returning to the palace as we speak to tell the king where you are."

The old woman saw the unhappiness on both the girls' faces and her heart clenched with pity for their impossible love.

A knight arrived before noon riding a magnificent chestnut mare with an expressive, pearl-colored face. Two more horses followed behind.

The knight dismounted and went to the princess. "Are you well, Princess Nazani?"

"Quite well," said Nazani. "This man and his mother have taken excellent care of me."

"Would you like to have a bowl of *dzhash* before returning?" asked the old woman. "Garin will water your horses while you eat."

The hungry knight accepted the offer, leaving Garin holding the reins of three horses.

Garin stroked the mare's pearly-white forehead. "You're an intelligent looking horse."

"Thank you," replied the horse.

Garin dropped the reins and stumbled back. "What?" She looked around. "Armen?" Her fishing buddy Armen was a jokester, always playing tricks. "Where are you hiding, Armen?"

"No Armen here, just me. My name is Lulizar." The mare nudged the reins on the ground. "Better grab these or the other two horses will wander off."

Garin picked up the reins, her eyes never leaving the horse. "You talk."

Lulizar snorted. "And here I thought you were a smart girl."

Garin glanced back at the house. "You know I'm a girl?"

"Of course. I can smell it."

Garin sniffed her armpit.

"Not there. Your cunt. Does the princess know?"

"No. What's the point? She's a princess, and I'm a poor nobody." Garin heaved a heavy sigh before leading the horses to a narrow creek beyond the fruit trees.

Lulizar knew a lovesick sigh when he heard one. "Did you deflower her yet? The girl needs a good fucking. Might tame her wild spirit a bit."

"How am I suppose to do that without a cock?"

Lulizar drank from the creek. "A strap-on," she said after drinking her fill.

"What?"

"Make one out of wood—not too huge but big enough to thrill."

Garin's mouth hung open.

"Nine inches ought to satisfy that hot little missy." Lulizar nudged Garin. "You always wanted a cock, right—close your mouth girl, I *know* these things—anyway I'm telling you how to have one. You *do* know what one looks like, don't you?"

Garin nodded, mouth still agape.

"The ones I've seen are carved smooth and attach to the body with a strap around the waist."

"I could be a man." Garin grinned for a moment before her elated expression fell. "The princess is leaving, it's too late."

"You're going with her. The king wants to personally thank and offer a reward to the person who found her."

Garin touched the spot where her cock should have been. "Wood is too hard. I can stuff some leather... make some testicles."

"Ah, just as I thought, you *are* a smart girl."

"But won't the princess discover the truth?"

"Eventually." The horse turned her head at the sound of the knight's call. "Come on, Garin. Let's take your ladylove home. But first, a word of advice. Do not ask the king for jewels or gold. Ask for me."

Sure enough, the knight told Garin to ride with them back to the palace. Garin raced inside to pack a rucksack. She paused to grab a cucumber from the table, then tied it low on her hips with a ribbon.

Not bad. It feels right. Why didn't I ever do this before?

Garin hitched up her trousers, grabbed the rucksack, and slung her quiver of arrows over her shoulders.

Princess Nazani was waiting for Garin outside the door. "I'm so glad we have a few more hours together." She hugged Garin tight, pressing their bodies together. "Oh." She giggled at Garin's arousal. "One more quick kiss."

The kiss wasn't quick, it was long and deep and wet. A kiss they both knew was the last one they would ever share.

Garin pulled away. "If the knight sees us kissing I'll get death not a reward."

A moment later, they emerged from the house. The princess gave the old woman a hug before mounting the horse.

As the horses trotted away, Garin looked over her shoulder at her mother. Her hand was on her cheek, a sad smile on her face.

It did not take long for the knight to suspect that the princess had fallen for the pretty-faced commoner. Both talked and laughed with a comfortable ease. Except for their different stations in life, they made a good match, their natures complementing each other's.

They were deep in the forest when Garin stopped the horse and signaled for quiet. She pulled an arrow from the quiver, threaded the bow, and let loose. Her aim, as always, was true, and struck the deer in the heart, killing it instantly.

"Dinner," said Garin to the impressed knight. She leapt down, bound the deer, then slung it over the horse, securing it with the strength and efficiency of a man.

They arrived at the palace, a towering stone structure with four turrets and tiled conical roofs. The king and queen stood at the entrance.

Princess Nazani ran into her parents' waiting arms and hugged them tight.

"We are forever in your debt," said the king to Garin. "Name your reward. Jewels? Gold?"

Garin looked at Nazani with longing, Nazani's taste still on Garin's lips. She scratched her chin like she often saw men do. "That's a tough decision."

Lulizar whinnied a reminder, which wasn't necessary. Garin planned on taking the mare's advice.

"I have no need for gold or jewels." Garin stroked Lulizar's forehead. "But I rather like this pearl-faced mare."

"Lulizar? She's past her prime," said the king.

Lulizar snorted in protest.

"She is strong, sure-footed, and fast, though." The king crossed his arms. "Are you certain that's *all* you want?"

I want your daughter but since I'm neither a prince nor a man I'll have to settle for the memory of our stolen kisses.

"Quite sure," said Garin. "It was reward enough to escort the princess home."

The queen whispered in the king's ear.

"Should I put the gold in the saddlebags then?" The king narrowed his eyes as he studied the lean youth before him.

"No, your majesty. I am content with Lulizar. Besides, how can I put a value on the princess? She is priceless, her beauty and virtue of incalculable worth."

Princess Nazani beamed at Garin, and Garin beamed back, their adoring looks noticed by the queen.

"Well said," nodded the king. "Take Lulizar to the stables, brush down your new horse, and join our feast."

After offering the deer to the king and queen, Garin followed the stable boy to Lulizar's stall.

"What are you going to do about Princess Nazani?" Lulizar stuck her muzzle into a bag of oats.

Garin shrugged and shook her head.

"Did I hear my name?" Nazani poked her head into the stall.

Garin glanced at Lulizar. "Just me. I like saying your name, it reminds me of—"

"Our kiss?" Nazani leaned against the wood slats. "You could have asked Father for *anything* and he would have given it to you. Why didn't you?"

"Because I want you." Garin put down the saddle and fenced Nazani in with her arms.

Nazani's head rested against the wood panel. "Kiss me again."

Garin leaned in and found Nazani's tongue was warm and demanding. Garin's hands roamed over Nazani's body, lingering at her breasts, caressing them despite the thick embroidered fabric.

"I want to feel your hands on my bare skin." Nazani's hand swept over the front of Garin's trousers. "I want to feel *this*." Her palm swooshed back and forth across his fake arousal.

"I want to taste *this*." Garin's hand wiggled between the folds of Nazani's dress.

Lulizar snorted.

"Taste?" Nazani's eyes lit up.

Garin knelt down, lifted Nazani's dress, and stroked Nazani's calves and thighs.

"That feels so good." Nazani hitched her skirt higher.

Garin's mouth grazed Nazani's inner thigh while Princess Nazani breathed loud, throaty groans. Garin kissed her dark downy mound, inhaled her musk.

Nazani shifted, spread her legs apart. "Do it. Lick me there."

Garin's tongue snugged inside, the taste of her first cunt releasing any inhibitions.

"Better than honey." Garin found Nazani's slick nub and swept her tongue over it, each sweet pass inciting Nazani's throaty coos. Garin herself was wet, her own cunt throbbing.

"Don't stop," said Nazani.

Stop? I can't. I'm so turned on by your groans my cunt aches.

Garin fanned wide Nazani's sex and marveled at her gloss. Garin's lust climbed upward, each lick and suck causing her own clit to swell.

My clit should be a cock.

When Nazani's cooing became raspy, Garin nuzzled deeper. Nazani smacked the wood slat partition between the stalls, the steady beats marking her ascent. She let loose a long, low, throaty squeal, her fists beating on Garin's shoulders, her legs trembling with the power of her first orgasm.

"I love you." Nazani panted. "I love you, I love you."

Garin stood and kissed her cheek. "I love you too, Princess Nazani."

Nazani smoothed her skirt. "I'm going to talk to my father right now. I'm going to tell him everything."

What?

Lulizar, who had been watching the whole time, swished her tail back and forth with frustration.

"What are you going to tell the king?" Garin licked Nazani's gloss from her lips.

"That I love you. That no one but you is capable of making me happy." Nazani walked through the gate.

"Horny?" asked Lulizar after Nazani was gone. "Better finish yourself off."

Garin leaned against the gate and rubbed her clit. It didn't take long until she shook with orgasmic relief. "Now what?"

"Better make a strap-on cock fast. Our princess is a shameless little miss." Lulizar nudged Garin. "Oh, don't look so worried. Everything will work out. Get a move on. You need a bath."

At the feast, Garin sat near enough to the royal table to see that Nazani's eyes sparkled with anticipation. Much as she loved the princess, this worried Garin, her lie a heavy rock on her heart.

At the end of the feast, the king stood and lifted his gold goblet. "As many of you already know, this honorable young man," he gestured to Garin, "returned my precious daughter unharmed. He refused my offer of gold and jewels. Said his reward was escorting the princess home. He asked only for one pearly faced mare. Even more impressive is what my daughter told me earlier this afternoon. Princess Nazani said Garin made her feel more wonderful than she ever felt before, that he ignited such a depth of feeling that she could not bear it if he left." The king's eyes met Garin's. "My daughter's happiness means everything to me, and so it is with great joy that I give her in marriage to Garin. Make her happy, young man, and you will want for nothing."

While the room thundered with applause, Garin's hand flew to her chest in terror. The guests took one look at Garin's shocked face and assumed it was joy.

What have I done? I've deceived my true love! What will Nazani do when she finds out I'm a woman? She'll never forgive me and the king will run a blade through my broken heart!

Garin met Nazani's triumphant smile despite the stab in her not-a-man heart. There were many congratulations, and the newly engaged couple wasn't able to speak in private, which suited Garin *and* the queen just fine.

The queen, seeing lust shining in her daughter's eyes, escorted Nazani to her chambers and locked her in. "It's for your own good." She turned the key. "Supervised visits until the wedding. You must remain pure."

Garin ran to the stables and told Lulizar what happened.

"Should I run away? Tell her I'm a woman? What should I do?"

"Make a strap-on," said Lulizar. "Fuck her good. It will all work out."

"If it doesn't?"

"I'm the fastest horse around."

While the king planned the seven-day celebration, the queen made sure Nazani and Garin were never left alone. She knew sexual yearning when she saw it. Though the queen was disappointed Nazani had fallen in love with a commoner, she was happy to discover how well suited they were. Their temperaments balanced each other's. Where Nazani was impetuous, Garin was cautious. Where Nazani was frivolous, Garin was sensible. Even more pleasing, the queen never heard Garin speak to or treat her daughter with anything but the utmost respect. Like equals. The queen was more impressed with this common lad than any arrogant prince.

When Garin wasn't attending court functions and parties, she locked her door and worked on the strap-on cock. She used butter-soft leather, stitched it meticulously, and stuffed the length until it was as hard as a real cock—the cock denied her by Nature. Securing it to the strap was the *real* challenge, but after several attempts she devised a holster of sorts, the shaft through a ring, a leather sack stuffed with two soft balls beneath, and a strap going around her waist and thighs. There was only one problem. Actually two.

"Nazani won't be able to see me naked," said Garin, modeling the strap-on for Lulizar.

"Tell her you're shy or that she'll be frightened by its size," said Lulizar.

"This false cock doesn't shoot cum either," said Garin.

"Or impregnate her," added Lulizar.

Make that *three* problems.

The morning of the wedding, Garin held her weeping mother.

"The king will hang you, or worse, when he discovers you're a woman." The old woman blew her nose. "I curse the day I found that girl."

"Don't say that, Mother. I love her."

"But does she really love *you*? The *woman* you?"

Mother doesn't understand. My flesh is woman, but my heart and head is man. I am both and neither.

Garin sighed and shook her head. "I don't know."

The wedding was the event of the year, hundreds of guests crowding into the cathedral. Garin had spent a week learning court protocol and wedding etiquette but nothing had prepared her for the first sight of her bride. Garin's heart leapt, Nazani's beauty and poise eliminating all but the most manly of feelings for a brief, wonderful moment.

I am the luckiest person alive. Nazani is mine. My future, with her. I will not let her down. I will love and protect her forever.

Garin blinked back tears, squared her shoulders, and enjoyed the dream that was doomed.

It was late when Garin and Nazani finally arrived at

their nuptial chambers, a room ablaze with candles and scented with flower petals and fragrant herbs.

"I want to make love by moonlight." Garin walked about the room and extinguished all the candles.

Nazani's arms wrapped around Garin. "Help me take off my wedding dress."

Garin lifted the loop of coins around Nazani's chin and removed her jeweled headpiece and veil, fanning her tresses over her shoulders. "I've been out of my mind with desire the entire day." Garin tossed the headpiece on the bed. "I can't wait much longer." Garin's tongue pushed between Nazani's lips, heartened by her enthusiastic response.

Garin pressed down through Nazani's embroidered dress, the curves of her body concealed beneath the layers.

"Let me just—" Nazani sighed.

"I want you *now*, wife." Garin eased her onto the bed.

Nazani rasped her approval as Garin pulled the wedding dress to her waist, then dipped into Nazani's pink gloss, already wet and hot, and glided two fingers back and forth until Nazani's hips began thrusting.

"You're mine now." Garin deepened the kiss. *At least until you discover the truth about me.*

The strap-on cock sprung from the vent between Garin's trouser legs. Like a real man, Garin held the base and guided it toward Nazani's tight wet cunt.

"I'll try to be gentle," Garin said feeling her own snatch moisten and squeeze.

"Shove it in!" Nazani grabbed Garin's ass. "Shove. It. In!"

Garin pushed, felt the resistance, felt it give, then plunged deep.

Nazani's head lifted off the bed. "You're huge!"

"Does it hurt?"

"It feels wonderful! Fuck me, husband."

Garin drove into Nazani hard and fast, the leather testicles rubbing against her own clit. Nazani's throaty rasps were a drug that pulled Garin from reality and into the fantasy of maleness, the strap-on cock seeming *real*.

Nazani growled her bliss, her orgasm sending Garin over the edge, her own clit erupting with release beneath the leather testicles. But unlike a real cock, the strap-on was always hard, and Garin kept driving into Nazani as she came again and again.

"No more, no more," the exhausted Nazani pleaded.

Garin lowered the wedding dress, then curled up beside Nazani, and they both fell into a satisfied sleep.

The next two nights, Nazani was too sore to fuck despite taking cool baths to soothe her well-fucked hole.

On the fourth night of the wedding celebration, Nazani announced her complete recovery.

"Leave the candles lit," said Nazani. "I want to see you naked and I want to see your cock."

Garin took off Nazani's headpiece and veil, and kissed the nape of her neck. "And I want to see you."

Nazani's dress was not easy to remove, and Garin used the slow undressing to tease her. Garin sprinkled kisses on Nazani's shoulders, nuzzled her neck, and suckled her breasts until the writhing Nazani begged to be fucked.

"Take off your clothes." Nazani undid the clasps of Garin's gold-embroidered *arkhaluk*.

She'll see my breasts!

Garin pulled down her trousers, glad the tunic fell to mid thigh and that her legs were thick and straight. "Get on your knees, wife."

Nazani squealed with delight, rolled over, and wiggled her succulent white ass. Garin bit into it and Nazani yelped.

Nazani shook her ass, the sweet flesh quivering like pudding. Garin's tongue ran over the curved mound and her fingertips glazed across Nazani's wet clit. Nazani's gloss was thick and fragrant with need.

"Do you want me? Are you ready?" Garin nibbled on her flesh.

Nazani looked over her shoulder. "Ready? My puss feels empty without you."

Garin thrust into her.

"Oh! I *like* it this way!"

Garin pushed deep into Nazani and leaned over to twiddle her nipples. They rocked and ground into each other, Nazani climaxing again and again, Garin temporarily forgetting the strap-on cock wasn't real.

"You're insatiable," Garin whispered in Nazani's ear as she slept.

Except for Nazani's pleas to see Garin naked, the fifth and sixth nights were the same, Nazani preferring to be entered from behind.

On the seventh night, the last day of the wedding celebration, Nazani stood with her hands on her hips.

"I demand to see your cock! I need to touch it. I want to taste it." Nazani gathered Garin's hands in her own and brought them to her lips, her eyes bright with love. "I know what you've been doing."

You do?

"Don't look so frightened." Nazani kissed Garin's fingers. "You wanted to make sure I focused only on my body, my pleasure. Mother told me this proved what a kind selfless man you are."

You told the queen?

"But now it's my turn to focus on you, to lick and caress *your* body."

Garin's heart raced, her mind in a panic. "My cock is so large you'll be frightened," she finally blurted out.

Nazani laughed. "Amazed is more likely." She tugged small scissors from a deep pocket in her dress. "Let me love you properly."

She ripped open Garin's trousers before Garin could stop her. The trousers dropped to the floor.

"What *is* this?" Nazani's eyes widened. "I don't understand. Where is your cock? Was it cut off? Did you have an accident as a child?"

Shame suffocated Garin's reply, her guilt a noose tightening around her neck.

Tell her! Show Nazani who you really are.

Garin unhooked the apparatus and held the strapon in her hand. With the other she spread herself wide. "I'm a woman."

Nazani backed away. "A woman? I've been fucking a woman? A woman's been licking my clit?" Her hand covered her mouth. "You...you...tricked me! You deceived me!"

"No, Nazani, I love you." Garin's hand patted her heart. "I am a man here. And here." She touched her head. "I *feel* like a man."

"You're a *woman*!" Nazani shook her head, tears

running down her cheeks, and fled from the room.

It seemed to Garin like only a moment passed before the king and queen stormed into the room, the princess wailing behind them.

The king looked at the strap-on Garin held and hurled a chair across the room. "You bastard!"

"I'm so sorry. I love your daughter. I really do." Garin collapsed on the floor crying and prepared herself to die.

"I'll kill you—" bellowed the king.

"No!" The queen stayed the king with an outstretched arm. "We will be the laughing stock of the kingdom if word of Garin's treachery gets out. I have a better idea."

They locked Garin in the room.

Garin picked up the scissors. *I deserve to die. Not only did I deceive my true love, I committed treason. My life was doomed the moment I realized I was a man trapped in a woman's body.*

Early the next morning, the king returned, his eyes hollowed from a sleepless night, and found Garin curled in a ball on the bed, the scissors laying next to the dismembered strap-on.

"I have a task for you, *son-in-law*," said the king. "The mare I gave you has a brother living in the forest. He's a wild stallion no one can subdue. Don't come back without him."

It was a fool's errand. One Garin could never hope to return from.

"Don't worry, I know where to find him," said Lulizar as Garin fitted the saddle over her the next morning. "Here's my plan."

After finding a necessary ingredient deep in the forest, Lulizar took Garin to the stallion's favorite grazing spot near a mountain stream.

Garin followed Lulizar's instructions exactly and scattered the narcotic weed she'd collected into the surrounding grass. It wasn't long before the stallion arrived. After that, it was easy. Garin threw the lead rope over the wild stallion's head and led the lethargic horse back to the palace.

The king was astonished when Garin returned with the wild stallion.

"You were lucky," said the king. "But tomorrow's task is more difficult. You will go to the home of the demons and collect the seven years of back taxes they owe me."

Princess Nazani burst into tears. "I'm so sorry, Garin," she moaned as the queen led her away.

"Don't worry," said Lulizar the next morning as Garin saddled her up. "I have a plan. The demons' mansion is next to a marble quarry. All we need is a mixture of saltpeter, charcoal, and sulfur to create an explosion. That should give you enough time to run inside the house and find their cache of gold."

Once again, Garin followed Lulizar's instructions. The thunderous blast shook the quarry. Rocks and boulders plunged into the quarry's depths. Every demon flew from the house screaming in horror and into the black smoke, dust clouds, and falling debris that left them disoriented and dazed. Garin ran inside the unguarded mansion, found the gold, and grabbed enough to pay seven years' worth of taxes. With interest.

Nazani wept with relief when Garin returned. "Stop, Father, I beg of you. I love her."

The king was amazed by Garin's fearlessness, but that didn't change what Garin had done. Garin *had* to die. And he knew one task his *son-in-law* would never survive. "Long before I was born, a she-devil stole my grandfather's gold rosary. Bring it back."

"Noooooo!" Nazani fell at her father's feet and clutched his legs. "The she-devil will cut out Garin's heart!"

"Garin made a fool of you, of all of us," said the king.

"Don't worry," said Lulizar the following morning. "I know where the she-devil lives and—"

"You have a plan," said Garin laughing.

But when they arrived at the she-devil's black marble palace, Garin had doubts.

"Just make sure to take a really good running leap from the window." Lulizar's tail swished away a pesky fly. "The window, there, overlooking the ravine."

"What if the she-devil catches me before I escape? What if I don't leap far enough? What if I miss the ledge? What if—"

Lulizar nudged Garin's shoulder. "You can do this. Have faith."

While Lulizar brayed outside, Garin crept into the mansion, slipped past the distracted demon guards, and tiptoed upstairs.

Outside, Lulizar continued creating a ruckus.

"What's got you spooked, you old mare?" shouted the she-devil from the window. "Go away, before I turn you into a worm."

In the room across the hall, Garin found the golden rosary in the enameled box on the sideboard. Just where Lulizar had said it would be.

The she-devil sniffed the air, the foul scent of human sweat accosting her sensitive nose. Following the putrid odor she turned from the window and found Garin with the rosary. "What is this thievery?" She hurtled across the hall, her eyes ablaze with wrath.

Garin ran, looping the rosary around her neck as she sprinted toward the window.

"Stop!" Arms covered in sharp scales reached out and swiped at Garin, tearing her sleeve.

Garin launched herself out over the window ledge and into the ravine below. The world blurred and spun, all senses and emotions eclipsed by the free fall.

Garin slammed down onto something solid. Her hands sprung out and hugged Lulizar's neck.

"Told you not to worry," said Lulizar, who had leapt through the air over the wide breach in the ledge.

"I curse you, thief!" shouted the she-devil as Lulizar galloped toward the tunnel that led out of the she-devil's territory. Seething with rage, she pronounced the vilest curse she could think of. "If you are a man, you are now a woman! If you are a woman, you are now a man!"

Garin groaned in pain, her stomach twisting as her womb shriveled and a cock sprouted between her legs.

"I'm a man!" cried Garin, his low voice a surprise. "A real man!" He shifted his new balls to a more comfortable position.

Lulizar galloped out of the tunnel and into the forest. "See? I told you I had a plan. I know this she-devil well, and that's her favorite curse."

Garin returned to the palace and the king saw the difference immediately—his smooth-faced and lean son-in-law had been replaced by a man with chin fuzz and muscled girth.

Nazani wept for joy when Garin told them what happened. The king and queen marveled at their good fortune. The curse was a blessing that would allow them to welcome the courageous and good-hearted Garin with open arms.

Nazani pulled her husband to her side. "I want to see your new cock," Nazani whispered in Garin's ear.

Garin scooped her up and ran all the way to their chamber, where he stripped off his clothes and grabbed his nine-inch cock.

"It's beautiful." Nazani kneeled before him and examined every inch, Garin groaning as she stroked.

A bead of cum leaked from Garin's cock and Nazani licked it off. She closed her mouth around the tip and sucked.

"It's not like my strap-on," said Garin. "I won't be able to fuck all night long."

"What's to stop you from fucking me and *then* using the strap-on?" Nazani cupped his balls as she swirled her tongue around his rigid length.

"Nothing at all," said Garin, easing her head away. "But first I want to fuck you."

They tore their clothes off, and Nazani lifted and spread her legs on the bed.

Garin grabbed her thighs and slid into her hot gloss, his pleasure so intense, so *right*, that his groan as he entered could be heard in the hall.

"What does it feel like?" asked Nazani.

"Paradise." Nazani was tight and hot and slick, and Garin's new cock swelled even larger, filling her up. "Like I'm finally home."

Garin thrust deep and withdrew slowly, enthralled by the marvel of sensations coursing though his body. Fast plunge. Slow withdraw. Again and again. He changed his rhythm. Slow entry and quick withdraw. He changed his rhythm again, each new thrust a discovery in sensation. "I'll need a lot of practice," said Garin.

Nazani was too close to climaxing to do anything but moan and buck. Once again her raspy sounds sent Garin over the edge and he hammered into her without control. He howled his release, felt cum pulse out, heard Nazani's throaty growl of pleasure. Garin gave her a few more thrusts and pulled out, his cock wet with cum.

"Keep fucking me with your leather cock," said Nazani.

Garin obliged his horny princess.

It didn't take long for the newlyweds to discover all sorts of ways to include the repaired strap-on into their daily lovemaking.

Garin and Nazani enjoyed a long happy marriage, ruled their own kingdom, and *always* consulted with Lulizar.

This cross-dressing transsexual ancient folktale comes from Armenia. Passed from generation to generation, Lulizar's name remains constant, while the others are merely identified as the king, queen, princess, old

woman, and daughter. A search through any Armenian folk story collection will invariably turn up a version of the Lulizar story. Many of the story elements suggest it predates Christian times. Therefore, it's safe to assume that over time the Christianized rosary, the final object retrieved, took the place of some pagan relic.

THE
VACATION FLING

"Damn, girl, the night's still early. You Americans need to learn how to party." Cousin Maria grabs my wrist and tugs me into the third nightclub of the evening.

I'm tired. A ten-hour flight from Los Angeles to Quito, Ecuador, plus the six-hour drive to Tena tends to mess with sleep patterns. I'm not complaining though, I'll sleep in late tomorrow.

"What do you think of our city?" Maria is amped up—it's not every day an American cousin visits.

"I love it so far." What else can I say? I've only been here for about four hours.

Tena is a mecca for the kayak, rafting, rain-forest hiking set (so not me!), its river a tributary to the Amazon, which for some reason is supposed to be really cool. Tena is also home to about fifty cousins on my mother's side. This trip is a graduation present. Four—okay, six—years of exams, papers, and textbooks done, over, *fini*. Career pending. Not sure what I'm going to do with my liberal studies degree yet. Maybe teach? Besides allowing me to do some sightseeing and meet all my cousins, I'm hoping this trip takes the sting out of a nasty breakup. I was expecting an engagement ring after graduation, not a love-you-but-I'm-not-ready-for-marriage text. But it was more than that. I didn't do it for him anymore. Our sex life was Blahsville. He stopped putting in any effort, and by that I mean he expected me to climb on top and do all the work. All. The. Time.

I look up at the neon sign over the door of the nightclub. CULEBRA NEGRA. Black Snake.

"It's *muy especial*," says Maria.

My other two cousins (whose English is not as good) nod energetically. My cousins are gorgeous, all smoldering dark eyes and curvaceous Latina bodies, their big breasts pushed high for maximum cleavage spillage. All three wear a different version of the same dress, painted-on tight, Barbie pink, and peekaboo-panty short. They're amazing. We've been drinking and dancing all night, and not one has complained about her feet in five-inch spike heels.

Standing next to my petite femme-fatale-dressed cousins, my five-foot, ten-inch height, black cotton dress, and flat sandals make me feel like a giant. But, thanks to my Norwegian dad, at least I'm a blonde-haired, blue-eyed giant.

Culebra Negra went for an all-black vibe: walls, floors, ceilings, tables, and chairs. Everything's painted black but the stage. Two enormous yellow snake eyes look out from the back wall, and a long red tongue slithers around the platform. I feel like Mowgli in *The Jungle Book* when he meets the giant snake Kaa.

My cousin scores a table near the front from some

hikers (sunburned Caucasians wearing trendy sweat-whisking gear) who look like they forgot to wear insect repellent.

"Did we miss the band?" The stage is set but nobody's there.

"They come on at eleven." Maria looks at her watch. "Any minute."

My cousins order a round of the house specialty, Snakebites—a shot of honey-flavored whiskey and a splash of lime juice.

"What's the name of the band?" I throw back the Snakebite. Yum.

"*Mono Suavo*. Smooth Monkey," says Cousin Rocio. "The singer is *muy caliente*."

The recorded dance music is replaced by a steady drumbeat, and the crowd starts clapping and thumping their feet. *Mono Suavo* walks out from behind the curtain. There's five of them, and except for one guy, they're all wearing black T-shirts with a Ray Ban–wearing monkey hanging from a tree branch emblazoned on the front. The back of the T-shirt has their name in a jungle font, the *M* and *S* like curling vines.

The guy in the loose black shirt and jeans is gorgeous. Movie-star sexy. A Latin hunk of smoldering sexuality. Bedroom eyes, square jaw, pillow-thick lips, ponytail, and just enough facial scruff to be a model for designer cologne. He's one of those guys you see and immediately think, *Bet he's wild in bed*. He lifts the guitar strap over his shoulder and flashes a killer grin at the audience.

The women hoot and holler. He smiles again, and this time it's shy, like he's humbled by their cheers. He adjusts his straw fedora, strums the guitar a few times, then turns to the band to discuss the set list.

I lean toward Maria. "What kind of music do they play?"

"Some of their own stuff. Some cover."

When the lead singer sits on the stool, the drummer begins. The ambient noise level drops, everyone waiting for the song.

His voice is amazing, a deep velvety baritone that seeps into your skin and soaks into your soul. It's sexy as hell, a voice you want whispering in your ear while fucking. The song is romantic but sad, about a man searching for a woman strong enough to peel away his protective layers so he can love fully. Or something like that. Translating Spanish songs isn't that easy for me.

My eyes close, and I let the song wash over me. His voice is cream: rich and smooth and decadent. He's like an overpriced frothy mocha, spreading heat through my body and awakening my senses.

When I open my eyes, I find him staring at me, and it feels like he sings the rest of the song just for me. After that, our eyes meet often. Maybe it's because I'm the only natural blonde in the room.

I don't know how many Snakebites I put down, but I'm pretty buzzed when the band finishes their set. The lead singer sets his guitar in a stand and makes a beeline for our table.

He steals a chair from a nearby table and slides it in next to mine. "*Hola*, blondie."

My cousins burst into giggles.

"Hi." Call me articulate.

He flashes me that killer smile, wide, bright, and

confident. "You from the US?" His English is excellent, my-private-school-teacher-was-an-American perfect.

"Yeah."

One glance at my cousins tells me they are horrified by my lack of flirting skills.

"I'm Marco." He extends his hand. "What's your name?"

"Angela." I put my hand in his—it's not a handshake, no up-and-down movement, just a soft, still hold—and a thousand bolts of sexual energy rocket up my arm and dive straight for my crotch. Holy shit. I gasp my surprise.

Marco holds my hand for too long and his Adam's apple bobs up and down. He feels it too. "Where are you from?"

"LA." I can't drag my eyes away from that gorgeous face.

"Having fun?" Marco directs his question to my cousins, who somehow manage to thrust out every inch of cleavage and sing the band's praises at the same time. "Think we're ready for Hollywood?" Marco leans close, his arm snaking around the top of my chair.

He smells divine, like fresh mountain water and a newly unfurled leaf. Most singers smell like booze and pot. Not that I've smelled a lot of singers.

"Your voice is amazing. Can I check out your Sound Cloud?"

"You can check out anything of mine." Marco stands, looks around, then glances at his watch. "Want a T-shirt?"

"Sure." I take Marco's hand—more sexual lightning bolts—and let him lead me away, all too aware of all the envious eyes tracking our progress across the room.

"Where are we going?" I ask as we weave our way through the crowd packed in the narrow hallway waiting to use the bathrooms.

"It's a room where bands can keep their stuff safe." Marco tugs a key from his pocket and opens the door. The band's instrument cases are lying about, as are four well-used backpacks. Two banged-up metal office chairs and a shiny music stand are pushed to the side.

Marco shuts the door, grabs a backpack, and plunges his hand inside. "Fuck it." He drops the pack and pulls me into his arms. "Did you feel it?" He lifts my hand and presses it to his chest.

"Feel what?" My heart is beating against my ribs like a four-year-old with a new drum set.

"*That*. Your touch is..." Marco exhales. "Electric." He runs his fingers down the length of my hair. "I thought you felt it too."

Maybe it's all the Snakebites that make me kiss him. Maybe it's my bruised self-esteem that causes my tongue to push inside and taste his gorgeousness. Maybe it's the feeling of being chosen in front of all those sexy women. Who cares? His lips are pillows, his tongue a bed of delights. I wrap my arms around his neck and sink into his mouth. We're devouring each other, thrusting and plunging and breathing into each other without control or finesse. I pull away, panting, my lips bruised. "Wow." No guy *ever* kissed me like that.

"Guess I have my answer." Marco puts his finger in my mouth. "Do you know 'Sabor a Mi'?"

I nod, sucking hard on his finger. It's my parents' favorite, a sappy song about carrying the taste of your lover with you for eternity, or something like that. It's played at every Latino wedding and anniversary party I've ever attended.

"We enjoy this love song for so long," Marco whisper-sings as my mouth sucks his finger.

My panties are wet. Not moist. Drenched.

Marco pulls his finger out and murmurs the next line, his whispered version so sexy I melt into him, my pelvis grinding into his hard-on.

"I carry your flavor..." His tongue pushes in my mouth and his hands roam over my B-cup-size breasts. "You also carry mine." Marco slips my dress strap over my shoulder, one pert breast and rock-hard nipple released from the confines of the built-in bra.

"Your tits are beautiful." Marco slips down the other strap, and my tits are ready for action.

Marco takes a nipple in his mouth and sucks like my tits give milk.

"Sweet Jesus." My legs wobble. The tug on my tits shoots into my cunt and makes my clit throb.

Marco switches sides, his hand still pulling and twisting the first one. *This* is how men need to suck tits. Like they mean it. With enough rough friction that its sweet agony makes your vagina clench.

It's not easy to unbutton his shirt, but I manage to undo enough to spread my hands across his hairless muscled pecs.

Lord help me, I don't want him to stop. My head rolls back. "Oh god."

Marco tugs up my dress, his fingers slipping beneath my panties. "Your pussy needs a cock."

"Yours," I say to the ceiling. "It needs yours."

His mouth chews my nipple while his fingers slip and

slide over my clit and into my fuck hole. Because that's what it is now. Vagina is too clinical. Kitty too precious. And there is nothing precious or clinical about what I want right now. My fuck hole wants a big Latino cock deep inside it. I unhitch his jeans and wiggle them over his slim hips.

Marco delivers, a massive cock escaping from his jeans and into my hand. "All yours."

"Sweet mother of god." I wrap my fingers around it.

His cock in my hand, Marco backs up and sits on the banged-up metal chair. "Take off your panties."

Reluctantly, I let go of his cock, slip off my panties, and drop the sodden silk into his waiting hand. Marco inhales deeply and groans, then shoves them into his shirt pocket. "Come here, my angel."

I step out of my dress and, standing over him, straddle his legs. His cock is poised like a rocket waiting to be launched.

"Fuck me, Angela."

I ease myself down onto him, his length packed into me. My vag walls squeeze and release around him. His size alone sends my clit into orbit. Marco grabs one tit and sucks on the other while I ride him.

"My angel, you're so fucking tight. And your smell! Damn girl, I wanna eat your pussy next." Marco latches onto a nipple and starts bucking, both hands cupped under my asscheeks as he lifts me up and down. "Ride me, baby, ride me hard," he says while switching tits.

I slam onto him, the force making me gasp. "Your cock feels so damn good."

Marco loosens more than my tongue—he rips away all restraint. I am woman, hear me orgasm!

"God, yes!" I ride him so hard the chair walks across the room with the force of our passion. "Fuck my pussy." I lean back, marveling at my stretched-out nipple clenched between his teeth.

Marco looks at me and grins, and I slam forward into him, my hand smashing his face into my tit. "Fuck yeah. Fuck yeah! I'm almost there. Oh god, soooo fucking close."

Marco snaps his head around when someone bangs on the door.

"Go away," growls Marco. "Keep going, my angel," he whispers into my ear.

"Marco! We're on in two." Damn band member.

Marco bites my earlobe. "Bet he's listening at the door. Heard us fucking. Give him what he wants. Sing for me."

Two more thrusts and my body bursts with pleasure. "Oh fucking yes!"

Marco bites on my nipple and another climax detonates over me, my cunt exploding like the last minute of a July 4th fireworks show. Marco comes hard while I'm still driving myself onto his cock, trying to ride the final shock waves of multiple orgasms.

"Holy fuck," I say pushing back his fedora. "You fuck like a god." My new religion, the Church of Marco.

"It's you who are fucking amazing." Marco kisses me deeply.

More door pounding. "We're on!"

Marco lifts me off, my thighs sticky from sweat, cum, and cunt. "I get off at four."

"Looks like you already got off." I step into my dress

and shimmy it up, returning the tank dress to its full upright and tit-hiding position.

Marco adjusts his fedora and snuggles next to me. "How the hell will I be able to perform knowing my cum is running down your leg?"

"You'll manage."

He pulls up his jeans, arranges his cock. "Four a.m.?"

"Not possible. My cousins...." I make an *I'm-at-their-mercy* face.

"We're here tomorrow." He buttons his shirt.

"Okay."

Marco crosses the room, puts his hand on the doorknob. "I'm not just a lead singer, you know. I'm a med student."

"Let me guess, gynecology?"

"Pediatrics," he says and opens the door.

I follow him down the hall and he's singing before he hits the stage. It's a lively beat that everyone starts dancing to.

"Everything all right?" Maria narrows her eyes.

"Where's the T-shirt?" Cousin Rocio is doing the perfect suspicious mom impression.

"They only had one. I wanted to get four, one for each of us. He'll have them tomorrow." Damn, I'm a smooth liar.

"You and he were kissing, *si*?" Maria pushes away the twenty empty Snakebite tumblers.

"Yeah. He's *really* good. *Muy bueno.*" I fan myself.

My cousins giggle and wiggle their long fuchsia-tipped fingers at me. "You're bad. Very naughty. *Muy travieso.*"

Maria checks her watch. "We have a lot of people to visit tomorrow. The uncles and aunts can't wait to meet you."

We get up to leave and Marco waves.

"*Mañana*," he calls out as we make our way out.

Someone's beating my head with a baseball hat. I open my eyes and Jesus on the cross swims into focus on the opposite wall. International flights and nightclubbing don't mix. Neither do headaches and sunlight. I tumble out of bed and drag myself to the mirror. Was last night a dream? Did I really fuck the lead singer of Mono Suavo during their break? The dried white flecks between my thighs reply in the affirmative. Roger that, Angela, you acted like a slut. I pull on a tank top and shorts, and tread down the stairs.

"Good afternoon, *mija*." My *abuela* picks up the remote and turns the volume down on the TV. She's watching a *novella*. Even without the sound I identify the plot. A woman in fake eyelashes and a push-up bra is screaming at a sexy bearded dude in a three-piece suit. Behind him, a dyed redhead with major cleavage spillage is pointing a long red pointy acrylic nail at her. Classic *novella*. Love, lust, and lots of adultery.

"Have fun?" *Abuela* asks in Spanish.

Cousin Maria is sprawled on the sofa, a soda in her hand. "How are you feeling?"

"Like the floor of one of those nightclubs you took me to." I accept a cup of coffee from the maid.

"Angela met a boy," blabs Maria in Spanish.

Abuela's eyes narrow. "What kind of boy? A good boy?" Two rapid-fire questions in Spanish.

"He's the lead singer of—"

"No no no!" *Abuela*'s "no" needs no translation. "No singer." She waves her hand. "Find a nice boy. One with money."

"He's not just a singer, he's a med student," I say in Spanish. The coffee isn't doing much to settle my stomach but the fried plantains the maid set down may.

Abuela's taupe-penciled eyebrows lift. "Ohhhh, a doctor. What's his name?"

"Marco."

Abuela screws her lips. "Does this Marco have a last name?"

"I forgot to ask." We were too busy fucking.

Abuela frowns. "Find out his last name. *All* his names." She turns back to her novella and raises the volume to old-deaf-people level.

"You know how it is with that generation," says Maria, aka Blanca Maria Esperanza Romero Navarro. "*Abuela* will be able to get his family's net worth and history by supper." She leans over and plucks a fried plantain from the plate. "He's really a medical student? Does he have any friends?"

"I'll ask." I sip the coffee.

"His fedora was very sexy. Wish more men wore hats like that."

Abuela's gray head swings around. "He wore a hat?"

Maria and I nod in unison.

Abuela lowers the volume so even I can't hear Redhead shouting at Fake Eyelashes. "Marco with no last name wears a hat? And he sings? What kind of music?"

"All kinds," says Maria. "He's better than Luis Miguel."

I cover my mouth to keep from laughing—the singer is a favorite of older Latinas everywhere.

Abuela glares at us. "Stay away from this man."

"Why?" I ask after Maria and I exchange an *Abuela's-gone-loco* look.

"This man sings and wears a hat and all the young women want him, *si*? I bet he's very handsome. Sexy." *Abuela* taps the top of her head. "He wears a hat to hide his blowhole. He's not a human, he's an Encantado. Stay away. Don't go back to that place."

Maria looks at the maid standing in the doorway. "Marta, did *Abuela* take her pills?"

"The pills are for my heart, which you are breaking." Abuela sits tall in her chair. "I'm not senile, Maria." *Abuela*'s eyes bore into mine. "Your singing doctor is an Encantado. He sings, he wears a hat, he's sexy. Stay away from the Encantado or he'll drag you into his watery home."

I look at Maria. "What is *Abuela* talking about?"

Maria opens her mouth but *Abuela* shuts her down with a torrent of Spanish.

"Did you get any of that?" asks Maria after *Abuela* is done.

"Not really," I say.

"Abuela says Encantado live as dolphins in the rivers but they transform into humans once they're on land. They wear a hat to cover their blowhole." Maria glances at *Abuela*, who nods encouragingly. "Evidently they're known for their singing, which makes all the girls fall in love with them. Encantado...enchanted...get it?"

"Yeah," I say, my cunt moistening as I recall the size of his enchantment.

"Once they lure their lovers to the river, they take them to Encante, some kind of underwater utopia."

"A shape-shifting dolphin?"

"*Si.*" Maria rolls her eyes. "She *really* doesn't want you to go back to Culebra Negro."

Abuela stands and points to the dining room table laden with way too much food for three women. "Eat. You're too skinny."

I eat my way through the day, each aunt serving a full spread of Ecuadorian dishes when I arrive at their houses. *Empanadas, lomo saltado, humitas, pan de yucca,* and *flan.* I'll be the size of a cow when I return to LA.

"It's just a story to scare virgins away from a ladies' man," says very fluent Cousin Agata when we stop by her house for the third meal of the day. Cousin Maria had told her *Abuela* thinks the lead singer of Mono Suavo is an Encantado because he wears a hat.

Agata shakes her head. "Anyway, I haven't seen any boto dolphins in the river for years."

By the time the sun goes down, I am ready to dance off all the calories I scarfed down.

"I assume we're going back to Culebra Negra." Maria sashays into the room wearing a red miniskirt and a white breasts-on-a-platter top.

"Of course." I unplug the curling iron. Tonight I'm wearing a full face of make up, a neckline-plunging cream-colored dress that barely covers my ass, and strappy silver heels. I want Marco to take one look at me and get a boner. "How do I look for dolphin man?"

We burst out laughing.

Abuela is waiting with crossed arms at the bottom of the stairs. "Don't go back to that nightclub."

Maria assures her we won't, and we dash out the door.

Maria starts the car. "Be careful, Angela."

"Why? *Abuela* got you spooked?"

"No, I just don't want you getting hurt."

Hurt? Marco's cock was sexual healing, *à la* that Marvin Gaye song.

"I'm not looking for a relationship. Just fun."

"That's fine as long as *Abuela* thinks you're an innocent virgin."

"If you can fool her so can I."

We arrive at Culebra Negra, find a tiny table in the back, and listen to a cringe-worthy version of Kesha's "TiK ToK" by the warm-up act.

My stomach is aflutter while I wait for Mono Suavo. Luckily a Snakebite tames my nervous excitement.

Another Snakebite later, Mono Suavo comes on. I sit on my hands to keep from waving like a starstruck groupie and wonder how he'll ever see me sitting way back here.

Marco begins the set with "Atlanta" by Stone Temple Pilots, a haunting song that starts my head swaying. Mid-verse, Marco stands and saunters toward my table. He holds out his hand and I take it and stand up, the rest of the lyrics sung just for me. Damn, no wonder singers get laid so easily. My panties are wet with wanting. The song ends too quickly, and Marco drops my hand but has a promise in his eyes.

"Wow," says Maria when I sit back down. "He is definitely into you."

After the set, Marco comes over and gives me a hug. "Missed you," he whispers in my ear.

"Yeah? Do you remember my name?"

Marco looks insulted. "Angela. With the wettest, tightest pussy this side of heaven." He leans in. "Got a minute?"

"Several."

Marco flashes his movie-star grin. "Come on."

I follow him as we wind around the tables and squeeze past the line of the red-lipstick brigade waiting for the bathroom.

"In here." He opens a door marked *prohibida la entrada*. No admittance.

Marco thrusts his tongue inside me and slams the door shut. We're kissing in a pitch-black void, tongue and lips the only sensations. His hand snakes around my neck and pulls me deeper. My tongue can't keep up with the speed and force of his. It's full-mouth lip-lock and my pussy's purring I want him so bad.

"We don't have long." His face suddenly lights up, the instant illumination from his lighter. "Suck me."

My ex never spoke like that. Good thing, because I would have laughed. But I'm not laughing now. His hungry-for-sex face and the deep tenor of his plea are freakin' foreplay.

I kneel down, unzip his jeans, and release his stiff cock. Marco lowers the flame, the glow spotlighting his cock and my face. Sexiest thing ever.

I wrap my hand around the base.

"Talk dirty to me, Angela."

I brush my lips across the head. "I'm gonna lick and suck your cock until cum fills my mouth."

Marco sighs and runs his fingers through my hair. "That's right."

My ex was unimpressed by my blow jobs; he claimed they lacked finesse, so I'm hoping Marco isn't disappointed.

"That's it, my angel, lick down the shaft, yeah, that's good, right there. Oh you're good, love when you whirl your tongue around like that. Where did you learn to give head like this?" He's saying all this while massaging my head, which feels so damn good I could suck on him for eternity.

"Stroke my balls, angel. Yeah. Like that. Go further back. Back. Back. Ooh, there."

I'm so blissed out from the head rub, sex talk, and fellatio, *I'm* moaning. My clit's gotta be the size of Texas.

"You like sucking cock. I can tell. Bet you love the taste of cum. You're gonna swallow it all, aren't you, every salty delicious drop of my cum. Take it all in, Angela. Deep-throat me."

He pulls my head forward and I open my throat to receive his full length.

"Damn, girl! Holy fuck!" His legs tremble.

I pull away, do it again, and he growls with pleasure, his head thrown back in delirium.

I pull his cock out and start stroking and licking again.

He has fistfuls of my hair. "Don't stop, angel, I'm so fucking close."

Marco's blowhole isn't on top of his head, it's out his cock. He spurts and spurts, and my mouth fills with cum. I swallow it all.

"Finish me." I'm still on my knees.

"No time." Marco flicks off the lighter, plunging us both into darkness. "Stay until we're done. I'll make it worth the wait."

"What about my cousin?"

"I just want you." Marco opens the door and I squint despite the dim hall light. "Where did you learn to suck dick like that?"

"You." I lick my lips, savoring his brine.

Marco blows me a kiss and disappears behind the door where we fucked yesterday, leaving me to make my way back to the table alone.

"What's with the disappearing act?" Maria narrows her eyes. "Your hair is all messed up."

I smooth it down. "Sorry."

"Can't he ask you on a proper date? Let him pursue you."

I didn't want to be chased. I wanted to be fucked.

Somehow I manage to convince Maria to leave without me after Mono Suavo announces it's their last song for the night. *Marco promised to take me home,* I say. *Yes, I know the way. Yes, he's trustworthy.*

A half hour later, Marco is driving me to his house.

"This isn't a house," I say as Marco parks in front of a dock on the Tena River.

"I'm Ecuadorian. We live with our parents until we get married. I'm not taking you there." Marco gets out of the car, opens my car door. "I told you I would make the wait worth your while."

We walk hand in hand to the dock's edge. The river is wide and the black water glistens in the moonlight.

"Ever fuck in a river?" Marco strips down, tosses his fedora in the water, pulls out his ponytail, and dives in. He emerges, arcs a stream of water from his mouth. "Come on in, Angela. Your pussy must be at least as wet as this river."

"Aren't there piranhas?"

"Only thing that's gonna feed on your pussy is me."

Marco starts scat singing the classic instrumental strip tease song so I do my best impression of a sexy stripper peeling off her dress. After twirling it and my panties around, I dive in.

Marco disappears underwater, then emerges by slithering up my body. "*Buenas noches*, my angel. I have a gift for you."

I wrap my legs around his hips and sink onto his cock. "I love your gifts."

I'm in lust. I can't help it. Marco makes me feel beautiful and sexy and adventurous. I don't know if he's marriage material but he's the perfect vacation fling.

Marco kisses slowly, his tongue unhurried and thorough. It's soft and sensuous, and mimics the pace of his thrusts. My legs tighten around him as my pleasure rises, and I run my hand through his hair.

I touch a bump on the top of his head. "What's this?"

"Birth mark." Marco grips my ass and stuffs his cock *deep*.

I groan and throw my head back. "Your cock is magic." My cunt pulses to a tempo that propels me into a glorious crescendo.

"Slow it down, angel." Marco caresses my ass, fingers my anus.

That's all it takes. I arch back and let the beginning of the orgasm wash over me. That's when I hear all the splashing.

Marco thrusts deep again. "Dolphins, nothing to worry about."

They're heading straight toward us, a hundred at

least, their pink skin glowing in the light of the moon.

"Enchanting, isn't it," he breathes in my ear. "Fucking the one you love in the midst of a family of dolphins."

He's thrusting faster now, prolonging my orgasm, his cock seeming to expand inside me. Wave after wave rushes over me. Marco holds tight.

Something brushes my legs. I open my eyes. Dolphins are everywhere, churning the water around us. One bumps my legs.

"Don't be frightened, Angela."

"You're an Encantado." Panic surges through my limbs as I try to wiggle away. I can't! His cock is stuck inside.

"Yeah." Marco nuzzles my neck. "You'll be happy." He begins moving inside me again. "I promise."

A sublime rush of pleasure floods my senses, my panic swept away in the tide of orgasm. I give myself over to wild abandon.

As my orgasm ebbs away, I look toward the dock—how did we get so far away—and see *Abuela* and Maria flailing their arms.

"You want this." Marco kisses me as we submerge.

I do.

The origin of the Encantado myth stems from the oral storytelling of indigenous peoples living near the Amazon and its tributaries. There is speculation about why the large native boto dolphins, with their pale human-

looking skin, might have become part of local folklore. Whether the Encantado myth was a way to explain an illegitimate pregnancy in an isolated tribe, an attempt by the elders to keep their youth away from the dangers of a flooding river, or a reaction to the dolphins' genitalia resembling human genitalia remains a mystery. Whatever the reason, don't take a dip in the Amazon after being seduced by a hot male or female singer with a beautiful voice.

AFLAME

"You disobeyed me, Bryn." Odin sat on his throne, legs splayed, one gnarled hand stroking his long white beard.

Bryn. Not Brynhild. The shield maiden knew Odin's tactic. The fiercest of all gods was about to deliver a terrible punishment.

Brynhild lifted her eyes to the ceiling, her attention fixed on the circular pattern of a million golden shields overhead, a military testament to Odin's strength and power.

Odin leaned forward. "For what possible reason would one of my most courageous Valkyrie defy a direct order?" Odin's voice rose above the ever-present clamor of battle-slain warriors, resounding off the walls of Valhalla.

The dead heroes stopped their sporting, drinking, and eating to hear Brynhild's reply.

"You asked me to *decide* the battle." Brynhild locked eyes with Odin. "I *decided* in favor of Agnar. King Hjalmgunnar is so old his ears are clogged with bushy white hair."

"You knew my preference!" thundered Odin.

Brynhild blinked. It was true. Except she knew Agnar would make the better king.

Odin beckoned Brynhild forward. "Bryn, your insolence gives me no choice. I must condemn you to life as a mortal."

Brynhild staggered back, her hand tearing at the chain mail she wore over her shirt and pants. "Anything but that."

Odin looked out from under his wild white brows. "You will stay in Hindarfell and wait until a mortal warrior crosses the flames surrounding the fortress to marry you. Come forward, Bryn. Now."

Brynhild took a deep breath and stepped toward his throne. Odin grabbed her hand, sticking it with a thorn he had concealed in his palm. She snatched her hand away, looked down at the bright-red bead of blood. She had only seconds to speak her mind before the poison doomed her to a deathlike sleep. "Only the most fearless man will *ever* wed me!"

"So be it," said Odin as Brynhild collapsed on the floor.

High atop a mountain a great fire raged year after year. Nothing dowsed Odin's flames, neither rain nor snow extinguishing a single flame. Behind Hindarfell's blazing walls, Brynhild slept. Though senseless to the time and the chain-mail-fused wool stuck to her skin, her body remained lithe and strong; her face, young and beautiful; her feisty spirit needing only to be awakened.

Passing through a forest of spruce and pine one autumn morning, the warrior Sigurd stopped his horse to consider the mountaintop inferno. The flames rose high into the air, as though licking at the heavens. Suspecting it was no ordinary fire, he galloped toward the blaze.

"I think this fire merits a closer look, don't you, Grani?"

Sigurd's horse snorted his approval.

The path was steep and narrow, and often blocked with fallen trees, yet Sigurd pressed onward. At the top, he patted Grani's neck.

"This is the work of the gods, maybe of Odin himself." Sigurd made a lap around the blaze and discovered the castle was made of shields that blazed with fire.

"Something of great value is inside," he said to Grani.

Grani agreed, her loud blowing a sign of the horse's curiosity.

Sigurd circled again, this time looking for any breach or opening. He almost missed seeing a way in, as the crackling, hissing flames nearly concealed the gap between the shields.

"You'll have to leap through the fire, Grani." Sigurd clicked his tongue to start forward but the horse stomped his foot.

"*Really?* The fire is *irritating?* Come on, Grani. I'm sure there's a bucket of oats inside for your troubles." Sigurd turned Grani around and found a place where they could get a running start. "Let's go." He clicked his tongue again.

The fearless horse took off fast and leaped through the flames and into the narrow gap in the wall. The castle's interior was untouched by the fire, no evidence of smoke or soot. Sigurd dismounted from his horse and walked through the chambers, impressed by the vaulted oak ceilings and the patterned stone floors. The furnishings were sparse, but the few carved chairs and tables were of superior quality. Round shields and kite shields of leather and metal hung on the walls, as did knives, long bows, flat bows, axes, spears, and helmets. A wide iron chandelier hung from the ceiling. Cups, cutlery, and plates were displayed in cupboards.

"Hello?" Sigurd's voice echoed in the cavernous space. "Anybody home?"

The castle was silent—not even the sound of the fire raging outside penetrated the walls.

Sigurd found a bag of oats in the scullery for Grani, and then mounted the wide staircase to the second floor. The first chamber was empty. So was the second.

"What's this?" Sigurd strode inside the third chamber.

A warrior dressed head to toe in full armor lay on a white stone slab in the middle of the room. A studded metal helmet fringed with chain mail concealed the face.

Sigurd pulled off the helmet. "What the—"

The warrior was a beautiful copper-haired maiden with rosy cheeks and slightly parted lips. Sigurd put his finger beneath her nose and felt the faintest breath of life. He fanned her copper mane over the slab, entranced by its silkiness and color. The maiden didn't move. He studied the chain mail encasing her. It was so formfitting it seemed grafted to her body.

"Which god did this to you? And what did you do to incur his wrath?"

Sigurd drew his sword from the sheath and sliced the first link at the neck.

Brynhild's eyes flew open. "Who are you?" The warrior leaning over her was tall and broad shouldered. His eyes, blue as a deep lake in the summer, peered out from beneath a heavy brow.

Sigurd removed his leather helmet and black hair tumbled to his shoulders. "Sigurd, son of Sigmund." His beard was trimmed and his mustache long and thick.

Brynhild's gaze traveled down the length of his brawny arm to the long sword in his hand. "You breached the wall of flames?"

"I certainly didn't drop from the sky." Sigurd scratched his beard. "Can you move?"

Brynhild rolled her head back and forth. "Only my head."

"I can cut this chain mail away but it will require your patience." Sigurd rotated his sword and leaned over to slice off another link at her neck. "Who are you?"

"Brynhild, I am a Valkyrie to Odin." She frowned. "*Was* a Valkyrie."

"Pissed off Odin, did you?"

"The god has an ego like you wouldn't believe."

"Well, he *is* Odin." Sigurd worked downward toward her sternum. "He gave me Grani. Best horse I ever had."

"He is often benevolent," said Brynhild. "If he likes you."

Sigurd looked up. "Guess he likes me."

Brynhild smiled, the warrior's manner putting her at ease. She also appreciated his steady hands and the care he took slicing away the chain mail that had merged with the lightweight wool beneath, which was plastered tightly to her skin.

"Mind if I take off my chain mail?" Sigurd glanced up. "This is going to take a while."

"I'm tough."

"You may be tough in spirit but your skin is as fragile as a mortal's now." Sigurd unclasped his wide leather belt, shrugged off his leather vest, and removed his chain mail. Wearing only boots, trousers, and tunic, he draped his armor over the chair. For such a large man he was graceful, his agile body built for battles and lovemaking. Despite the loose tunic, Brynhild knew he possessed a muscular physique.

Sigurd pushed up his sleeves, his forearms thick with black fuzz. "All right then." He sat on the platform again and began slicing where he had left off, right down the center of Brynhild's armor.

"Right arm first," said Brynhild. The thought of the warrior seeing her naked breasts while her limbs and torso were covered made her *very* uncomfortable.

"Good idea." Sigurd shifted about on the platform and severed the link at her wrist, which he noticed was as delicate and white as snow.

Brynhild watched as he sliced, relief flooding her body as he gently pried the chain mail away from her slender, pale forearm. When he removed the fused links at her elbow, Brynhild bent her arm and grabbed his hand.

"How can I show my gratitude for your breaking the chains and releasing me?"

"You're still stuck." Sigurd tapped the flat side of the

blade on her upper arm. "Let's discuss your gratitude when I'm finished."

"Fair enough." Brynhild released her hold, then wiggled and stretched her fingers. "They still work."

"Not only that, they're strong and soft." Sigurd peeled away more severed chain mail.

Sigurd's own hands were rough and calloused, a warrior's hands that made Brynhild's heart beat fast whenever he touched her.

"What's it like?" Sigurd sliced his way toward Brynhild's shoulder.

"Well, it's a bit boring."

Sigurd looked up. "Choosing who lives and dies in battle is *boring*?"

"Oh, *that*. You mean my position as a Valkyrie."

They held each other's gaze, blue and gray eyes recognizing a kindred spirit who had witnessed the horror and satisfaction of battle.

"Why do *you* stab one in the heart and another the leg?" asked Brynhild.

"It's not the same. My actions are determined by weaponry and my enemy's proximity. I act on instinct. A shield maiden *chooses*."

Brynhild sighed. "My choice is instinctual. Age, skill, future, family; none of these matter when I attend a battle." She laid her hand over her chain-mail-covered heart. "I feel the choice here."

"Do you grieve for those that are doomed to die?"

"More often I feel grief for the men who must live to battle a lifetime of sickness, disease, hunger, cowardice, injuries, hatred, deceit, and infidelity."

Sigurd peeled away the cut chain mail encasing her

shoulder. "That's life. A man must learn to cope with life's troubles or suffer from the worst malady of all, fear."

"You consider yourself a fearless man?"

"I like to think so." Sigurd's gaze roamed over Brynhild's body. "Leg or left arm?"

"Leg."

Sigurd removed Brynhild's leather shoe and wiggled off her wool sock. Next he flicked at the taut links snugged tight around her ankle. A bright droplet of blood appeared.

"I nicked you," said Sigurd.

"I don't feel anything. Let me see."

Sigurd touched it and transferred the scarlet bead to Brynhild's outstretched hand.

"The fluid of mortality," she said before wiping it on the chain mail.

"You would think the gods might have given us tougher skin to protect such a precious liquid." Sigurd's tunic whisked back and forth across Brynhild's bare feet as he cut the chain mail on her leg.

Brynhild giggled.

"Ticklish?" He peeled away the links from her shapely calf.

"So *that's* what it feels like."

"Mortal skin is fragile but it does have its benefits." Sigurd sliced higher and pried back the chain mail to expose several inches of her luscious thigh. He shifted about, concerned she would see the bulge made by his stiff cock.

"What's wrong?" asked Brynhild.

"Nothing? Why?"

"Your breathing is shallow."

"I'm fine. Never better." Sigurd sliced and several links crumbled away. He peeled it back very slowly, his fingertips grazing her creamy skin.

His feathery touch felt better than the caress of a breeze. Brynhild sucked in her breath.

"Are *you* okay?" he asked.

Brynhild touched his cheek. "Mortal skin is sensitive."

"Did I hurt you?"

"No, it feels good." Her face grew hot and she looked away.

Sigurd cleared his throat and pulled away more chain mail. He wiped sweat from his forehead—controlling himself was proving more difficult than not slaying an enemy. He wanted to kiss her thigh, lick her leg from ankle to—

Sigurd cleared his throat again.

"Other arm." Brynhild pushed his sword left. She knew warriors like Sigurd were just as bold and aggressive with their lovers as they were on the battlefield. And why not? What woman would turn down a strapping hulk with the fortitude to fuck all night long?

Sigurd moved to the other side of the platform and drew his long blade across the links binding her left wrist. Brynhild thought the attention he paid to gently removing her chain mail had changed somehow, the tedious process now proving to be both pleasurable and frustrating. Each inch Sigurd removed warmed her body despite the cool autumn weather.

Sigurd straightened his back, his eyes wide with

amazement. "*Karlvagn*." He touched the pattern of freckles shaped like a ladle on her forearm. "How many other constellations are on your skin?"

"All the ones that guide man." She held up her right arm.

"There is the goddess Freya's." Sigurd traced the freckles forming a smaller ladle, then gazed at Brynhild's naked leg. "Here is *fiskikarlar*." He tapped the three large freckles in a row above her knee. "Our gods are clever to devise such a map." Sigurd set a quick kiss on *fiskikarlar*.

Brynhild gasped, his lips on her skin like a gale blowing through her body, a storm gathering inside her.

He jerked up. "I don't know what came over me."

Brynhild tried to control her breathing. "I suggest you pay equal homage to the other constellations."

One side of Sigurd's mouth lifted in a rakish grin. "Of course, Bryn."

She suppressed a smile. She was Bryn now, was she?

Sigurd lowered his head to her left arm, his beard tickling her skin as he kissed *Karlvagn*. This kiss was slower, more deliberate. His lips made full contact. No longer Odin's shield maiden, she was now a mortal woman with a woman's yearnings for a man. Her skin tingled, her body as charged as the air awaiting the first lightning strike. Sigurd returned to the other side of the platform, his head hovering over the freckled *fiskikarlar*. One eyebrow was cocked, not from waiting on her permission but with admiration.

Bryn sucked in air with anticipation. Sigurd set his warm, calloused hands on either side of her thigh and lowered his head.

The first lightning strike jolted her body the moment Sigurd's lips brushed over the freckles on her thigh. The jolt drove deep inside and scorched the valley between her legs. Her bottom clenched when his tongue flicked across the constellation.

Sigurd lifted his head, his pupils dilated with lust. Bryn grabbed his head and pulled him forward and over her body. Sigurd kissed her and she parted her lips so he could explore her mouth. He tasted like a warrior: of mead and pine and strength and valor.

"You taste like spring," Sigurd said before thrusting his tongue back inside.

The kiss deepened, grew insistent, two fearless warriors sporting, testing limitations. Bryn knew no limits; her lips and tongue met each parry. When his tongue wrestled hers, she wrestled more. When his teeth nipped at her lip, she nipped back.

Breathing heavily, Sigurd's round biceps flexed as he lifted himself up. "Is there something more I should know about Odin's punishment?"

"Why? Are you afraid?"

"Never." Sigurd narrowed his eyes. "Are you?"

Odin had condemned Brynhild to a mortal life with a mortal husband. So far, Sigurd seemed to be the perfect man. Fear? She was eager to see how this all played out. "The only thing I fear is that you won't kiss me like that again."

Sigurd dropped his mouth to hers, this time his hands wandering up her bare arms and over her chain-mail-clad torso.

Sigurd rose up again. "I've work to do." He picked up his discarded sword, pulled off her left boot and sock, and cut through the chain mail on her left ankle. Each inch of skin he freed he kissed.

Bryn's sighs distracted him, as did her outstretched hand reaching for his cock. Sigurd was glad she couldn't reach it. He was so horny he was certain to explode if she did. He freed her shin, then licked her from ankle to knee. He moved to her right leg and did the same, this time his tongue moving over her knee and up her inner thigh.

The lust storm raging inside of Bryn made her squirm as lightning bolts rumbled through her. No matter what part of her body he touched, each kiss warmed the valley between her thighs. Even her chain mail felt hot to the touch. She wanted him to hurry. To slow down. To never stop.

Sigurd moved over the apex between her legs and exhaled. His hot breath permeated the chain mail and wool and copper thatch of curls that protected her virginity. To Bryn, his breath felt like a *föhn*, the warm wind blowing down a mountainside. But instead of drying her valley it made her wet. Sigurd exhaled again and Bryn moaned, her head rolling from side to side.

Sigurd's *föhn* wafted a third time, her valley now steamy with desire.

"Remove the rest of my chain mail." Bryn's voice was part command, part plead.

"With pleasure." Sigurd straddled her, his knees at her hips, and sliced the chain mail between her breasts.

Bryn reached out and pressed her hand against the tunic to feel his solid cock.

"Easy now, Bryn. I need steady hands."

Bryn didn't care. The loose tunic and pants allowed

for an almost unhampered opportunity to determine his impressive length and girth.

Sigurd stopped slicing and kissed her, his tongue more insistent with her every stroke.

"This is a challenge I don't think I can win," Sigurd said coming up for air.

"You surrender?" Bryn's left hand slid between his legs, annoyed by the layers of wool preventing a real grasp of his tight sac.

"Never." Sigurd resumed cutting, his attention fixed on freeing her torso despite Bryn fondling his sac and the smooth skin behind.

Sigurd was a warrior, used to fighting for an entire day without rest or food, but this battle made him weak. Bryn pushed away the tunic and moved her palm up and down against his rigid shaft. She was pleased by his heated desire, evident even through the wool pants.

"By the gods, Bryn, how am I supposed to free you when you're doing that?"

"Afraid you'll spill your seed in my hand and not my valley?"

"I fear nothing, least of all a shield maiden so eager for cock she can't let go."

Bryn pumped faster. As in battle, Sigurd centered himself, thrusting aside all distractions, and focused. A man's lust is not easily conquered.

But Sigurd was no ordinary man.

So while Bryn's hand worked his cock, Sigurd concentrated on his task. The woven chain mail crumbled away to reveal Bryn's pert breast, which was shaped like a wide chalice, a small nipple sticking out like the nob in the middle of his shield.

Sigurd lowered his head and, with the tip of his tongue, traced the circumference of her areola. Bryn moaned and dropped his cock. Sigurd's lips brushed across her rigid nipple and then latched on and pulled it into his mouth.

Bryn's arms wrapped around him and smashed his face against her breast. The storm descended into her valley, each tug on her nipple spinning the whirlwind ever faster.

"I am defeated," she whimpered while Sigurd sucked her breast and caressed her thigh.

Sigurd lifted his head. "Not until you see the heavens, Bryn." He sliced the links on the other side and stopped often to taste her tongue, suck a nipple, or puff his warm breath into her valley.

Bryn swept away the pieces of chain mail at her sides and clutched Sigurd's buttocks, which flexed as she massaged them.

Sigurd released the left breast, as perfect as the right. "Now I know why you're called shield maidens. Two cover your body." He latched on to the left, his hand rolling the right nipple between thumb and forefinger.

Her shield maiden duty felt like lifetimes ago. "I belong to Freya now."

Freya was the goddess of love and fertility, and the sorceress concerned with fleshly pursuits.

Sigurd's body stretched out over Bryn's, his mouth and hands wandering from her lips to her breasts. Bryn's hand moved over his back, firm muscly ropes stretching from hips to shoulders. Not one ounce of extra flesh could she feel, his every muscle battle honed for endurance and strength.

Sigurd tore his lips away from the heat of her mouth, picked up his sword, and gazed at the beauty before him. Bryn's chest rose and fell, ragged breaths matching his own. He sliced away the links at her navel, loosened the chain mail and peeled it from her slim body. Now all that stood between their pleasure was a girdle of fused chain mail. The greatest gift was yet to be unwrapped.

He stopped slicing at the pubis to admire the freckles making up another constellation. "The Mouth of the Wolf. Very fitting." He peeled away more chain mail, the first glimpse of her copper coils making his cock jerk. He brushed across her damp thatch and felt her shudder.

"Get. It. Off," Bryn urged.

A six-inch swath remained. Two layers welded over the entrance of her valley. Sigurd stood and stretched his arms, his gaze traveling up and down Bryn's near-naked body.

"What are you doing?" She lifted herself up on her elbows.

"Savoring the moment." With a fluid movement, Sigurd drew his tunic over his head. Next he removed his boots and trousers. His cock stood ready and poised to conquer Bryn's cunt. Sigurd hefted his sword and touched the tip. "Needs sharpening." He removed the small whetstone wrapped to his belt, spit on it, then drew the blade tip across.

"Afraid the dull blade will knick me?"

"I don't know fear, Bryn." He didn't dare look up, his composure almost gone. "But I know my sword."

"Seems like a blunt weapon." Bryn pointed to his cock.

"Blunt and effective."

Suddenly Bryn's eyes widened. "Are you married?"

"Never found the right woman...until now."

She smiled and her heart warmed with the first twinges of love. "Do you want to know the rest of Odin's punishment?"

"Already guessed." Sigurd felt the blade's edge. "Ready?"

"I've been ready since my right arm was free."

Sigurd lowered his sword between her legs and sliced, teasing away the iron chastity belt bit by bit, the scent of her valley escaping through the chinks. He paused midway to suck Bryn's nipples, her squirming and pleading swelling his cock even more.

Sigurd snipped away the last of it and dropped the sharp, jagged fragments onto the floor. Then he lowered his face to her copper valley and tasted her dew.

Bryn sucked air through her teeth and her legs snugged around his back.

Sigurd burrowed deep, found her nub, and tongued it well, polishing it like any beloved weapon. His fingers climbed up her ankles, over her legs, and across her stomach to grab hold of each pink bud.

"This is an ambush," Bryn said, her body awhirl, her valley drenched with lust. The pleasure was sharper than any blade, more overpowering than any warship.

Sigurd lifted his head, his beard glistening with her lust. "Then I'll change maneuvers." With speed and agility he shifted his body and hers, and Bryn found herself sitting astride him, his solid cock awaiting her command.

Bryn rubbed her cunt over his length as Sigurd drew

her close and suckled her breasts. Back and forth she glided over him, her thoughts only on the whirlwind centered on her clit.

Sigurd groaned. Her wet cunt slithering across his cock was more excruciating than a knife wound. Yet again, he called on his warrior training, willed himself to concentrate and check his eruption before he taught this virgin how to fuck.

Bryn's breath was coming in quick loud pants that fluctuated in tempo and pitch. She was lost to sensation and Sigurd knew better than to rush her journey home, knew the best way to make her his own for a lifetime. He suckled harder and Bryn whimpered, slid faster, then let loose a war cry. Sigurd shifted ever so slightly, pushed past her virginity, and sunk into her womanhood.

Bryn cried out, a deep guttural exhalation. She was air and light and wind and heavens and her body was without boundaries. She rode Sigurd's cock. Each plunge kept her aloft and gave her more bliss than she'd ever felt as a Valkyrie.

Sigurd's victory was eclipsed by his own uncontrollable lust. He gripped her ass and guided her rhythm.

"Better . . . than . . . riding . . . a . . . horse." Her breasts jiggled with each plunge. She spread her thighs, each fall onto his cock pushing him deeper, each thrust bringing her closer to the Northern Lights above.

Sigurd was a berserker now, his mind in a lust trance, his cock ramming into the maiden with a single aggressive purpose. His fierceness catapulted Bryn skyward and her body shook with ecstasy again, which in turn hurled Sigurd into joining her. Together they rode homeward.

Bryn fell atop him and her face nuzzled into his neck. "I am conquered."

Sigurd swept her copper hair away from her face and kissed her salty forehead. "And here I thought *you* had conquered *me*."

"Then we are both victorious." Bryn crossed her leg over his. "I will teach you many runes for sailing, warring, philosophizing, speech-making, and healing if you like."

Sigurd hugged her tight; the wisdom of a Valkyrie was great. "Will you marry me?"

"I couldn't possibly marry anyone else."

The story of Brynhild and Sigurd doesn't end here. In fact, their story has enough deception, betrayal, jealousy, and magic to be worthy of any best-selling novel. The thirteenth-century Völsunga Saga *dishes it all. There are also plenty of Norse poems about their romance, and composer Richard Wagner took their story to a new level in his opera cycle,* Der Ring des Nibelungen.

GOOD
MEDICINE

"He's all yours now." Momma lifts her wrinkled hand from the hospital bed and points a bony finger at the latest doctor.

The doctor looks up from the clipboard and flashes me a heart-stopping grin. Damn! My own doctor is a Filipino woman half my size. Momma scores a gorgeous black man with a killer smile and swoon-worthy liquid brown eyes. He's got a clean-cut low fade and a short beard. From the way his scrubs hang from his broad shoulders and his biceps peek out from under his sleeves, I know he lifts weights. Lord, have mercy. I need a doctor like this.

"Hi. Liyana. I'm the daughter." I extend my hand. Every time I visit Momma there's a different doctor assigned to her case. Momma has seen all kinds of specialists. None find a reason for her wide assortment of complaints. Her pain, sometimes a sharp stab, sometimes a lingering burning sensation, travels from stomach to head to heart to big toe. And back again. Maybe this doctor will understand. There's nothing *physically* wrong with Momma.

"Dr. Nkosi." The doctor clasps my hand. His grip is smooth, strong, and warm. Comforting and confident. "Your mother was just telling me all about you."

"She ought to be telling you about her symptoms." I look past him and at Momma, who looks all too pleased with herself.

"I told Dr. Nkosi you work too hard," Momma says with pride. "Always helping our people. Never taking a day off."

That's not true. I only work half a day Saturday and take off all Sunday. My workweek is long though. I'm an estate attorney. Wills, trusts, probate, that kind of stuff. I also volunteer my legal services for a nonprofit organization that helps African immigrants and refugees. I love showing the high-school-age children how to apply for all the educational programs they are eligible for. My husband, Michael, is a workaholic too, a successful real estate developer currently gentrifying downtown. We don't have children yet (there's still time) but our spacious home in the foothills is ready for a pool and a swing set.

"That husband of hers. Ooooooh." Momma shakes her head. "Bad news."

"Momma, please."

Momma dislikes Michael. Always has. Says he's not trustworthy. Says he has a roving eye. Momma's right about the roving eye. But Michael only *looks*. He doesn't touch. Hell, I take a long look when a sexy man walks by. Or stands in front of me in scrubs.

Dr. Nkosi looks down at the clipboard. "Your mom has TB nodules on her lungs from when she had it as a child. The state requires several tests to determine it's not a reoccurrence before we can release her. Standard procedure. We should have the results in about a week. During that time, I'll run some other tests." He sets down the clipboard, moves around the side of the bed, and takes his stethoscope from around his neck. "Sometimes *not* finding anything terminates the curse."

"Momma!" I rub my temples. "You told him?"

"Of course I told him." Momma breathes deeply while Dr. Nkosi checks her heart.

"I'm sorry." I'm so embarrassed. "Momma really believes a woman cursed her."

"A witch with black *muti*," says Momma.

Muti is medicine. Black *muti* is poison. White *muti* heals.

Dr. Nkosi puts the stethoscope around his neck again. "You don't believe in *muti*?"

"I believe that *she* believes." I cannot *believe* I'm having this conversation. "Can you refer me to someone with white *muti*?" I roll my eyes.

Dr. Nkosi gives me a look somewhere between pity and compassion. "*Muti* is powerful. Do not scorn the old ways."

Dr. Nkosi has more years of education than I do, so I figure his statement as a physiological understanding of the link between body and mind, not as a cultural ideology.

"When did you come to the US?" I ask.

"Same time as you." He holds Momma's small wrinkled hand in his big one. "Try to get some sleep, Thadie."

His intimate gesture and use of Momma's first name strikes me as odd. Maybe he has a way with grouchy old women.

"It's good to meet you, Liyana." Dr. Nkosi comes around to shake my hand again. "I'm sure we'll see each other again soon."

"Do you like him?" Momma says after he leaves.

"I like him if you do." I raise the bed, fluff her pillow, and help her get comfortable. "Do you want to watch TV?"

"No, my mind is too busy for that nonsense."

I kiss her too-cool cheek. "I'll bring your housecoat."

"I don't want that thing. Bring my blanket."

I know which one. It's a brightly colored Zulu print purchased from a vendor at a craft fair. My phone beeps. "I have to go. I'll stay all day tomorrow, I promise." I told the center's director Momma came first this week.

"You going back to the office?"

"Yeah." I kiss her cheek again. It's a small lie. This whole thing with Momma makes me realize I need to start looking into some long-term care options. Her mind is going. It was bad enough when she "confessed" to being a witch last year, but now this whole business with another witch cursing her with black *muti* has me wondering if it's the onset of dementia.

It's raining when I leave the hospital. Great. The freeways will be damn slow. Southern Californians don't know how to drive in the rain.

After a too-long commute, I turn into the driveway just as a lightning bolt brightens the sky. Rain sweeps across the front yard.

I'm about to pull under the portico but some damn bird is in the way. A bird the size of a turkey. Its feathers are tannish pink and it has a long black beak like a woodpecker but a whole lot bigger. It's a predatory-looking bird—even its feathers fanning out from the back of its head are badass. A fugitive from the zoo no doubt. Last year it was a peacock.

My foot hits the brake and I wait while the bird cocks its head, spreads wide iridescent wings, and soars low over the yard.

I pull under the portico, get out of the car, and unlock the front door. The rain's coming down so hard and fast I can hear it inside the house. It's a comforting sound that makes me want to make a cup of tea. Michael's carbon fiber Zero Halliburton briefcase is in the foyer so I know he's home already. He's got the TV on upstairs. Porn by the sound of it. Michael loves his porn.

I set my purse on the table, kick off my heels, and tread upstairs. About halfway up, I stop. Michael has the volume turned up loud. All I hear is "Fuck me, *fuck* me, fuck me with your huge cock. Oh yeah, deeper bae, deeper. So fucking good."

"God your tits are amazing." It's Michael's voice.

I freeze. Skin, blood, heart. I'm frozen with rage.

"Ohhh, Mikey, your cock is gonna make me squirt." It's a *real* voice.

Mikey? My muscles thaw enough for me to creep forward.

"You like big cocks, don't you? Like them deep inside your tight cunt."

This is Michael? The man never says two words when we have sex.

The idiots didn't even bother to shut the bedroom door, so I peek around.

Some blonde bitch with cheap extensions is riding

my husband like she's on a mechanical bull. One hand is waving in the air, the other pushing down on the top of his clean-shaved head. Michael's got his paws on each one of her watermelon-sized implants as they bounce up and down. She's a rich girl, has her Chanel bag on my dresser and five-inch red-soled Louboutins near the bed.

"I'm gonna fuck your tits next," Michael says.

"Fuck my tits. Fuck my ass. Fuck my mouth. Just fucking *fuck* me!"

And he does. The man never fucked *me* like that. A few halfhearted thrusts are all I ever get. He's fucking this girl like he's auditioning for a porn movie.

I pull my phone from my pocket and tap VIDEO. I need proof, evidence, a bargaining chip.

Michael rolls the girl over and spreads her legs wide.

"Fuck yeah! Fuck yeah! Harder! Harder! Fuck me hard!"

This video will come in handy if she's married.

"Is this hard enough for you? My cock is a sledge-hammer, bae."

It's like a bad porn movie. It *is* a bad porn movie. Weird thing though, I'm turned on. Mad as hell and yet my panties are wet.

Rich Bitch orgasms. Loud. Putting-on-a-show loud. Michael too. We've been married for ten years and he only ever whimpers. Now he's moaning and groaning and giving Rich Bitch all the cred.

Michael pulls out his cheatin' cock and shoves it between her collagen lips. Rich Bitch slurps his cum, and then Michael gets on all fours and shoves his ass in her face. Damn, Michael. I turn off the video.

I slide the phone in my skirt pocket and move around

the door. Michael sees me right away. Rich Bitch doesn't, she's too busy stroking his semi-hard cock and licking a dark, dark place.

"Fuck." Michael swats the girl's hand away and sits down.

Rich Bitch looks confused. She tucks a strand of hair behind her ear. "Are we having a threesome?"

Michael opens his mouth.

"No." I cut him off. "I'm his wife. Get the fuck out of my house."

Rich Bitch rolls her eyes, wipes her mouth on my sheets, slides off the bed, and wiggles into her lime-green Versace dress like she has all the time in the world.

"Liyana..." Michael stands, comes toward me, arms wide. "Baby..."

I hold my hand up. "No."

Rich Bitch slings her Chanel bag over her shoulder, scoops up her Louboutins, and saunters toward me. "He's even better than my friends said." She smirks and walks past.

I want to tear her extensions out. Rip off her fake eyelashes. Stick her stilettos through my husband's cheating heart.

I don't.

My fists clench so hard my nails dig into my palms. Last thing I need is for her to press assault-and-battery charges.

"Paris!" Michael grabs his clothes and runs after her.

"Where are you going?" I ask.

"I need to drive Paris home." Michael traipses down the stairs.

"Yeah. Do that. Don't bother coming back." I keep

my voice in check. Don't want to give Paris the rich bitch the satisfaction of seeing me go all Crazy Wife.

Michael throws on his T-shirt and hoists up his pants while Rich Bitch checks her phone. If she takes a photo to put on Instagram I'm going to lose it. #GotCaught

"Nice meeting you," she calls as Michael pushes her out the door.

I snap. The next thing I know I'm looking at a broken lamp, torn-off sheets, and the mattress against the wall.

I stagger down the stairs, consider smashing Michael's fish tank in the family room, and head for the kitchen.

One vodka, three ice cubes, and a lemon wedge later I open the French doors and plop my ass on the chair under the covered patio. It's still raining, not as heavy, just a steady shower that cools the air. I need cooling off because there are things to think about. Should I get tested for STDs? How many women has Michael fucked? Can I afford this house on my own? Will he ask for alimony? Who's the best divorce attorney in town? How could I have been so stupid?

I saw the signs. Late-night meetings. Refusing to tell me the passcode for his phone. Texting clients during evenings and weekends. Lots of business trips. I should have confronted him, but I didn't want to be *that* kind of wife.

I lift the glass to my lips. Empty already. I go inside and make another, then grab the vodka bottle as I walk back outside.

The odd-looking bird is standing on the edge of the patio.

"Shoo." I wave the vodka bottle at him.

The bird hops closer. It must have escaped from the zoo—it's way too friendly.

"Don't have any food for you. Unless you want to peck out my husband's eyes when he comes home."

The bird stretches its neck and waddles forward. It has webbed feet.

"Maybe I *do* have food for you."

I walk inside and use a large clear pitcher to capture one of Michael's three-thousand-dollar clarion angelfish. It's gorgeous but aggressive and territorial. Like Michael, named for an angel but nonetheless a predator.

"Here you go." I empty the pitcher and the fish falls to the ground.

The angelfish flops once before the bird scoops it into its long black beak and swallows it whole. The bird looks at me and starts calling. It's a staccato sound that ends with a long squawk.

"You want another? I've got one more."

The bird eats that one too. I feel better and the bird looks happy.

"That's it. Fish tank empty." I set the pitcher on the table.

The bird walks to the end of the patio, spreads its great wings, and lifts off into the air. It circles twice around the yard before disappearing over the top of our neighbor's eucalyptus trees.

The doorbell gives me a start. Drink in hand, I walk inside and look at the video doorbell mounted inside the kitchen. Dr. Nkosi waves at the camera.

This can't be good.

I press the speaker. "Is Momma okay?"

"She's fine. I'd like to talk to you about her."

"It's not a good time."

"That's why she sent me." Dr. Nkosi rubs the back of his neck.

"It's *really* not a good time." What the hell did Momma say to him?

Dr. Nkosi leans close to the camera. "How many doctors do you know who make house calls?"

Good point.

"Be there in a sec." I check the mirror and wipe away a mascara smudge. Still looks like I've been crying, though.

"Thank you," he says when I open the front door.

He's wearing gray slacks and a white linen shirt, the top button undone and sleeves rolled to his elbows. He looks younger without the doctor duds. Even sexier since the clothes accentuate his fine body.

"You want anything to drink?" I say, passing the kitchen. "Water, tea?" I jiggle my glass to clink the ice cubes. "Vodka?"

"No thanks."

I take him outside and we sit down at the table. It's raining hard again, which matches the torrent I need to weep.

I brush away a tear. "Sorry. Bad day. Found my husband with another woman when I got home."

"Thadie never liked him."

I squint at the doctor over the rim of my glass. "Do you know Momma personally?"

"We've been friends a long time." Dr. Nkosi folds his hands in his lap.

"She never mentioned you."

"Why would she?"

"Um...just how do you know Momma?" I get the feeling he knows a lot more about me than he's letting on.

"Thadie and my momma are in the same club." He tilts his head. "The Zulu women's group that meets once a week."

"Oh, *that* group."

Momma has been going to meetings once a week for years. Her Zulu Sisters, she calls them. Every few months she asks me to go with her. Says daughters and granddaughters are welcome. I've never been.

Dr. Nkosi looks out over the yard. "Thadie saw it coming."

"It?"

"Finding out about Michael's betrayal in the worst way possible. She had a vision."

Momma and her visions! Most were just logical predictions, although a few were disturbingly accurate surprises, like the Jesus-praising client who stabbed her husband to death.

I finish my second glass. "So Momma convinced you to come here to do *what* exactly?"

"Get revenge." He says this without a trace of humor.

Not only do I think Momma is going senile, I'm beginning to have my doubts about Dr. Nkosi.

"What kind would you like?" He rubs his hands together and then bursts out laughing.

I laugh too. The man had me going for a moment. "Right now? Death. A painful death." I look into my empty glass. "Tomorrow I'll just want the house."

"No chance of reconciliation?" His eyebrows lift.

"No. I've been deluding myself long enough."

Dr. Nkosi is quiet, his eyes doing all the speaking. *Talk to me,* they say. *Unburden yourself.*

"Our sex life's been tepid for years." I push the glass away. "Michael always complained. Said I was too uptight. Not creative." I pull the phone from my skirt pocket, hit PLAY, and slide it toward him.

Dr. Nkosi would make a perfect poker player. His face betrays nothing. "Why are you showing me this?"

"Is that what it's supposed to be like?"

"Sure, why not?" Dr. Nkosi stands, pushes in the chair.

I get up. "Tell Momma thanks but I need to work this out on my own. Tell her she was right about Michael." I walk Dr. Nkosi to the foyer but instead of opening the front door I turn to face him. "Since we watched porn together I think it's only fair I know your name."

"Shaka."

It's a Zulu name.

Shaka stands close. "I *am* here for you." He cups my cheek. "You're a beautiful, smart woman, too good for Michael. You need a faithful man who respects and adores you." He bends over and sets a soft kiss on my lips.

I don't pull back. Enjoy the moment. Shaka pulls away, those sexy eyes asking a question I already know the answer to.

I part my lips and move forward. This kiss starts soft, cautious, and I wrap my arms around his neck. Our tongues meet, tasting and exploring with rising fervor. He tastes delicious, and the scent of his skin makes me weak.

Our mouths smash together. Who needs air? I haven't been kissed like this since college. My panties are wet. Maybe watching the video got us both riled up. Maybe it's the vodka. I don't care. This man wants me!

Shaka's fingers slip beneath my blouse and grab a handful of breast. He groans and pins me against the wall. He's ripped. I discover just how sculpted his muscles are as my hands work their way down his hard body. He rubs his cock against my stomach.

"Do you want me?" He breathes into my ear.

"God yes." This is crazy. What am I doing?

Shaka pushes me to my knees and unzips his pants. His cock springs out, black and bold and beautiful. He's bigger than Michael and not circumcised. My lips close over the head of his cock and suck. My hand rides up and down his length. My cunt pulses, my thighs trembling I'm so fucking horny.

Shaka strokes my cheek. "Liyana, you're amazing. Your mouth is blowing my mind."

I wiggle my tongue over his smoothness.

"Your husband is an idiot. You're fucking incredible." He groans loudly and my clit throbs harder. "Girl, I'm not coming in your mouth. You need a real man's cock inside you." He tugs me up, pushes my skirt to my waist, and takes me against the wall.

I'm whimpering it feels so damn fine. His cock thrusts hard and I swear my cunt is dripping. My legs hitch around his waist and my arms hold tight.

"Fuck me." The words are freeing. Stimulating and arousing. "Fuck me."

"You need a good fucking. It's the best kind of *muti*. Tell me what you want, Liyana."

"I want..." I groan, my transition from *horny* to *almost there* taking me by total surprise *"Fuck."*

Shaka goes deep, each plunge rubbing my back against the wall.

"Like that?" Shaka bites my earlobe. "Your cunt is so damn wet and tight, I can't hold out much longer."

I'm panting now, the thick weight of pre-climax making me writhe. "I'm coming. Oh god, I'm coming!"

"Oh girl—"

I explode, pulse my juices all over him. My limbs shake and my ass tingles.

"Fuck, yeah." Shaka shouts, trembles, and burrows his head into my neck. "So fucking good."

I burst into tears and slide down to the floor.

"That bad?" Shaka pulls up his pants and zipper.

I'm panting, trying to catch my breath, my cunt still pounding. I want more. Lots more.

Shaka knows this. He drops to his knees, sticks two fingers inside and lowers his head to my clit. So fresh from orgasm, it only takes a few licks for me to come again. My ass clenches and lifts off the floor, but Shaka keeps licking. I come again and again. Each orgasm brings a fresh torrent of tears. Years of pent-up sexual frustration unleashed as he laps at my cunt.

Breathless, I push him away. "No more."

Shaka gathers me close and we sit like that for a few moments while thunder shakes the house and lightning illuminates the foyer.

"You need to leave," I say.

"Are you sure? I'll stay all night if you want."

"No, I don't know when Michael is coming back." I scrape my fingers across his short beard. "We need to talk."

Shaka helps me to my feet and his lips graze mine. "I'm here for you. Don't forget that."

"Yeah, you make one hell of a house call. I think you jump started my healing process."

"The right *muti* is powerful." He winks and shuts the door behind him.

Michael comes home an hour later. We talk. Or rather, he accuses me of not meeting his needs. It's my fault. I won't suck him back up after he comes. I won't give him a rim job. I won't let him ass-fuck me. I don't talk dirty, I don't...and on and on. I tell him to leave. He refuses. He tells me he intends to collect alimony because I earn more on paper. He's glad I never got pregnant. I'd be a terrible mother. He sits there with his arms crossed and tells me he's not leaving the house.

I get up, throw a change of clothes in a duffle and walk out the front door. I stay at a swanky hotel, order room service, and book a morning spa appointment for the next day. A little pampering is in order. I think about calling Shaka but don't. Alone time is what I need. And a good divorce attorney.

In the middle of the night I wake up, my dream about Shaka making me orgasm in my sleep. He unleashed something inside me and it scares me. After a breakfast of eggs Benedict on the terrace and a harmony-promoting massage in the spa, I head home.

I feel good. My head is clear. I know what I need to do. I have the video.

The bird is in the driveway again. Sheesh, I probably shouldn't have fed it. I honk the horn but it only flies as far as the stucco wall at the edge of our property.

Michael walks out of the house. He's dragging luggage behind him.

I turn off the car. "Glad you came to your senses."

"You're a fucking crazy bitch." He throws a suitcase into the BMW's trunk.

"I'm crazy? You're the one doing the nasty with Paris the ass licker."

"Don't play innocent with me. You told your mom to put a curse on me."

"I have no idea what you're talking about."

Michael pulls up his T-shirt. There are long gashes on his back. "Fucking bird tried to kill me last night while I was outside in the hot tub. I know your mom sent it. I'm leaving all right?"

"A bird?"

Just then that bird swoops under the portico, wings wide, claws outstretched, and knocks him across his head.

Michael covers his head and dives into the front seat. "Fuck you, Liyana. Tell your crazy ass mother to go to hell!" He slams the door.

I rap on the window. "Momma is in the hospital. How dare you."

Michael rolls down the window a crack. "She called and threatened me. Said if I didn't leave the house she'd sic her lightning bird on me. Crazy Zulu bitch."

The bird swoops down over the car. The car window goes up and Michael gives me the finger as he drives away. The bird is following him, swooping and diving around the car as he turns into the street.

I dial the hospital and ask for Momma's room. "Did you call Michael last night?"

"You're welcome, Liyana. It's time that man knows who he's dealing with." Momma sounds especially energetic for being cursed. "I sent my impundulu after him. He was more than eager to help you. Good thing you fed him. That made a big impression."

The impundulu, or lightning bird, is a powerful magic bird that serves witches. But it's not *real*.

Or is it?

The large bird returns, swoops down, and sits near the door. My blood runs cold.

"Momma, it's here, looking at me."

"Good. You need to learn how to control it."

"Why?"

"It's my bird. Has been for forty years. My momma passed it to me. Now I give it to you."

Momma is crazy. I never saw this bird growing up. "Momma..."

"An impundulu is passed from mother to daughter. It's time you learn the old ways."

Keeping an eye on the bird, I walk backward into the house, the phone pressed to my ear, and shut the door. The bird flies away. "I'll call you back." I need to call the zoo.

"Fine." Momma hangs up on me.

I'm in the kitchen making coffee and holding for zoo personnel when the doorbell rings. It's Shaka. He's in a polo shirt and shorts.

"What's wrong?" he asks when I open the door.

"Momma..." I shake my head. "Never mind." I close the door behind me after searching the yard for the bird. "Michael left."

Shaka gathers me into his arms. "See? Everything will work out for the best."

We kiss. Nothing tentative about it. Just demanding tongues and groping hands.

"I need some of your good medicine again," I say.

"You've been starved for too long." Shaka picks me up and carries me to the couch, his lips nibbling at my neck. "I recommend a thirty-day intensive prescription." He removes my top, slips off my bra straps, and sucks on my tits.

Hell, the man wastes no time. One pull on my tits and I'm wet.

"Your breasts are gorgeous." Shaka draws out the nipples between his teeth.

The arousing sting races down my body and burrows into my twat. It's like my tits and clit are connected by an erogenous thread.

"Bite them again," I say.

Shaka chews, amping up the sting the more I moan. He shimmies my jeans down and peels off my panties.

I spread my wet cunt. "Eat me."

Shaka dances his fingers over me, plunges his finger deep inside, and brings it to my mouth. "Taste your magic."

I suck on his finger, the taste making me quiver with desire. He dips in again and I suck my cunt juices off.

"Damn girl, my cock is so hard it hurts." Shaka takes off his shorts, holds his cock. "It fucking *aches* for you."

I want his cock everywhere. In my mouth. In my cunt. In my hand. I can't decide.

Shaka decides for me.

He pushes his cock into my mouth and finger-fucks me. His thumb rubs my clit as his finger reaches for my G-spot. I come without warning. Squirt my climax out. I never did *that* before. I pull his cock from my mouth, already salty with precum.

"Fuck me, Shaka."

"Let me hear you, Liyana." He lifts my legs in the air and glides in.

He's hammering into me, so deep and hard I'm bouncing on the sofa, my nails raking down his back; hollering at how fucking good it is to get so thoroughly fucked, I'm lost to time and space.

By the time his body jolts with orgasm, we're on the floor, the vase of flowers knocked over, one of my legs lifted over my head. My cunt is bruised and raw, but I feel extraordinary. The shackles of shame and inhibition are torn away. Like every inch of my skin is alive, pulsating with energy.

We nestle together on the floor, catching our breath, our bodies slick with sweat and lust.

"You released my inner sex goddess." I trace a finger up his chest.

"I released more than that." He kisses the top of my head. "I'm yours now. You own me."

I giggle.

"I mean it, Liyana. You control me. I am the impundulu. This is my human form. Your grandmothers have passed me from mother to daughter for five hundred years."

I push him away and sit up, my heart pounding in my ears.

Shaka grins. "It's time to confront your destiny. Embrace the old ways."

It's tempting. *Really* tempting.

The lightning bird is a mythological magical creature of many South African peoples. It's a fearsome yet respected bird that helps witches and witch doctors with magic. Good or bad.

SEVEN NIGHTS

The supplicant is the last one for the day but he is art-less, his cock hammering into me without rhythm or concern for my sexual pleasure. I moan loudly. *Really* loudly. That gets most men off faster. Hope he didn't have too much ale before coming to the temple. Ale-addled men take *forever*.

Goddess Inanna, make him spill his seed already! I've got things to do. Friends to visit.

The supplicant's nasal snorting quickens. *Finally.* I tighten my vaginal walls and squeeze his miserable little cock.

"Shamhat." That voice.

I roll my head left, my eyes traveling up and up to the gorgeous face of the mighty King Gilgamesh. Standing beside him, a wide-eyed stranger stares at the ritual.

Gilgamesh slaps the supplicant's shoulders. "Go. Now. I have business with Shamhat."

The senseless supplicant keeps humping. He's too far gone, already in that climactic place between awareness and orgasm. Gilgamesh seizes the supplicant under his arm and flings him to the ground. Drops of cum on my belly, over the platform, and across the floor point the way to the supplicant's crumbled figure a few feet away. Flying ejaculation. Now *that* must have been an interesting sensation.

Gilgamesh nudges the supplicant's linen kilt with the tip of his sandal-clad foot. "Your worship to Inanna is complete."

With his body prone and forehead touching the floor, the supplicant reaches out and snatches the cloth.

"Go," said Gilgamesh.

Dismissed, the supplicant crawls backward, his forehead scraping the floor.

"*Go!*"

The supplicant scrambles up and flees down the cavernous temple gallery.

Gilgamesh inspires fear and devotion. Fear mostly. Though he is perfect in strength he *does* tend to lord over his people like a wild bull.

I take Gilgamesh's outstretched hand. "Mouth pleasure?"

I give the best blow jobs in the world. Gilgamesh's claim, not mine. Who am I to disagree? Although I admit, my tongue is superior; it can knot a string. My mouth is special too; large enough to accommodate Gilgamesh's enormous cock. And my full lips are shaped for oral pleasure, creating a spellbinding suction that brings supplicants from faraway cities.

Actually, my whole body is perfectly suited for my job as temple prostitute. My vagina is as tight as a virgin's. I keep it snug with two exercises, squeezing the muscles that control my pee and holding a small weighted ball inside my vagina. I can bring a man to orgasm just by constricting my vagina. Wide soft hips, thick long hair, and generous bouncy breasts tipped with golden areolas add to my beauty. I'm the most requested temple prostitute for a reason.

I must tilt my head to look at Gilgamesh. He's taller and bigger than any man I've ever seen. He is dressed formally today, his long hair curled, his cheeks shaved, his beard trimmed, and he's adorned with golden rings, armbands, earrings, and necklaces. Gilgamesh is beyond gorgeous with twinkling brown eyes, a strong nose, and a wide mouth set on an angled face. A face of arrogance and brute strength. The face of a demigod. Gilgamesh is two-thirds god, one-third mortal.

Gilgamesh grins, eyes twinkling with impishness, and strides down the gallery. I follow him, as does the other man, whose lion's pelt skirt indicates he is a trapper by trade.

As we walk, the men and women we pass drop to the ground, prostrate and silent. When we reach the terrace overlooking the great city of Uruk, Gilgamesh stretches his arm and points to the grassy wilderness that extends from the city walls to the uplands in the far off distance. "This man," he nods to the trapper, "came to me with an extraordinary story."

I glance at the unremarkable trapper. So much for mouth-fucking Gilgamesh. Maybe he wants a threesome. I've sucked two cocks before. I've also fucked two cocks. But Gilgamesh isn't a share-the-hole kind of guy.

"He was trapping, setting out snares and digging pits as always, but this time when he returned for his quarry he found the snares disabled and the pits filled."

"Interesting." Not really. But I have to say something.

"Curious who might be undoing his work, the trapper waited by a large waterhole visited by both trappers and animals. He saw a man, a wild man running with the gazelles like he was part of the herd."

"The wild man sprang the traps," I said.

Gilgamesh nodded. "This man runs as fast as the gazelles, grazes alongside of them, and speaks their unfathomable language. I dreamt of this wild man so of course I was not surprised by this news." Gilgamesh takes my hand and kisses the palm. "Tame this beast man, Shamhat. You are the only one who can. After you civilize him, bring him to me."

I blink, unsure if I heard correctly. "Tame a wild man? How?"

Gilgamesh brushes his fingers across my bare breasts. "Like all women tame men. Take off your robe, show your breasts, spread your sex, and work your charms."

"I'll do it." No one says no to Gilgamesh.

Gilgamesh pulls aside his linen loincloth. "After this."

I kneel down, wrap both hands around his enormous cock, and whirl my tongue over his rosy crown. It's an honor to service him in any capacity. His cock is the stuff of legends, his sexual prowess known throughout the lands. As king, Gilgamesh always exercises his right at every wedding to ravish the bride before the husband does. I feel sorry for the brides. Once you've been fucked by Gilgamesh it's difficult to endure inferior sex with lesser endowed and unskilled husbands. Gilgamesh has fucked every temple prostitute many times over. Sometimes he wants us to get on our hands and knees in a row so he can go from one to the other. He satisfies us all. He might be one-third man but his cock is full god. How else can he bring a woman to orgasm so easily? Giving him mouth pleasure is no different. His divine cock makes me climax every time!

Gilgamesh sighs and lays a gentle hand on my head while my lips, tongue, and hands work his cock. His arousal is an aphrodisiac, and already my cunt is wet. I drag my gaze away from his powerful brown thighs and look into his eyes. He grins, accustomed to the adoration he incites in both men and women.

"It's a pleasure watching you, Shamhat," says Gilgamesh. He nudges the trapper. "If she can't tame the wild man, no one can."

The trapper, whose erect cock peeks out under his pelt, hasn't blinked since I started.

"Ahhh, that's it." Gilgamesh winds my hair around his arm several times.

I'm used to this. It's how he controls me.

I'm usually the one in control, so Gilgamesh's dominance thrills me, my vag responding to his supremacy by oozing honey. My lustful whimpering inflames him and he tugs my hair to slow my artistry. He's close now, but he likes to draw out the pleasure. Like a pot on low heat, he wants to simmer for as long as possible. It's what causes his orgasms to be robust and mighty and prolonged. Just listening to Gilgamesh orgasm is enough to incite my own. He always shakes his head back and forth and roars like a lion.

It's difficult to slow myself when my clit begs for release but I'm a professional. Gilgamesh wants slow. He gets slooooooow.

Gilgamesh yanks my hair. "You're a tease, Shamhat."

He pushes his cock into the back of my throat and I gag. I don't have to gag. I just do because he likes it.

"What's that?" He's grinning.

"Just doing my job." But my words are too garbled by his thrusting cock for him to understand.

I pull him in and out, my lips clamped around his length, sucking, slurping, and swirling my tongue over and under his most sensitive spots. I hear his final ascent, long low exhalations that quicken my own climb to paradise. I slow even more, in control once again, and keep him simmering . . . simmering . . . simmering . . .

Gilgamesh thrashes his head back and forth and loudly hails his arrival to paradise. Cum fills my mouth. A demigod's cum. A goblet of salty nectar that makes me climax. Gilgamesh takes several slow breaths as I extract every last drop of cum from his divine cock. I squeeze his testicles and the head of his cock, and lick off more.

"Always a pleasure, Gilgamesh." I glance at the trapper. He's got a handful of cum in his hands and he's looking sheepish.

Gilgamesh helps me to my feet. (He's so thoughtful.)

"I'd fuck you all day but we both have work to do." Gilgamesh slaps the trapper's back. "I'd wipe off that cum before you escort my favorite prostitute to the waterhole."

The trapper drags his hand over the pelt skirt.

"Does this wild man have a name?" I ask.

"I named him Enkidu because I believe goddess Aruru made him from a pinch of clay." Gilgamesh kisses my cheek. "Make me proud, Shamhat."

"I will."

I follow the hunter from Inanna's Temple and stop at his small home where he gathers supplies.

"Can I fuck you?" he asks while filling animal skins with ale.

"Not unless you go to Inanna's Temple to pay tribute." Men are always looking for a freebie. "Or you're Gilgamesh."

"I should have pretended to be a wild man." He stuffs the ale skins into a bag and slings it over his shoulders. "Does it pay well?"

I lift up my arms, adorned with thick bands of gold and strings of jewels, and wiggle my ring-laden fingers. "What do you think?"

"I think I should have been born with a cunt." The trapper laughs and stacks a second sack onto the first. "Let's go."

"What about lions?" I say as we walk through the city gates.

The trapper points at his cum-crusted pelt. "Lions are no match for me."

The journey takes three days. We leave the road the first day. Walk a narrow path through the grasslands the second. Follow a game trail the third. We see many deer, hear a boar rooting in the grass, and skirt around the vultures feasting on a rotting leopard carcass. Only one old lion crosses our path and the trapper kills him with ease.

The wild man's waterhole is not visible until we crest a small hill. It's a large blue oasis in the midst of grasslands, scrub, and a scattering of cedar trees. A herd of ostriches is bending their long necks to the water as we scramble down the hillside.

The wilderness is a lonely place. The endless blue sky offers no shade. The trapper provides no interesting conversation. And the night sky and nocturnal noises frighten me. I'll be glad to get this task over with. I miss the sounds and smells of food and people.

We set up a small camp behind a thick tangle of brush under a cedar tree and wait. One day passes with no wild man sightings. On the second day a cloud of dust in the distance gives us hope. *Finally*, a herd of gazelles arrives when the sun is high overhead.

"There he is." The hunter points to a man running with the herd.

Enkidu matches the trapper's description perfectly. The wild man is tall, maybe as tall as Gilgamesh, but he is leaner, his limbs knotted with lithe muscles. A runner's body. His dark brown hair hangs in tangled clumps to his back and his matted beard touches his navel. Dust and filth conceal his skin color.

"Don't scare him away," says the trapper. "Let him come to you."

I have a plan. One that involves fucking a *clean* wild man, not a filthy sweaty one.

I rise from my crouching position and move slowly toward the far side of the waterhole. I comb through my braids with my fingers, shake out my long tresses. I remove my sandals next. At the edge of the waterhole I remove my robe and spread it over the ground.

The water is cool and clear, and feels good splashed on my skin. From the corner of my eye I watch Enkidu. He moves through the herd, slapping the gazelles' hind-quarters to move them away as he heads toward me.

I pretend not to notice and walk deeper into the

waterhole until I submerge. I rise like a goddess, the water droplets catching the sunlight and making my skin sparkle. There's something about a wet woman that men love.

Enkidu stands at the edge and gawks. His cock is erect. Good. Wild or civilized, men are all the same.

I smell Enkidu from here. He stinks worse than a beast. I walk toward him until the water only reaches my thighs.

Showtime.

I spread the folds of my sex. I'm hairless (a job requirement) so he sees every pink ridge and rosy crest.

Enkidu splashes into the water, pausing when the water is at his knees.

Nope. Not clean enough.

I smile and giggle and dive into the water. Enkidu is gone when I surface. My head swivels about.

"Enkidu?"

A hand clamps around my ankle. Enkidu leaps from the water and laughs. He's only *slightly* less foul smelling.

I arch my back and push out my breasts. Enkidu is a wild man but he's not stupid. He sets both hands upon them with a kind of reverence.

"Shamhat." I touch the valley between my breasts.

Enkidu tilts his head and gives my breasts a gentle squeeze.

"Shamhat." I say again.

"Shamhat." His voice is deep and raspy. A sexy, manly voice.

I dive back into the water. Hope he follows.

He does. He thinks it's a game. He touches my

breasts. I giggle and dive into the water. He follows. By the seventh dunking the stink and dirt are gone, his face is clean, and his golden brown skin glistens.

Enkidu is handsome, with intelligent brown eyes that taper at the corners and a strong hooked nose with wide nostrils. A face of strength, dignity, and intelligence. This favor for Gilgamesh may not be so bad after all.

He follows like a lost puppy as I walk backward out of the waterhole, and yet when I lie on my robe he just stands over me. The wild man's cock is impressive. Not as big as Gilgamesh's but big enough to amaze women and make men jealous.

I spread my thighs and pat the ground between them. Enkidu sits on his haunches and sniffs. Like an animal catching the scent of a female in heat, he advances with caution.

Letting him rut like a dog is out of the question. So uncivilized! I direct his approach, guide him inside, and wrap my legs around him. He pushes inside with a low guttural moan. He feels good. I like big cocks. Prefer the way they fill me. I feel complete. Whole. Divine.

My hands glide over Enkidu's expansive sharp shoulders, roam over the ridges of his back, and cup his hard buttocks. He's a novice. I'll have to teach him everything. But that's okay. Virgin men are a pleasure to instruct in the art of fucking. Most are eager to understand the secrets of a woman's body. They realize having erotic skill gets them more women. Only brutes don't care about a woman's pleasure.

I treat Enkidu like a virginal youth. I let his hands wander, encouraging him with sighs, since any man who's lived among wild beasts must be attuned to the slightest sound and movement.

Enkidu is a quick learner. My breasts enthrall him, and when I guide his head to them he latches on. Thank Inanna this diversion slows his wild thrusting. I rock my hips, control his rhythm, and Enkidu succumbs to my tempo. He grunts like an animal and when he *does* look at me his eyes are lust-glazed. He snorts his orgasm, pushes deep inside, and collapses on me. I wrap him in my arms and wait for him to fall asleep.

"Shamhat," the hunter calls quietly from behind the tree. "What should I do?"

"Leave us be awhile. It will take more than one coupling."

"How many?"

How do I know? I'm good, but it's going to take more than one fabulous Shamhat-style fuck to convince a wild man to join civilization. "Wait for us at the shepherd's camp."

"I'll leave enough food and ale for a week." The trapper crept away.

Enkidu is out, snoring with sexual satisfaction.

I make good use of this time to study his face. A shave, beard grooming, haircut, nourishing oils, and clothes are all he needs to join the civilized world. Haircut first. It's too matted for a comb. I pull a bit of straw caught in the snarled mess and Enkidu's eyes fly open.

"Hello, Enkidu." I touch his hairy cheek.

He tries wiggling between my thighs but I stand and walk to the cedar tree where the trapper and I made camp. Enkidu, of course, trails close behind.

I drink from the ale-filled skin. "Ale." I hand it to him.

He mimics my actions, smacking his lips after a few hearty chugs. Enkidu's standing so close to me, his hard cock pokes my belly.

"More fucking?" I ask.

Enkidu's head turns away, his gaze on the gazelles near the waterhole.

"We need to work on your eye contact, Enkidu," I say. "Good thing I know how." I pour ale over his cock and his head snaps back around. I kneel down and give him a Shamhat Special.

It works like a charm. (Even better than the charms the shamans sell at the market.) Enkidu cannot take his eyes off me as my mouth and hands work his cock.

"You like?"

Enkidu's eyes shine with adoration. "Like."

A blow job inspires Enkidu's first word. Why am I not surprised?

Enkidu doesn't take long, and cum fills my mouth after a few slurping sucks.

"Like," says Enkidu watching as I rummage through the sack stuffed with barley cakes, lentils, chickpeas, and cucumbers.

After grabbing a handful of chickpeas and a barley cake, I return to the edge of the waterhole and sit down. I tear off a piece and eat, share a piece with Enkidu. He studies it, mushes the dough between his fingers and takes a tentative nibble.

"It's good." I tear off another piece.

"Good." He clears his throat. "Good. Like."

Our first meal together. So far I've taught the wild

man how to eat and drink, and say two words. Not too bad for one day. After we eat the chickpeas I rinse my mouth in the waterhole. Enkidu does the same.

Kissing time.

I put my lips to his cheek and he pulls away. Maybe he thinks I'm going to eat him. I try again. Same response. I take his hand in mine, rub it against my cheek, and kiss the top. Enkidu tilts his head. His cock tilts too. Out and up. This is a good start.

Enkidu imitates my actions and I giggle.

"Like," he says.

"Like," I say and kiss his cheek.

He kisses back.

"Good." This time I kiss his lips.

Enkidu holds them still, unsure but curious. I push my tongue into his mouth and his eyes grow wide.

I kiss him again, thrust in my tongue.

This time Enkidu responds. So does his cock. It's bobbing about like it's looking for something.

I must admit, teaching Enkidu how to kiss makes my sex slick with desire. He kisses for the sheer pleasure of it. No expectations. He takes his time exploring my mouth, sometimes substituting his finger for his tongue. The sun is going down when he pulls away to sniff. He smells my desire.

I lie back and spread my legs, and Enkidu pushes in. After a few thrusts, I lift my legs over his shoulders.

"Good," he says, duplicating the first tempo I taught him.

I reach around and cup his testicles. He yelps with surprise, then purrs with pleasure as I stroke.

His orgasm is more intense this time—his loud grunts

startling a bird in a nearby tree—and while cum rolls out of my sex, he sits back and gazes at me with amazement.

He learns three more words—ale, water, and gazelle—before we go to sleep.

He wakes me twice to fuck.

He sleeps through the sunrise, no surprise there, but I get up, my mind preoccupied with thoughts. Civilized worries. Which words do I teach next? What happens if he runs away? What if I fail to civilize Enkidu? Will Gilgamesh be angry with me?

I'm making a porridge of barley, garlic, and lentils when I see him stretching like a leopard. Enkidu points to his erect cock.

"I'm sure you have one every morning."

"Good."

"We'll 'good' later. Eat this and then let's do something about your hair."

I know better than to bring out a knife—it looks too much like a pointy horn or lion's canines—so I show him how to comb my hair.

Enkidu buries his nose in my tresses. "Mmmm. Shamhat."

"Your turn." I tug on the ends of his snarled mess.

Enkidu shakes his head. He looks embarrassed. This is upsetting. Enkidu is pure, a son of nature, and yet in one day I make him feel inferior. I never imagined there were drawbacks to being civilized.

While Enkidu watches the gazelles grazing on the far side of the waterhole, I get a knife out of the sack and pull a few blades of grass from the ground.

"Enkidu." Once I get his attention, I cut a few blades of grass. "I'll cut your hair."

He turns away, a sad faraway look in his eyes. I'm losing him.

I put down the knife, stand in front of him, and jump, flinging my arms around his neck and my legs around his waist. He laughs, surprised, and I plunge my sex onto his ever-erect cock.

The faraway look vanishes. Gazelles forgotten.

He loves this position. He strides around the cedar tree, walks to the waterhole and back. The second lap around the tree is much slower. He stops and grunts, jiggling my ass to thrust deep.

Later, the gazelles ignored, Enkidu lets me cut his hair. I cut his beard, too, but he'll need a barber before we go to Uruk.

"You're very handsome. Like a god," I say.

Enkidu's hands roam around his head, rub his square jawline, and he shrugs.

"Come on." I pull his arm.

We race to the waterhole and splash around like children. Later, I comb his hair.

Enkidu no longer looks like a wild man. One problem solved.

The third day is much like the second. I teach him more words and we fuck three times.

It's the morning of the fourth day, and Enkidu stares at me with a troubled look.

"What is it, Enkidu?"

He shakes his head, frustrated to express what must be complex thoughts.

Animals convey fear, aggression, and affection with their bodies. So do we, so I pantomime a few things—eating, swimming, Enkidu's peeing (he bursts out laughing). "Act it out, Enkidu. I will give you the words."

Enkidu drops to the ground, pantomimes fucking, grunts several times, points to his cock and then points to my sex. Easy enough.

"Your seed goes inside me."

Enkidu rolls on his back, spreads his legs and points at me again. He shakes his head and frowns.

Praise Inanna, is the wild man concerned because I don't ejaculate? Is he aware enough to realize I haven't climaxed? Enkidu might not know language or customs but his heart is in the right place. That makes him more civilized than most men.

Time for the next lesson. I straddle his face and spread my sex.

Enkidu inhales my cunt. "Good."

His fingers explore the valley and ridges slowly as though memorizing it. When he touches my clit I purr my pleasure. Enkidu is a thorough and careful explorer, his fingers probing all the way to my anus. He grabs my ass, scoots me forward, and laps his tongue back and forth. Hail the wild man. He is attuned to the slightest change in scent, sound, and movement. A lifetime of relying on instincts and senses make him an attentive and exceptional lover. Every "oh" and "ah," every flinch or tensed muscle, he responds to. My cunt goes from moist to dripping (from purring to moaning) in no time.

He knows how to tease. Whirling and suckling and slurping and lapping, keeping me on the edge of paradise—bringing me forward, holding me back—until my entire bottom (from slit to anus) is a wet quivering valley of carnal tension.

It is oral pleasure without boundaries, preconceptions, or misinformation. His honest hunger is so pure and voracious that my whole being is lost. I am nature and beast. I am gods and demons.

My thighs squeeze his head. My body twists and jerks. My voice screams praises to the heavens. I spin and tumble, orgasm after orgasm lifting me up and over the cliffs of reason.

I want cock!

I shimmy down, wrap my hand around his cock. It's sticky with cum. My pleasure made him orgasm, and yet my wild man is still hard.

"Fucking good," says Enkidu as I sink onto his length.

It is fucking good. I am a temple prostitute no longer. I am a woman. A wild woman in need of wild-man sex.

If we fucked a lot before, we fuck more now. Six times a day. I don't know who's hornier. I show him every position I know. Enkidu even comes up with a few of his own. Being impaled backward on his cock while he stands is my favorite. We fuck in the waterhole, in the grass, and hanging from the cedar tree (good thing he's very strong).

Strange how such fucking awakens Enkidu's intellect. His hunger for knowledge is as voracious as his sexual appetite. He's like a giant python, unhinging its jaws to swallow a goat whole.

I show him in which direction Uruk lies, draw symbols in the sand, teach him about the gods and demons. Once he learns enough words he asks questions.

How many people make up a herd? *It depends on the size of the city.*

Is there an alpha? *His name is Gilgamesh. He's the king and stronger than you. (Enkidu snorts at the improbability of this.)*

Do all men wear clothes tied at their waists? *Yes, and sandals, armbands, bracelets, and rings, and their hair and beards are braided.*

Will you braid mine? *Of course, Enkidu.*

What do people do all day? *They have jobs, like baking, brewing ale, carpentry, and farming.*

What's your job? *I perform rituals in Inanna's Temple.*

"There are festivals every day," I say before he asks what a ritual is. "People dance and sing and eat and drink with their friends."

"Are we friends?"

"Yes." I hope he doesn't ask me to explain friendship.

"I want to be friends with the alpha, this Gilgamesh."

"I think you will be good friends. You are alike in many ways."

The morning of the seventh day, the earth trembles beneath us.

Enkidu leaps to his feet. "My herd is leaving. I must go, Shamhat." He takes off running.

I draw my knees to my chest and watch Enkidu race through the grass. I failed. The wild man cannot be tamed.

The gazelles change direction as Enkidu approaches. He chases after them. They veer away, the herd sprinting and leaping over rocks and shrubs. Enkidu can't keep up with their flight over the hill. At the hilltop, Enkidu stops, his hands on his hips, and looks over his shoulder at me, then back at the retreating herd. He paces the hilltop for several moments.

Both sadness and happiness fight for control in my heart as I watch him walk back to me. The child of nature is now a man of civilization.

"My herd ran away from me. They don't know me anymore." Enkidu sits beside me. "I smell different."

"Why do you want to run wild with gazelles when you can race with man?"

"Is that a job? Like baker or carpenter?"

"No, but you will find your place soon enough." I run my fingers through his wavy brown hair. "There's a shepherd's camp two days from here. It's time you made more friends."

Enkidu nuzzles his head in my neck and inhales my scent. "Let's fuck first."

This time Enkidu teaches *me* about fucking.

I thought I knew it all, yet he shows me how to abandon oneself to absolute sensation. He fucks me from behind first, thrusting slowing, his fingers rubbing my clit. He withdraws, sucks on my clit, and finger-fucks me while I'm on my back, my hands pulling my ankles toward my head. My cunt is his feast, and his tongue flutters, his lips torment, and his fingers plunge until I babble like a savage. He enters me like this, plowing so fast and deep, I can't tell one climax from the next. He pulls out and aims his cock at my open mouth. I catch his cum, swallowing it all.

"Good?" he asks.

"You're a god, Enkidu."

Enkidu is different now. Like dry farmland saturated with nourishing rain. His mind is fertile, his personality taking root, his confidence ripening like an orchard of pomegranate trees. Enkidu will be Gilgamesh's greatest harvest.

The four-thousand-year-old Epic of Gilgamesh *was transcribed from clay cuneiform tablets. Shamhat and Enkidu appear in the first tablet. The next eleven recount the adventures of Gilgamesh and his friend Enkidu as they battle fearsome creatures and discover the truth about man's eternal struggle.*

ABOUT
THE AUTHOR

AUTUMN BARDOT writes erotica, historical fiction, paranormal romance, and even academic literary essays. She has a bachelor of arts in English literature. Her day job and family keep her busy so she spends every spare minute writing her next novel. She lives with her husband and rescue pooch in the Los Angeles area. Which mythical lover are you? Take the quiz at www.autumnbardot.com/lover-quiz/

You can connect with Autumn at www.autumnbardot. com, and on Goodreads, Instagram, and Twitter at @ autumnbardot.